Finding Mr. Right

Sweetheart Falls Book 1

By Emmy-Lou James

Published by JEM Family Publications
Cover Design by German Creative
Chapter Header designed by Emmy-Lou James

Paperback ISBN: 979-8-89379-296-6
EPUB ISBN: 979-8-89379-297-3
eBook ISBN: 979-8-89379-291-1

Printed in Canada
First Edition April 2024

To all the aspiring romance authors out there.

Have faith, believe in yourself.

Your words matter.
You matter.

Give yourself permission to write your story, and get it done!

Acknowledgements

The Devereaux family have been a part of my family since 2015, and as I've travelled the paths of their stories, they've become like a family to me. The journey to publishing their stories though come down to the amazing support of the people in my life, and I'd like to take this chance to thank them. Each have not only been part of that support network, but also beta readers, critique partners, proof-readers, cheerleaders, counsellors, and so much more.

Jim, you're the light of my life, and whilst I know there were times you wondered if I'd ever actually hit the publish button, it's because of you that I was able. Your belief that I'd get across the line, even with the rollercoaster life we live, never wavered. I appreciate everything you do!

Steph, my incredible daughter who has pushed me these last few weeks to just "make this happen, get it done!" (*that will be my epitaph!*). You're an amazing person and have always had such complete confidence in my abilities as a writer, and a mom, even when I question myself. I'm so lucky to have you!

Judy, who is the most awesome friend and accountability partner— even when I take off around the world and struggle to keep up! I love when you pick up the phone, or answer What's App calls with "So, are we going to jump up and down and celebrate you finally pressing that publish button yet?!" Man, I miss coffee mornings with you!

Mom, thank you for nurturing my love of books, and for sharing reads with me over the years. It's exciting to finally have my first book complete, and to share it with you. I know you don't read romance, so thank you for putting up with my fluffy bunny world to read through these stories. Your proofreading and feedback are really appreciated. My next goal is to get a copy of one my books in your library!

Jo, thanks for being there when I doubted myself. You've always boosted me up when I've been unsure and questioning myself. I hope that I can repay the compliment when you need it!

My wider writing community in New Zealand, including the Canterbury Writers, Canterbury Romance Writers', Romance Writers of New Zealand, and North Canterbury Writers' who I miss so much!! And who, over the years have shared their own experiences to help develop my own writing skills. Travelling means that I'm often out of the loop, but I'm so grateful for each and every one of your support. You all rock!

To my boys, and Rosella, the fact I'm finally publishing this I hope shows you all that anything is possible if you keep working toward it. Don't give up, don't let people steal your dreams, and always strive to get to the finish line—the journey's worth it!

For my readers, I hope you fall in love with the Devereaux's in the same way I have. Thank you, for reading.

Overview

Freshly divorced, and determined to start anew, Savannah Devereaux is navigating life as a single mother to her twin daughters in the bustling New York City. The last thing on her mind is romance, especially with Mac Mackenzie, a charming Kiwi who oozes sex appeal. Add into that he's her brother's best friend and business partner, and it sums up every reason why she needs to steer clear.

When her ex crashes a fundraiser, she's hosting and bids on her services in an auction, Savannah finds herself swept off her feet, by the irresistible, Mac.

From coffee dates to late-night texts, and steamy nights between the sheets, Savannah soon realizes that her whirlwind romance with Mac is more than she bargained for. As family secrets unveil, and their chemistry intensifies, Savannah and Mac find themselves navigating a rocky road to love.

Can Savannah overcome her past and embrace a future with Mac, or will their undeniable connection be overshadowed by the challenges that lie ahead?

Trigger Warning: This novel contains a scene featuring domestic abuse that may be distressing or triggering for some readers. Reader discretion is advised.

DEVEREAUX FAMILY

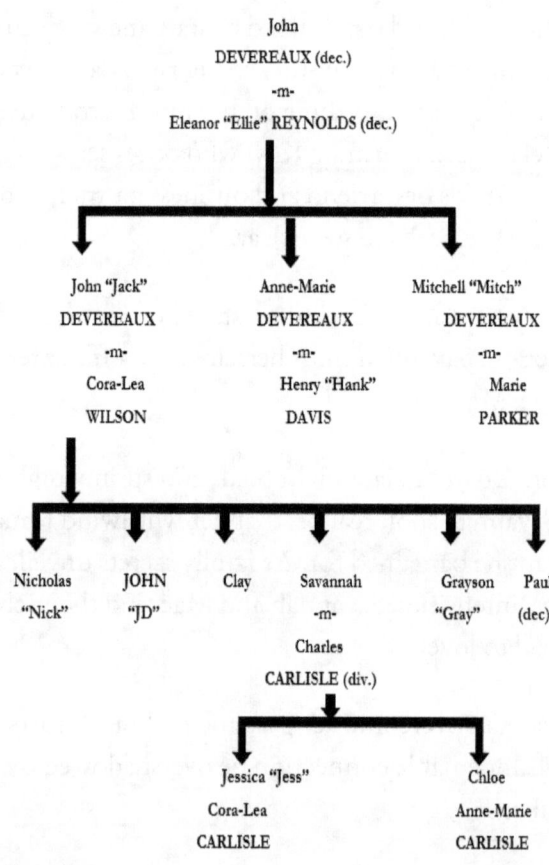

John
DEVEREAUX (dec.)

-m-

Eleanor "Ellie" REYNOLDS (dec.)

John "Jack"
DEVEREAUX
-m-
Cora-Lea
WILSON

Anne-Marie
DEVEREAUX
-m-
Henry "Hank"
DAVIS

Mitchell "Mitch"
DEVEREAUX
-m-
Marie
PARKER

Nicholas
"Nick"

JOHN
"JD"

Clay

Savannah
-m-
Charles
CARLISLE (div.)

Grayson
"Gray"

Paul
(dec)

Jessica "Jess"
Cora-Lea
CARLISLE

Chloe
Anne-Marie
CARLISLE

Dec – Deceased

Div – Divorced

MACKENZIE FAMILY

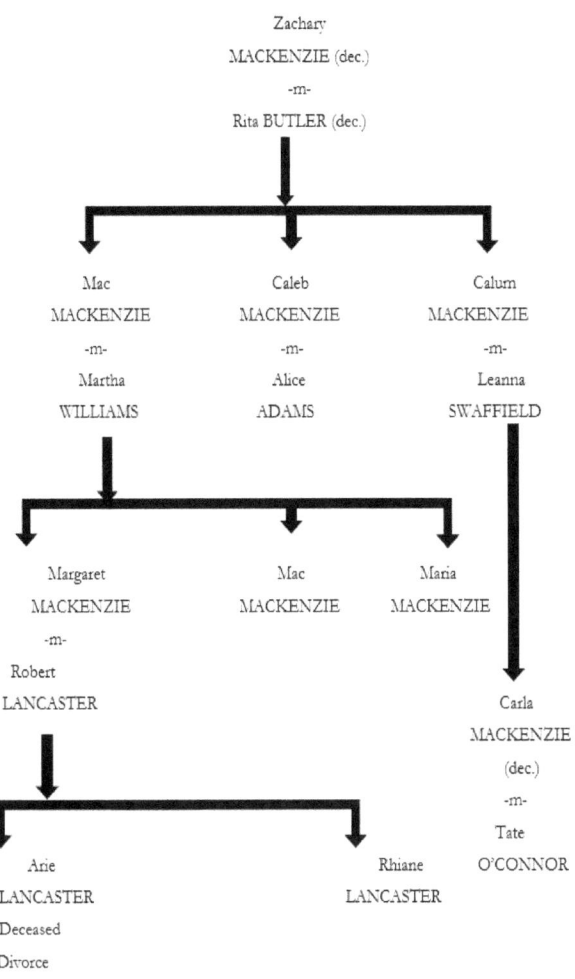

Zachary
MACKENZIE (dec.)
-m-
Rita BUTLER (dec.)

Mac MACKENZIE	Caleb MACKENZIE	Calum MACKENZIE
-m-	-m-	-m-
Martha WILLIAMS	Alice ADAMS	Leanna SWAFFIELD

Margaret MACKENZIE	Mac MACKENZIE	Maria MACKENZIE
-m-		
Robert LANCASTER		

Carla
MACKENZIE
(dec.)
-m-
Tate
O'CONNOR

Arie LANCASTER	Rhiane LANCASTER

Dec. – Deceased

Div. – Divorce

Table of Contents

Chapter One

SAVANNAH

SAVANNAH DEVEREAUX stepped into the Fifth Avenue rooftop bar, eyes sparkling with wonder. Three months of hard graft, and here she was. The space had transformed into a glittering tableau.

Decadent blacks and reds, highlights with gold and crystal filled the room.

The curtains, furniture, and décor were all selected by Savannah and her friend Felicity, working in just the way they'd envisaged.

In any other circumstances, the colors may have appeared gaudy. But here, now, there was an exquisite sense of opulence, enhanced by the sheer volume of glittering wealth they would entertain tonight.

Suave tuxedo-clad men, young and old, engaged in deep conversation. Women, in the latest fashions in every style and color, added a new level of exquisite to the room. Among them, smart-suited servers carried trays laden with sparkling champagne flutes, or hors d'oeuvres.

Savannah's smile widened, and the butterflies she'd experienced earlier dispersed.

The urge to whoop with excitement was so strong that she fought to hold it at bay. Thank goodness the nerves of the past weeks were now forgotten.

She stepped aside as two middle-aged gentlemen entered, and she smiled, dipping her head in acknowledgement.

One she recognized to be a local senator. The other, the star of a recent blockbuster Hollywood action movie. Two glamorous women followed in their wake. One wore a stunning gold dress, the other black. Both enhanced with dazzling jewelry, the effect— breath-taking.

"This is happening," she murmured. "This is really, really happening."

She brushed the front and side of her glittering silver gown, self-conscious amid the throng of designer frocks, the fingers of one hand worrying the three and a half carat diamond and sapphire pendant at her throat.

A smile played at her lips.

"You'll be great, my darling," Cora-Lea Devereaux said earlier in the evening. Her mother stood behind her before the antique mahogany framed vanity mirror in her bedroom, fastening the heirloom pendant around her neck, the belief in her eyes resonating the pride she'd so often shown in Savannah and her five siblings.

Savannah's eyes misted at the memory. She knew that same pride reflected in her own eyes at the achievements of her own girls. It didn't matter how old she got, that parental approval was always something she'd sought. Even in the murkiest days of her marriage.

"If there's anyone who can pull this off, sweetheart, it's you."

Savannah chuckled. "You're biased, Mom," she'd replied. "You believe I can do anything?"

Her mom's knowing grin responded to the statement.

"Every one of my babies can achieve whatever they put their mind to. As can yours."

Savannah's eyes shimmered.

The reminder reinforced just how much rode on this evening.

This must work, too much relied on it.

She needed to lay to rest the ghost of the past few years once and for all, and this was her opportunity to achieve just that.

A finger tapped her on the shoulder, and she was grateful that she had held back a startled yelp.

"Oh my god," a familiar female voice said from behind.

Savannah grinned and turned to find her brother's best friend, beaming at her. "This is incredible, Sav." Gwen gushed, sweeping her into a bear hug.

"Isn't it?" she replied, speaking into Gwen's shoulder. "I can hardly believe it!"

"Nicks so proud. Honest, when you said you'd organize this, we imagined nothing on this scale."

Savannah pulled back, eying the diminutive form of Gwen. At a little over five feet, she was petite, despite a titan of a personality. In the time she'd known her, Savannah found herself in awe of the petite woman.

"I didn't either," she replied. "It kind of..." she shrugged, "ran away from me."

Gwen chuckled.

"Well, if you continue creating events like this, it's safe to say you'll have a fully booked calendar for the next five years. It's incredible!"

Ever one to err on the side of caution, Savannah retorted. "Don't get too confident. Both you and Nick ensured that this subject is a political hot potato."

She gestured to where the Governor of New York stood talking to a group of men near the bar. The senator who had passed her moments earlier there, too.

"No politician would miss the chance to grab some spotlight, especially with the primaries on the horizon."

Another laugh, and Gwen shrugged.

"Well, if it worked—good!"

They fell silent, their gaze taking in the ever-growing crowd.

It would be so easy for Savannah to fail, and New York was an unforgiving city.

She gave a mental head shake, dispersing the predicted ripple of uncertainty, her shoulders straightening on a deep, cleansing breath.

This would work. Too much depended on it.

Tonight, she dispersed the demons of the past once and for all. It's my time to shine.

"Uh oh," Gwen groaned, flicking a sympathetic glance Savannah's way. "Someone needs rescuing."

Savannah frowned, but followed her gaze, and came to stop on her brother, Nick. Mimicking Gwen's earlier eye roll, she too groaned, shaking her head in disbelief.

Nick, engaged in an animated conversation with the governor, and a group of men, seemed oblivious to a growing interest around them. The series of nods, causing more than a little unease.

"Go," Savannah gestured. "Please, tell him not to rock the boat tonight."

Gwen chuckled.

"Knowing how he feels about the foundation? Yeah." There was no missing the sarcasm in her voice. "That's going to be easy."

Savannah understood both Gwen's and Nick's pain.

Tonight was all about the foundation the pair established. It was impossible not to become infuriated at the funding cuts that made it necessary.

In a post-pandemic world, the country, if not the world, was in a state of crises, with homelessness, mental health, and drugs, all out of control, and encampments found across cities and towns over the country.

It wasn't just homes that were in short supply, though. Access to affordable healthcare, and many times, healthcare full stop, reached critically low levels. It was that which inspired Nick and Gwen to create Access2Care, bringing a series of pop-up clinics in and around the worst affected parts of the city.

Nick, and Gwen, both ER surgeons, had been on the frontline too long. They'd proved a match made in heaven though when it came to raising the profile of these issues. Where politicians had failed to find resolutions, they'd found themselves frequently in the pair's cross hairs, bringing about temporary solutions. But only providing only a temporary fix for an arterial bleed, and tonight focused on raising enough funds to navigate through the remaining winter when their resources were crucially needed.

Access2Care needed tonight to be a success more than she did, and there was nothing Savannah would do to jeopardize that.

She grinned as Gwen swept away, strutting toward Nick with a determined tilt to her chin.

There was a reason Nick called her his own personal firebrand. They weren't your usual couple. In fact, there was no romance at all, early on there had, but they'd slipped into the friendzone, their friendship built on mutual respect and trust, and it clearly worked.

That friendship had continued to flourish beyond their university days, and into their careers.

Savannah smiled as she watched the petite brunette tap Nick on the shoulder, her side-eye unmistakable to anyone who knew her.

Yes, she could be fiery as all hell when required, but that was the perfect complement to Nick's easy-going personality.

Yes, Gwen would pull him into line, of that Savannah was certain.

But in truth, Nick wouldn't mess this up, either.

Success was vital.

Distracted by another celebrity couple, Savannah continued her perusal, and her stomach performed a series of nervous acrobatic flips. A fluttering dance, as her eyes roved over the growing glamorous assembly. The room now pulsated with a vibrant mix of celebrities, city officials, business executives, and the crème de la crème of local society, creating an atmosphere that promised to live up to expectations as the fundraiser of the year.

Actors and actresses mingled with pop stars and influencers, and new money seamlessly intertwined with New York's old societal elite.

She'd almost completed her sweep when she froze. Her own gaze catching that of a man at the far side of the bar. Something familiar about him causing her to start.

She frowned, unable to break the gaze, all too aware of his intense scrutiny.

Who was he?

She dipped her head, acknowledging him, studying him a little more.

Most men in the room maintained immaculate grooming, sporting short and styled hair, but this guy showcased a mass of dark curls tumbling down over his forehead. It provided him with a messy, boyish appearance, contrasting with the neat, trimmed beard.

His olive skin, almost Mediterranean-like, gave him the look of someone who worked in the sun—someone who might chase the waves on a beach rather than a city office. A stark contradiction to most of the attendees tonight.

For the briefest moment, it was as though the world disappeared. Even as the thought permeated her mind. As though the band disappeared as well.

The music faded; the voices gone. Just two strangers in this world of opulence.

He stood motionless, one hand gripping a half-filled frosted champagne flute. His other shrugged into the pocket of his suit pants. The effect, casual, his expression—anything but.

Her brow creased deeper, but that gaze held. And try as she might, she could do nothing to break the spell.

A confused smile tugged at her lips, her own frown deepening, and he returned his own—a light, boyish smile, his eyes twinkling. The air left her lungs in a rush, the air between them somehow suspended.

Dry mouthed, her tongue slid out, running across the length of her lower lip to moisten it. She repeated the action with her upper lip, then pursed them, her head cocked to one side, fascinated.

Blood thundered through her ears, her heart pounding against the inside of her ribs, and she rested her hand over it. As though in doing so, she might steady it.

The sensation was tantamount to a locomotive picking up speed, dangerously close to veering out of control.

He's gorgeous.

She froze, wondering from where the thought had come.

And the last complication you need in your life. Eyes off!

The thought was enough to draw her back to the present, the steady thrum of the guest's chatter, gentle jazz music pulling her back to the present.

She swallowed, surprised at the strength of emotion she'd experienced.

Still curiosity tugged at her, and she narrowed her eyes, watching as he glanced at his companion. His brow furrowed as he considered whatever his companion said.

He answered and nodded his head in affirmation before glancing back in her direction.

It was in that moment she glimpsed the companion.

She stilled, her breath hitched in her throat, and her brows furrowed further.

Clay?

No—it couldn't be. He was in New Zealand. Wasn't he?

Her gaze fixed on him, and when he glanced to his side, she gasped.

It is!

A rush of excitement blended with disbelief surged through her and propelled her toward him. Eyes shimmering with joy, the unexpected presence of her twin brother injecting a happiness into her that had been absent for too long.

She paused behind him and tapped his shoulder. Unable to contain her whoop of delight when he turned.

"How did you slip into the country without me knowing, you sneak?"

Chapter Two

MAC

MAC MACKENZIE saw her the moment she entered the room. The silver of her figure-hugging dress shimmered in the dim light of the bar, the gentle grey chiffon of the skirt accentuating curves that ought to be illegal.

For long seconds, he watched. An elegant sentinel, surveying the room with an air of watchful aloofness. Her blonde hair swept off her face and rolled into a tight chignon atop her head. The shimmering tiara affixed to the chignon adding a sense of enchantment, creating an aura of a modern-day Disney princess.

Mac swallowed hard, his heart pounding in his chest as he continued to watch, unable to tear his gaze away from the mesmerizing sight before him.

To describe her as stunning would be an understatement—she was drop dead gorgeous.

"We're aiming to have the Bora Bora resort open in time for mid-October," Clay's voice interjected, breaking Mac's trance. He glanced at his best friend and business partner, nodding as he continued. "A bit later than we'd wanted. Unfortunately, the pandemic put the brakes on us for a while."

A hush fell over the group as people nodded in understanding. The agreement on the challenges the pandemics brought, were universal. Yet, for Mac, the room seemed to have narrowed its focus, fixated on the captivating presence of the woman who stood in the open doorway.

"With Mac on board, we navigated a lot of the bureaucracy, which gathered the momentum."

Mac nodded, distracted.

There was nothing he ever enjoyed about these kinds of events. Over the years, he had witnessed more than enough ostentatious displays of wealth.

Every time, it felt nothing but a charade for those fortunate enough to possess wealth and was often an opportunity to assert their superiority of those less fortunate.

To Mac, it often seemed like the wealthy were just showing off, more concerned with stroking their egos than truly giving back. He saw their glamor as nothing but a mask, and he preferred to keep his distance from it all.

At home in New Zealand, his family had maintained their estate for more than one hundred and fifty years, with several other businesses across the country, so he was not new to city fundraisers. He'd attended many in Wellington and Auckland, a handful on South Island and several in Australia and other South Pacific regions.

But this New York experience took the concept to a whole new level, reinforcing how far he was from the comfort and small-town feel of home.

This was opulence like nothing he'd known.

The only reason he'd opted to attend tonight was because this was Clay's sister's event. Not to mention the perfect opportunity to network and promote the resorts. It was this kind of clientele they wanted to attract, whether he liked it, or not.

He took a sip of the ice-cold champagne. Enjoying the taste and smooth texture as he swallowed, his attention once again drawn to the blonde.

Engaged in conversation, she shared a moment with the petite brunette who Clay introduced earlier as Gwen, his brother Nick's best friend and work colleague, and the two driving the whole Access2Care organization tonight would raise funds for.

He observed the easy interaction with fascination. Their familiarity was clear, an ease that spoke of a shared history, and for the briefest moment, a sense of familiarity flickered.

As if he would recognize anyone here. He'd been in New York for twenty-four hours, and despite all the years he'd known Clay, he'd met Nick and JD, his brothers and Gwen. This trip would see him introduced to Clays, parents,

Gwen departed, leaving the blonde to navigate the room solo. Her fingers caressed the sparkling pendant at her throat, a solitary figure amid the elegant affair.

The moment her gaze met his, it was as though someone took a sledgehammer to him. Knocking him off kilter as he stilled, his breath somehow suspended.

It took everything in him not to let out a low whistle. The primal response so uncharacteristic, he wondered if it were his jetlag-addled mind.

For a long moment, he held her gaze, wondering who she was. Some socialite? Hollywood starlet? Who cared? He could not tear his gaze away.

She was—mesmerizing.

"Top of the line, luxurious retreat in the heart of a dark sky reserve—trust me, it doesn't get any better—hey Mac?"

Mac frowned, distracted.

"Sorry?" he asked, trying, and failing to sound interested in the conversation.

It was out of character, and he struggled to focus.

Clay repeated what he'd just said, and Mac grinned, turning his attention back to the conversation. "Most beautiful place in the world."

Clay was trying to involve him in the conversation, but in that moment, he couldn't have cared less.

He smiled at a young red head, her arm anchored around an elderly gentleman of perhaps, seventy. Silver thinning hair, and a wiry moustache that gave him the look of a retired military commander, although Mac recognized as a New York based entrepreneur and scientist.

"Oh darling, can you imagine, a Christmas in the Antipodes?" she purred. "We must book."

Clay laughed. "You'd better get in quick then, Monica!"

A flash of silver appeared in Mac's periphery, and he glanced up in time to see the dazzling blonde striding toward them. She paused behind Clay and tapped him on the shoulder.

Jealousy twisted in his gut.

The instantaneous pang taking him unawares as Clay turned to meet sapphire blue eyes. Eyes that were like... he glanced from one to the other and closed his eyes.

Disbelief coursed through him, followed by a ripple of disappointment.

He hadn't for one moment considered she may be the elusive Savannah. But when he opened his eyes to see Clay lift the smiling woman and swing her in an exuberant circle. It was impossible not to see the unbidden joy between the siblings.

He'd known she'd be here, and now, as he studied the two, it was impossible to ignore the similarities.

They shared the same deep blue eyes and pale skin. Their blonde hair and dimples appeared in their cheeks when they smiled. Even the lilt in their voice shared that same distinct tone that endeared Clay to Mac's family a decade earlier.

"I can't believe you're here." Savannah reached up to brush her fingers across Clay's cheek, as though to ensure he was real. The smile of delight still shimmering in her eyes.

"Mom said you were staying on in New Zealand for a few months." She scowled. "In fact, Mom said you were looking at making it a little more permanent."

Clay's chagrined expression confirmed those words, and Mac felt a pang of surprise. How on earth had Clay considered this without even discussing it with his twin?

"I figured it couldn't hurt to surprise you," he replied, adding in a whisper. "The rest we can talk about later. Tonight, you're the focus."

He gestured to the room, the pride in his voice clear. "This is amazing, Sav!"

Savannah's cheeks turned an endearing shade of pink, and she averted her eyes, the flicker of uncertainty clear.

"Ssshhhh," she whispered, glancing around. "Don't say that— the evening hasn't started yet! Knock on wood."

Clay laughed.

"I thought you grew out of that Ju-Ju stuff!"

He turned to Mac, who was watching the interaction with fascination.

"Mac, you finally get to meet Savannah," he grinned, gesturing from one to the other. "Savannah, meet Mac. Mac, meet my baby sister."

Savannah gasped.

"Excuse me!"

"It's true. I'm the older sibling," Clay continued.

"By fifteen minutes, be gone with you. That hardly makes a coffee break!"

"I seem to remember Mom arguing that logi... ouch!" he yelped, the twinkle of mischief in his eyes something seldom seen in public. "Still got the elbow huh!"

13

He rolled his eyes when she jabbed his upper arm, but she was no longer looking at her brother. Instead, her curious gaze now focused on Mac.

Mac extended his hand, his gaze locking onto those mesmerizing pools of shimmering blue. "It's great to put a name to the face," he said with a warm smile. As her hand met his, he felt the softness of her fingers wrapping around his, sending a sudden jolt of awareness surging through him like an electric shock.

The contact lingered, leaving an imprint that extended beyond the physical connection, creating a charged atmosphere between them.

Savannah withdrew her hand, the visible acknowledgement of the shared sensation undeniable as her eye widened, mirroring the startled expression of a doe caught in the glare of headlights.

She cleared her throat, closing her eyes as if attempting to regain composure.

Was it only him who'd noticed it? Clay appeared oblivious, and the rest of the party ignored the interaction.

"I need to get on. There's still so much to organize." She turned to Clay. "We'll catch up later," she declared. "Promise?"

With Clay's nod, she pivoted and glided away, leaving Mac in a state of shell shock, the aftermath of their brief encounter lingering in the air.

He watched as she walked away, pausing when another woman rushed toward her, clipboard in hand. The two women engaged in a rapid discussion before disappearing through a door at the other end of the room—but not before she'd cast one last glance his way, flickering from him to Clay and back again.

How many times had Clay talked of her?

He'd described the tom-boy sister who'd foregone her graduate studies, opting instead to support the husband who did not deserve her? To become the mother of twins and show every one of her family just how strong she was in the aftermath of a bitter divorce?

He turned his attention back to Clay, unable to deny the belief that this trip to the US had taken on a whole new meaning.

This was going to be a trip he'd never forget, for all the wrong reasons.

Chapter Three

SAVANNAH

"Wow, what a night," Felicity bubbled, two hours later.

Her best friend, and neighbor, was a steadfast presence in her life, supporting her not just through the divorce, but also during the subsequent weeks and months. Savannah, delving into her burgeoning event business, found Felicity invaluable, and as a result, she had brought her on board.

Savannah had long been aware that in doing so, it helped Felicity build her cupcake baking side hustle, without the strict hours of her previous position, and perhaps, this wouldn't be long term. Irrespective though, they'd become more like business partners, working side by side with their common goal. No sign of a hierarchy between the two.

Their friendship flourished, and Savannah's daughters always embraced her as an honorary aunt, the result of which had seen the planning of tonight's event turned into an unexpected joy.

As the first of the evening's auctions concluded, they stood side by side. Watching the room filled with laughter. Then once again, Savannah's gaze gravitated toward Mac.

The moment their eyes met; that spark of intrigue ignited once more. Heat tinged her cheeks and her hand rose, brushing one self-consciously. She smiled, the smallest smile, and an unexpected surge of awareness quickened her pulse.

Even with four male siblings, men were a puzzle to her. Charles, her ex-husband, was her only long-term partner, and her body's visceral response to Mac's gaze bewildered her. Her physical reaction to Charles had been nothing like this. It wasn't just a physical reaction, this drowned out all other sounds, leaving only the two of them in that moment, and the irrationality of it scared her.

No. It terrified her.

The man was a stranger, and yet, when he looked at her, it was as though she'd known him before.

She swallowed the golf ball sized lump in her throat, a feverish heat spreading through her. Mac shifted his focus back to the table, engaging with her siblings, and she observed him with fascination. His Kiwi lilt, genuine smile, and easy interaction with her family seemed as natural as though he'd been family forever.

It seemed absurd Clay and he had friends for so long, and yet they were only just meeting him. The fact he lived a world away answered it in short, but he'd been a part of family conversations for years, and it was as though they'd known him all along.

A wave of familiar sadness twisted in her stomach. It was a stark contrast to Charles, who never integrated into her family's close bond.

Resentment clouded her thoughts, and she scowled at Charles intruding into her mind.

There was a reason he'd never fit in.

And tonight, there was no time or space in her mind for him to occupy her thoughts—or ever, for that matter. He deserved no real estate in her mind.

Every time she allowed it, he won just that little bit more.

"Do I see five?" Pete Saunders, the celebrity auctioneer, called out.

"Yes, great. How about five-five?" he continued, his words tumbling out at a speed that left Savannah's mind spinning. "Oh, this is good. This is very good. Judge Anderson, it looks like you've got someone eager to enjoy your company. Do you think everyone knows you've got tight pockets?"

"Does anybody here know I'd give him away for free?" Mary Anderson, the judge's wife quipped. An attractive, silver-haired woman in her mid-sixties, she side-eyed her husband and the comment sparked raucous laughter throughout the room. "My goodness, if I'd known it was this easy, I'd have auctioned him off twenty years ago."

The judge scowled at his wife, but the twinkle of humor in his eyes was unmistakable as she squeezed his hand.

"Mary, we're trying to raise money for an exceptional cause, not give away freebies," Pete admonished. "C'mon now—play the game."

"Ah, well, if that's the case—six," she called, winking at her husband, and stroking his arm.

"Now you're getting it," Pete grinned. "Anyone got seven?"

"Ah, to heck with it, I'll go all in. Ten!" Mary called.

"Wow, guys. Looks like Judge Anderson lost control of the purse strings. Anyone going to better that?"

"Mary's going to outbid anyone who tries," somebody called out, causing another peel of laughter, and Pete brought the hammer down.

"Looks as though you get to take your husband home," he grinned. "Just make sure you get your money's worth, okay?"

Savannah gasped.

"Ten thousand. We just exceeded our target, with one more auction to go, right?"

They had divided the auctions into three. The first had been for the tangible donations they'd received, including a set of custom-engraved high-end golf clubs, accompanied by private lessons with Andrew Peterson, a renowned golf pro. An exotic car experience, including a weekend rental of a top-tier luxury car, complete with chauffeur. A unique custom designed piece of jewelry designed by a renowned New York jeweler, with a personal touch; and a series of gift baskets.

The second, intangible auction, including a series of VIP spa day. A personal stylist session, a private celebrity chef experience, including classes, and gourmet dinner for the winner and guest, and finally a fitness retreat at a luxury resort in Lake Tahoe. After those first lots were auctioned off, the evening took a hilarious turn, and it was that, which led to where they were now.

Felicity nodded, wide-eyed.

"There's still one more lot to go."

Savannah frowned, glancing at her run sheet, and scrutinizing it, as she tried to figure what she'd missed. "That was the last..." Her words trailed off as Pete took up the microphone again.

"And the last of this auctions lots—we're offering our gracious host and organizer, Savannah Devereaux."

Savannah's jaw dropped as all eyes turned her way, cringing at the attention.

This isn't happening.

He continued. "As you've seen from this evening, she's darned good at what she does. So, if you have an evening event, a party, or something that needs organizing—you're safe to say she's your go-to."

Her breath ramped up a notch, close to hyperventilating, and it took everything in her to keep any element of control.

She glared at Felicity, who smiled and shrugged wide-eyed. "Figured it would be a great way to promote the new business."

The words didn't compute straight away, and Savannah closed her eyes, forcing her breath to settle before glancing back at the stage. She'd coordinated most of the evening on the down low.

Nick and Gwen MC'd, with Pete overseeing the auction aspects, so she'd been able to focus on logistics. As a result, she'd remained invisible, but for occasional introductions. She'd wanted the evening to shine before pushing on to new projects. Now, with all attention upon her, she cringed in the limelight's glare, aware of the focus of everybody in the room.

This was the last thing she'd expected, and her nerves prickled, a sheen of sweat marring her brow. Years of constant criticism left her more than a little insecure, terrified of failure, the specter of imposter syndrome hounding her for weeks in the lead up.

As a result, she'd focused on working behind the scenes, putting the various players into place to ensure that would remain the case for the entire event. The degree of its success, though, had never been expected, and whilst they'd need the business, the last thing she wanted was to be the focal point, in any shape or form.

The hilarious turn the second auction took had added a series of unexpected lots, and she'd laughed alongside everyone else as they'd auctioned Senator Bradford off to his political opponent. He'd become a car valet for a neat twenty thousand dollars. Judge Saunders, a federal judge in the New York circuit would become a golf caddie for a day. The conditions, that he didn't play, or offer any of his anecdotal advice, for a neat nine thousand dollars.

Holly Matthews, a local socialite, and influencer would work as a housekeeper for billionaire Bill Affleck for a week, with the promise of no social media posts for a week. The fact she'd recently broadcast a series of podcasts on his business ethics would make for an interesting follow up.

Jeez, Bernie Johnston bought his own mistress for twenty thousand after going into an all-out bidding war with two partners from opposing law firms. On all counts, it had led to the single-most comical exchanges of the evening.

Putting herself into the bidding war wasn't.

Now, with the shoe on the other foot, Savannah's teeth clamped over her lower lip, her hand coming up to rub the back of her neck. She reached unconsciously for the necklace, fingering the sapphire as though it were a touchstone.   Oh, for the world to open and swallow her now.

This was her debut. She hoped to pick up a lot of business from it, but like this. This wasn't what she'd planned.

Savannah glanced back to her own table, her siblings aware of her discomfort, worry etched across each one of their faces, and then she met Mac's.

She'd only spoken a few times throughout the evening. Their interactions were anything but personal. But as she met his eyes, she realized there was no worry, only—her frown deepened—reassurance?

Her uncertainty eased, and she dipped her head, wondering just how a simple look could achieve that?

A gentle sense of confidence beginning to take hold.

There was no logic. There'd be time to dwell later.

She glanced back at Pete, ignoring the rest of the room, aware that if she did, she'd crumble.

"Stay strong." She murmured. "You've got this!"

Later, she'd have it out with Felicity. It was difficult enough to step onto the entrepreneurial stage in this city, let alone leave herself wide open to....

No, not now. This isn't the time, she chastised herself.

"Let's start with two, shall we?" Pete began, winking at her. She offered a nervous smile in response, her hands balling into fists at her side, every muscle taut. "We've all seen how good she is at this job. Do we have two?"

A hand raised.

"Two five?"

Another, in the far corner of the room. Savannah couldn't see whose.

"Yes, And three? C'mon, we can do better than this. You guys have how many soirees a month?"

"Four!" a female voice piped up, adding, "She'll rock the pink ribbon dinner."

Felicity grinned at Savannah. "See!" she hissed. "You'll have bookings until Christmas."

Even as she heard those words, a sense of unease prickled, and she fought not to hush Felicity. Something was wrong, but what?

"Ten," a voice interrupted from the back of the room, and that unease set in.

Her blood turned to ice in her veins. The hairs on the back of her neck on end at the familiar poison in that tone.

Charles?

Chapter Four

SAVANNAH

Savannah squinted, trying to make out where Charles was.

No. No. No.

Not now.

Not here.

Savannah's head whirled.

Where was he? How did she not notice him here tonight? He was not on the guest list. She'd have noticed.

Eleven months had passed since their divorce, but he'd spent those eleven months attempting to mess with either her or their daughters' lives.

Despite that, she'd held her head high, determined to move beyond the trauma of the past few years.

It hadn't been easy.

Dread knotted her gut, a flash of anger close on its heels, and she sat motionless, barely able to breathe. Uncertain of how to react.

A wave of nausea slammed into her, her earlier apprehension manifesting into something much worse, and it took everything not to bolt from the room.

No. No sign of weakness, she reiterated. Show him nothing, and he can't hurt you.

"Ten," Pete let out a shrill wolf-whistle and, in his finest Southern drawl, added. "Now that, sir, that's mighty generous. Any improvements…"

"Ten five," Savannah turned back to the table, grateful at the familiarity of Clay's voice, the icy edge unusual in her casual, fun-loving brother. She met his gaze, dipping her head in an almost imperceptible nod of thanks. Like any of the brothers would allow Charles to come out on top.

Keep it cool, Clay, she urged. The last thing she needed was a scene, although it was clear Charles felt differently.

"Eleven?" Pete yelled. "This is getting interesting."

"Twelve," Charles called.

"Twenty." Clay cut in.

"Twenty thousand dollars! Pheweee, we already hit the foundation's target, but looks as though we're going for doubles. Keep it going!"

Pete spoke fast, wrapped up in the developing drama.

"Always was good at squeezing every dollar out of a guy," Charles jeered.

The scraping of chair legs on the wooden parquet flooring echoed through the room seconds before it crashed to the floor, and Clay was on his feet, striding in Charles' direction.

Savannah's breath hitched, panic clawing at every inch of her, then a wave of relief followed as Mac's firm hand closed around her brother's upper arm.

What was he doing?

Clay glared back at him, scowling, when Mac muttered something.

His jaw set as he nodded.

Thank you, she murmured, resisting the urge to blow out a sigh of relief. Grateful for Mac's intervention, but Charles was not done.

"Twenty-five," Charles shouted, and Savannah squeezed her eyes closed. Her arms came around her torso, gripping her elbows, a vicious tremor rippling through her.

Damn you, she thought. She didn't verbalize it, that would only fuel Charles' game.

Dear God, why was this happening tonight of all nights?

It was her nightmare come true.

More than a few times in her life, she'd wanted the ground to open and swallow her, but right here, right now, she wanted the world to stop so she could get off.

"One hundred thousand dollars."

Savannah's heart stilled, her breath caught in her throat, homing in on the sound of the Kiwi accent now so familiar. Her eyes opened, her jaw dropping in an audible gasp, and for the second time in as many minutes, she gaped in Mac's direction.

She wasn't alone.

The stunned gasps that filled the room turned into a raft of incredulous chatter.

"One hundred thousand doll…" Pete's voice rose a pitch, his bark of laughter holding a hint of disbelief. "Did I hear right?"

"You did," Mac replied, meeting Savannah's wide-eyed gaze before looking daggers in Charles's direction. "And I'll double it if someone kicks the scumbag out."

A snicker sounded from behind, and Savannah turned in time to catch a young woman flush and hide her face. Too numb to respond.

Pete still reeling, croaked. "One hundred…." He shook his head. "You've got to have one helluva party planned, bud…"

"Damned right he will," Charles yelled. Savannah scrunched up her eyes, still unable to make out where Charles was. "With her on her back."

In an instant Mac moved across the room, Clay right beside him at the same time Charles stood, and for the first time, she saw him. Charles, the man she'd married, divorced, and now existed in her nightmares.

Charles pulled his chair in front of him, the defensive gesture a direct contradiction to his combative glare.

Coward.

Savannah rushed in their direction, barely considering the ramifications of her actions. She thrust herself in front of Mac, whispering with urgency. "Not tonight, please," she pled. "Don't rise to it. He's not worth it."

"Truth hurts, does it, Sav?" Charles goaded, in that far-too-familiar, supercilious, condescending tone he reserved just for her.

"You need to leave. Now."

The icy chill in her voice surprised even her. It might have been a stranger speaking, but for the glacial threads of anger running through her veins. The initial fear now replaced with unbidden fury. She did everything to appear calm. Nerves frazzled; it would be a cold day in hell before she'd give him any satisfaction in seeing how his antics affected her.

A deadly hush settled over the room. All eyes their way.

Charles sneered, his face transforming, as he returned her icy smile with sheer venom.

"I intend to, darling. It was hardly difficult to achieve what I needed."

Savannah's pulse thundered, blood roaring through her ears, and she stepped forward, jabbing a finger into Charles' chest.

"You bastard," she hissed, in as low growl.

Contempt flashed in her eyes. Anger permeating her with icy tendrils. How dare he. "You couldn't help yourself, could you? Couldn't even give me this?"

She waved an arm, gesturing at the room, giving Mac the opportunity he'd been waiting for, and he pushed past her, reaching for Charles.

Charles was too quick, shoving the chair forward with such force it crunched against Savannah's shins, and she let out a startled cry of pain.

He scurried back toward the door, tripping over his feet as he did, and grabbing for a chair to avoid falling. It proved just the distraction Mac needed, and she watched him close in and grab Charles by the scruff of the neck, dragging him to his feet and toward the door.

"Get your hands off me. There are witnesses. I'll sue you so bad the next three generations of your family will have nothing," he ground out, almost hysterically.

Mac tensed and muttered something Savannah couldn't hear. Whatever he'd said, though, Charles' shoulders slumped, but not before he glared over Mac's shoulder, sending Savannah a deadly glare that she recognized as a promise.

A small whimper escaped her before she could stop it, and the chill that followed froze her to the core.

No. This wasn't supposed to be happening. Not now. Not tonight.

As Mac shoved the door open, Charles sneered.

"Good luck on getting your money's worth. She might do enough for a hundred bucks. One hundred thous..." he waved his hand as a magician would with a magic trick. "Ppppffff, the slut saw you coming, you fool."

Chapter Five

MAC

In the elevator lobby, Mac maintained his hold on Charles for long enough to punch the down button, ignoring the writhing and stream of curses, as he tried to lay a punch on him.

His initial impression of the man was surprised.

Charles Carlisle was unassuming at first glance, with a slender build and a non-descript appearance that seemed more fitting for a library than a courtroom.

He stood around five nine, to Mac's six feet two, his mousey brown hair receding to reveal a wide forehead, and a pair of wire-rimmed glasses perched on his nose.

There was something else though, something that set Mac's teeth on edge, and it was nothing to do with what he'd done to Savannah, but everything to do with the smug sense of entitlement that oozed from every pore.

Or perhaps it was the flash of anger behind his eyes?

Either way, he looked nothing like Mac imagined.

He released his hold on Charles, grateful that Clay and JD stood before the swing doors to the bar. It didn't stop Charles' attempt to return, and Clay shoved him back. Mac, without thinking, twisted him into an armlock.

"I dare you," Clay growled in that same tone as Savannah. "Give me one reason. There aren't witnesses here, Carlisle."

The elevator door slid open, and Mac shoved Charles in, kicking his glasses to the back of the elevator when they fell off, giving him not opportunity to squirm free.

Seething anger gripped him.

He'd seen fear in Savannah's eyes.

Not just fear, terror.

In the same moment he'd rushed Charles, he'd fought the need to go to her, to ensure she was okay, needing to put as much distance between her and her ex as possible.

She wasn't okay. That was obvious. It wasn't just terror. He'd seen hurt, disbelief and anger too, grateful because the last expression had been anger. It made it a sight easier to drag Charles out of there and away, and to give her a chance to rescue the event. All evening she'd been the consummate professional, and it had been clear from that first moment, she was in control, and competent, with an underlying confidence rarely seen in a new business venture.

He frowned, wondering how he'd become so invested so fast. All evening he'd watched as she moved from table to table, talking with a warmth and understanding that was authentic, not forced.

And then...

Mac blinked, realizing the elevator doors were closed, and Clay pressed the button for the lobby. So close to Charles, the man squirmed.

"Not so sure now?" he jeered when Charles attempted to back up but was halted by Mac at his back. "Is this what you were like when you were married?"

Charles sneered.

"Like any of you gave a damn. You were quick enough to turn your back when she married me."

Clay froze.

"Turn our backs? Is that what you think we did?"

"Well, you didn't send any wedding cards or invites to the house. In fact, as I recall, you couldn't stay far enough away."

Clay swallowed, his pulse thumping at the side of his neck, and Mac glanced down to where his friends' fists balled at his sides. It took a lot to rile him. He was one of the single most balanced people he knew. But now, he understood the anger.

If one of his sisters faced this, Mac wasn't sure he would have been this civilized. He'd have likely dangled Charles off the bar roof until he swore, he'd never, ever come near her again. He stood back, allowing Clay to say what needed to be said. Home truths that were well overdue, and when he stopped, Charles shook himself free of Mac's grip. He stepped toward Clay, who stood towering over the smaller man.

"Don't try threatening me, Carlisle," he warned, his voice dripping the same venom Savannah had only moments earlier. He used Charles' last name with the same condescending tone that he'd used when speaking to his ex-wife. "I have far more resources than you'll ever have, and I'll make damned sure you never work in this city again—let alone run for office."

Charles's eyes widened.

He lunged forward, but not before Mac caught his arm and shoved him against the elevator wall, pinning him by the throat as he stared into wide grey eyes, the fear emanating from him, palpable.

"No," he spoke with a deadly calm, holding Charles' scathing gaze.

"You don't get to throw your weight around—got it?"

In that moment, though, Charles' eyes widened, his brows knitting into a deep frown.

His head tilted to one side.

"You her latest conquest?"

He writhed, attempting to get clear of Mac's grip, but Mac gripped tighter.

"I'm nobody's conquest," Mac snarled, white hot fury taking hold.

Until now, he'd acted as a barrier and a defender. Now, though, anger overwhelmed him as the knowledge of just how this one insignificant person affected Clay's family—in just the way Carla's had his own.

It was wrong. On so many levels. Not just regarding Savannah, but in the way he'd created such a clear divide between a family united.

How could he treat the woman he'd married, born children with, and spent a life with, with such malice?

He glared at Charles; his lip curled with contempt. "But I promise you something, mate." He emphasized the word. Mac eye-balled the man. "I just became your worst nightmare."

The more Charles writhed, the tighter Mac gripped, and he kicked out at Mac's shin.

Mac side-stepped. "Give it your best shot, Chuckles," he sneered, so close to Charles' face he smelled the stale scent of alcohol mingled with tobacco. "Although, come to think of it—I'm not your type, am I."

The other man frowned, confused, and Mac continued.

"You go for defenseless women who won't hit back—is that right?"

This time Charles roared, red-faced with rage, and in the same moment the elevator pinged, arrived at the ground floor. The doors slid open a second later, and Mac propelled him into the lobby and toward the front doors.

"Not just defenseless either, aye? You get yourself all tanked up and then go for it—too cowardly to even say what you mean sober—is that right?"

He talked as he moved, Clay flanking him as security guards, briefed on what happened, opened the front doors.

He'd seen the security team move in upstairs, but Clay held them off, determined to deal with the unfolding issue, and Mac understood why. He'd wanted the family to deal with this.

By the looks of it, it was long overdue, but they'd make up time. He felt their eyes had been opened wide this evening, and he prayed Savannah would out of her ex's toxic reach at last. It was clear more was happening beyond what the family saw, or possibly knew.

Even as he thought it, pain arced through him, the familiar ache, one he'd known to long.

He knew instinctively that this was the way things had panned out for his cousin and look how that ended.

He closed his eyes, as though shutting out the flood of memories, forcing himself to focus.

He couldn't change the past, but he'd sure as hell deal with the now.

Until now, it was clear she'd played her cards close to her chest.

Mac shoved Charles out of the front door and onto the sidewalk.

At the same moment, a yellow cab pulled up, and Clay spoke to the driver, offering him a folded wad of cash, then opened the rear door.

"You need to get out of here while you can still walk," he growled, his eyes black with rage. "That was a nice try, but you knew it would be impossible to tear Savannah down. All you achieved tonight was to reinforce the opinions of everyone here that you are a sociopathic narcissist, with a vile capacity to undermine those around you."

He manhandled Charles into the car at the same moment as a camera flashed, and Clay muttered a colorful curse. Something else

Savannah wouldn't need, but it was too late to worry about it now. They'd deal later.

"Be glad we put you in a cab and didn't throw you into the gutter where you belong." Clay snarled as he slammed the cab door closed and dusted off his hand, turning to glare at the paparazzi photographer, whose camera continued to snap.

Mac left him moments clearing up that mess, as he turned to find Nick and JD, arms crossed, leaning against the wall with smug expressions, a stark contrast to the anger he'd seen before.

"Well, he handled that well, aye Nick," JD grinned. "We came down thinking you'd need help."

"Mmmm," Nick replied with raised brows. "Almost too well..." he side-eyed JD, raising his brows as he added. "I reckon he'll do."

Mac didn't bother asking for an explanation, heading for the elevators and back upstairs, some protective streak driving him back to make sure she was okay. Or as okay as it was possible to be under the circumstances.

For reasons he did not understand, he had invested in Savannah Devereaux's happiness, even after this small amount of time. How she'd feel, he had no clue. But on the most primal level, he knew that if he was near, and as long as he breathed, Charles Carlisle would never pull a stunt like that again—ever.

Chapter Six

SAVANNAH

Savannah city beyond with unseeing eyes.

Mortification and anger rendered her speechless, and she'd left the room with all eyes on her, needing space to compose her shell-shocked soul.

Even now, twenty minutes later, her entire body shook, and she tilted her head back, allowing a guttural moan to escape.

The professional in her hadn't allowed her to leave the building, although the thought of disappearing appealed right now.

Timbuktu wouldn't be far enough, though.

She leaned against the railing, eyes closed, the dull throb of a headache thumping at her temple.

"You, okay?"

She froze at the sound of his voice.

"Fine," she snapped, regretting the impulsive response.

He was not to blame for Charles' theatrics.

"Anyone would understand if you weren't. That was unforgivable."

"Thanks."

He joined her, both gazing out over the city.

"He's gone I take it?"

Mac nodded. It had been hard not to see what happened on the sidewalk below. Just five floors up, it was amazing how sound carried, and the paparazzi had been the icing on the cake.

"I don't understand why he can't just move on," Savannah said, in a hushed whisper.

"You're better off away from him, that's for certain."

A small, humorless laugh escaped Savannah. "You reckon?"

"Anyone who could pull a stunt like that? Especially at a charity event planned by someone he claimed to have loved. Is at the very least unhinged, and at worst, a nasty piece of work." Mac replied.

"That's a lot politer than I would have put it," a bitter chuckle ripped through Savannah. "I'd call him a lowlife, sociopathic, narcissistic pig, who finds pleasure in destroying other people's lives — but then, I've known that a long time."

"That works," Mac replied. "Is it better?"

"What?"

"Calling him out for what he is?"

"Not really." Savannah laughed, grateful for the momentary light relief. "But it's the best I've got, and oh boy, it's long overdue."

Mac didn't respond straight away, and she waited for him to speak again. The gentle lilt of his accent already soothed her frazzled nerves, and she studied him.

"You didn't have to..." she started, staring up at a chopper hovering above the skyline, before glancing down to where her hands gripped the railing. "Do that."

"Do what?"

"Step in like that—I'm not some helpless damsel in distress. I can look after myself."

Mac's breath stilled in his throat, and she turned to face him. There was no fight in her eyes, a strange sense of calm transcending so that she was eerily at peace.

"Is that what you thought that was?"

When Savannah first saw him earlier, it was impossible not to note how he stood out from the crowd. The mass of unkempt curls. That from the moment she'd met him, he fought the urge to reach out and tangle her hands through them.

Such a contrast to the neat, groomed beard, and perhaps reflected his personality?

She frowned.

Unsure of where that thought came.

"I think his performance was more than just vindictive," Mac interrupted her thoughts, and she blinked. "I think he's more concerned about you being a success. By the sounds of it, he kept you in his shadow for a long time—besides, I'd say you gave as good as you got. It took balls to come back at him like that. Not to mention..."

He glanced behind him, gesturing to the bar inside.

"Few people could pull off a gala on this scale as their debut. Especially in a city like this." He waited for a response, and when one didn't come, said, "That takes courage—and bucket loads of confidence."

Savannah lifted her chin, eying Mac, surprised at the ripple of pride that gripped her with his appraisal.

"Thanks." Her cheeks reddened, despite the pride, and she glanced at him with more than a little self-consciousness.

"It's not a gratuitous compliment, Savannah," he said. "I mean it. Take this as a victory. If he lashed out in such a public way, he's threatened right now."

Savannah let those words sink in. It seemed there wasn't a week to pass by without Charles stirring up trouble, but what he'd done tonight took it to a whole new level. When they married, she took on every role: wife, homemaker, hostess, and personal assistant. Her life planned from the moment she woke in the morning, until the moment she collapsed, exhausted, into bed each night.

With their daughters, those roles expanded, to include mom, taxi driver, frequent nurse, and cheerleader. Somewhere, amid the chaos, she'd lost sight of her own identity.

It wasn't until after their girls that the fractures in their relationship became apparent. But it took a notorious #MeToo court case, involving a famous Hollywood agent, to widen the chasm between them into an unbridgeable gulf.

The revelation of his affair with a young intern from his office landing the final blow and sealing the fate for their marriage— divorce inevitable in the aftermath.

She frowned at the path her thoughts took, and eyed Mac with curious eyes.

"I want to believe that" she replied, wondering why she was discussing this with him.

He was a stranger. Except, it didn't feel that way. He wasn't a stranger. She was aware of that on the most primal level from that first moment. And while a part of her wanted to run for the hills, another part of her wanted to learn everything about him. Which may well be absurd, but for the fact, on an instinctual level, she trusted him.

She trusted her brothers and knew from a lifetime of experience that they'd all chosen friends with care. It was only she who'd missed out on the trait. Clay and Mac were friends for years. That spoke volumes.

She eyed Mac, thoughtfully.

"Every time he pulls a stunt like this, I find myself back at square one. The anger takes hold like ..." She waved her hand, a gesture of futility. "It's like an all-encompassing poison that filters through my veins ... toxic. Not healthy!"

"Then you're letting him win."

His words were blunt, and she blinked, aware of their truth, but in that same breath resenting the ease of his appraisal. She answered, though.

"'I know ... I want to move on—start living again." She gestured toward the door, desperation in her tone. "That's what this is—I needed to find myself. Not only for me, but for Jess and Chloe."

Her daughters were her life, and oh, she missed them.

After much argument, she'd consented to them spending the Fall break with her parents in Sweetheart Falls, and they'd left just two days earlier.

The next two weeks would drag.

The thought of being away from them for that long was an anathema. After much begging, and promises that they'd call every evening, though, Savannah realized that the break would afford her the much-needed time and space for this event.

Their daily phone calls reassured her it was the right decision.

The small town, home of her family for over two hundred years, had a way of working right into the soul. She wanted them both to experience that small town life over the chaos that was New York.

At least, that's how she justified it to herself.

Still, being apart gnawed at her. She'd loved being a full-time mom, even in the darkest depths of her marriage.

"Is it working?"

She blinked, realizing she'd been so deep in contemplation she'd lost track of their conversation.

"Sorry?"

"The finding yourself?"

It seemed an absurd question from a stranger, and she tilted her head to one side, observing Mac.

"How do you do that?" she asked, returning question to question.

"What?"

"You just seem to…" her words trailed off, and she turned toward the city, uncertain about continuing this line of conversation. It was as though he was inside her head, understanding her thoughts processes, pre-empting the very questions she was asking herself. As though he knew her as well as she did herself, except that was impossible.

Mac, however, wasn't ready to let it go. He placed a hand on her shoulder, and she jerked back in surprise. The jolt of awareness, not for the first time this evening, stealing her breath.

"I… I'm sorry," Mac began.

She shook her head, unable to find words. That unexpected surge of attraction heightened.

Her nerves frayed, the adrenalin rush from the evening's success erased by Charles' stunt. Yet, standing beside Mac, she sensed he would never treat her, or any woman, the way Charles did.

You don't know the guy, Savannah. Your behavior is irrational.

It made no difference, though.

In that moment, whatever unfolded seemed more primal than any experience she'd ever encountered before.

It's chemistry, a voice whispered in her mind.

But, right then, she yearned for something more—a desire to be held, to be respected. To be loved.

Even if it was just for a fleeting moment, she craved someone to embrace her, providing emotional support. The weight of loneliness lingered for far too long. It couldn't hurt. Could it?

Instinct told her she Mac had the potential to be the person to take her through, and beyond.

In the same breath, though — it was the last thing she needed to — wasn't it?

She swallowed, flicked her tongue out to moisten dry lips. As if on autopilot she reached out, lifting a hand to brush away the errant curl that fell across his forehead, never for a moment losing his gaze.

She inhaled the already-familiar scent of his cologne, spice with a hint of sandalwood, filling her senses, and she stepped a little closer. So close, she saw the crow's feet at the corners of his eyes, noticing for the first time the little flecks of gold in those warm green eyes.

Mac's hand closed around her wrist, stopping her mid-movement. The blazing heat in his eyes was so hot that for a moment she wanted to run—fast. Only, she couldn't have if she tried. She wanted what came next.

"Sor ..." she started, but said no more, her words stolen as his warm, soft mouth closed over hers.

Savannah moaned, attempting to shake her wrist free. Any hint of common sense gone as she melted against him, the strong rhythmic beat of his heart, resonating against her palm when she rested it against his chest.

Mac's hand came to her cheek, but then he hesitated, pulling back, chilling her where before there'd been warmth. He hissed through clenched teeth.

"I'm sorry. That was ..."

She wasn't ready to give up on this.

Not yet.

Aroused in ways she hadn't been for way too long, not to mention grateful for the distraction, she reached out.

"No. Not sorry."

She wanted more. For whatever baffling, irrational reason it was, she needed more.

"Kiss me," she urged.

Mac didn't need asking again. His lips claimed hers in a kiss that was slower this time.

Tender and restrained.

Searching.

"SAV!"

Clay's urgent voice shattered the moment, and Savannah stepped back. Hesitant, her gaze still starry-eyed, her thoughts in disarray, she cleared her throat.

"Here!" she called, hoping that her twin wouldn't notice the dazed state she found herself in.

Her trembling fingers brushed over her lips, now swollen and sensitive. The glazed look in her eyes spoke of a storm within, and she closed them, taking a deep, steadying breath.

Mac lifted his hand to rub across the spot on her lips that she'd touched seconds earlier, and Savannah gasped. The electric current of awareness surged through her.

She'd heard of chemistry before, but this experience was a whole new level.

"You're good, princess, don't worry. We'll talk about this later," Mac reassured her at the same moment Clay rounded the corner.

"There you are. We were worried sick." Clay studied Savannah's face, then smiled. "He's gone—and he won't be back."

"Clay, you didn't..." Savannah's words trailed off, a mix of confusion and concern in her eyes.

"Use violence? Not us, no. Cowardly, little shit picks on women, but put a man—or three—in front of him and he doesn't like it one bit." Savannah grimaced as Clay grinned at Mac. "No, correct that. One furious, Kiwi, and he near as peed in his pants."

Mac snickered, but Savannah shook her head.

"The last thing I need is him causing trouble for you—or" she glanced up at Mac, wide-eyed. "You. It's why I haven't involved you all. You go all macho, like I'm the annoying little sister who needs protecting or rescuing every time."

"How did you get on with that?" Clay shot back with characteristic speed.

Not about to let him get the last word, she retorted.

"I divorced him."

She didn't expect the roar of laughter that exploded from Clay, nor when he put his hands up, the gesture of surrender that followed.

"Okay, okay. We'll discuss this later," he said, adding, "Right now, you have a party to see through, and a business to salvage."

He scrutinized her expression.

"Show them what Savannah Devereaux can do under pressure. Then we all head back to my place for a Devereaux-debrief and a few drinks—yes?"

She smiled then, realizing that her twin brother had just done what he always did. His capacity to calm her, something he'd spent their life doing—at least until she'd been married.

Her brain may be frazzled from the events of the evening, not to mention the hot-as-hell Kiwi stood beside them. But Clay achieved the impossible, as always.

"I love you, brother," she grinned, raising her fist, and he bumped it with his own.

"That's the girl."

She headed back inside, catching his wink, her head still spinning from Mac's kiss. Despite the whirlwind of emotions, she was determined to rock the rest of this evening. Reflections were for later. For now, she'd finished this night on a high.

It would be a snowy day in hell before she allowed Charles Carlisle to have any influence on her life again. Let alone their kids. Tomorrow would begin with a police report for the breach of his injunction. After that, she and the girls would move on. She'd make sure none of them ever looked back. Never would Savannah or her girls ever be his, or anyone's victim again.

Chapter Seven

MAC

"How in the hell did I stop myself from doing violence?" Clay asked as Savannah left them to return to the bar.

"No idea. He's a bigger S.O.B. than you reckoned."

Clay shook his head, moving to the railing where Savannah had stood moments earlier, and glanced out over the city, wondering how the scent of her fragrance still lingered, a sensuous reminder of where she'd been.

"That crossed my mind too," he grimaced. "You know, we all had concerns, but what I saw tonight, I can't help but wonder if there was more."

Mac turned to face him.

"In what way?" He'd considered the same, so to hear his friend vocalize it reignited the anger once again.

In his mind, he kept reliving the moment his lips met Savannah's, the way her cheeks flushed with heat, eyes hazed, and in the next breath, he'd find himself transported back to that look of desolation that came prior, the mixture of hurt, confusion, and disbelief.

And with the memory, the protectiveness slammed back into place.

He forced himself to focus, jaw taut, as he stared straight at Clay. He had a sneaky suspicion where this went.

"I mean, we're a close family. Have always been that way. He gaslit her, made her believe she was no longer a part of the family. We lost count of how many times we tried to get through to her. But there was something else today. Ruthless. Like…"

His words trailed off, but Mac didn't let them remain unspoken.

"You mean that you're concerned this escalated tonight? Or that he's hit her before?"

Clay didn't answer right away, processing the thoughts, but Mac felt the tension in his friend.

"Perhaps both? Alarm bells are screaming. The fact he did this. And in an arena that included his peers. It doesn't sit right.

Mac nodded. Yes, that was where his own thoughts went.

There'd been so much malice in Charles' behavior, and he'd seen Savannah flinch, the terror in her eyes when Charles glared at her, as though she'd expected him to…

Mac shook his head. Why would he?

There were judges, lawyers, advocates, and more than a few of Charles's own clients present tonight, so he'd taken a massive risk generating such a scene. Add into that the negative publicity during the #MeToo case, his reputation tarnished.

This—this would be enough to destroy his career—so why?

He frowned.

There was no doubt this was a factor that didn't sit right, but in the same breath, it was one that needed to be considered, if only to keep Savannah—and her girls—safe.

The door opened, and Felicity peered around.

"Hey, Savannah asked if you guys can come help," she smiled. "We're pulling the last auction forward, see if we can't get this night over with no more high drama."

"All good. We'll be right..." he frowned and glanced at Mac and then back at Felicity. "Hey, Flick," he referred to her with the name the family used for her. "How's Charles been with Savannah?"

Felicity froze. Her gaze darted from Clay to Mac and back again. "I... I uh..." she glanced behind as though to make sure she was alone. "Clay, I can't..."

"After tonight, you can."

Clay opened the door and gestured for her to come through. Closing it behind her.

"What he did tonight was out of character, or so we believed—but something doesn't sit."

Felicity nodded, and Mac saw the flicker of her eyes.

"This isn't an interrogation," Clay added. "We just want to figure how we deal with what comes next."

"Next?" Felicity winced, glancing behind. "Savannah wants to deal with it. She..." she glanced behind, checking the door once more. "She took out an injunction—he's been a nuisance for months, but she's determined..." Her words came out in a tumble, and instinct told Mac that she hated speaking without Savannah's consent. In the same breath, though, the danger Charles posed was real.

Mac had seen it with his cousin... He froze... Slamming his eyes shut as the memory of Carla played over in his mind. The wreck of the once beautiful twenty-five-year-old battered to within an inch of her life. The tubes, the bleeps of the hospital machines, the flat line when they'd switched off life support a month later.

To this day, he heard the tears of her two toddlers as they called for their mama and the gavel slam down when the judge sentenced her estranged husband to twenty-five years.

It hadn't been enough. Twenty-five years for a life taken. One year for each of her life—a bargain for the ex. There'd been no justice that day.

Was this what it had been like for Carla?

Could Charles pose the same threat to Savannah?

The temperature seemed to drop by ten degrees.

Felicity glanced between them. "Look, she's my best friend. I don't like what happened any more than you do. And I do my best to be there when he's around—there's a reason I still have the apartment opposite you realize. After my parents..." Her expression flickered. "After my parents died, I saved enough to leave New York, set up somewhere else," a bitter laugh ripped from her, and she took a deep breath, as though clearing her mind before speaking again. "But I couldn't leave Savannah or the girls. Not while he's still around. I won't."

She glanced down at her hands, intertwining her fingers, nervous. "He's not been violent. He's just..." she shrugged, glancing up at Clay. "He's awful—doesn't turn up for the days he's supposed to visit with the girls, make nuisance calls, spreads vicious rumors, withheld alimony," a bitter laugh exploded from her. "Saw several events bookings cancelled before tonight because of his calls, and..."

Her words drifted off, and this time Clay cut in.

"What? Tell me, I can't do anything if I go in blind."

"A few weeks ago, he started sending threatening texts and emails. He turns up outside the girls' school and sits outside the apartment at all hours. That's when she got the injunction." Felicity finished.

Clay let out an audible exhale, throwing his head backward to gaze up at the sky, shaking it with disbelief. For Mac, Felicity's words came like a full blow to the solar plexus, knocking the wind right out of him. He'd looked into those beautiful blue eyes and seen Savannah's fear, but she'd assuaged his worry with the sheer resolve she'd shown. That this had been going on for months...

Felicity interrupted his train of thought.

"I need to go back in. I've said too much. And you...she needs us all on board. This discussion needs to happen later, okay?"

Felicity glanced between Clay and Mac, eliciting a nod out of them both, and then walked back through the doors from which she'd come. Mac waited until the door closed before he spoke again.

"Did you have an inkling how bad it was?" he asked, aware of what the answer would be.

"No," Clay replied. "Had I, the son of a bitch, I'd have buried him years ago."

It was rare to hear Clay's voice drop to the chill it did, and Mac eyed his friend with worried eyes.

"Do the family?"

"Christ no, if there was any inkling, I'd have said something. This has escalated, I'm sure of it."

The two fell silent for long moments, playing over just what had happened before Mac spoke again.

"I've known you ten years," he said, clapping Clay on the shoulder. "How did we go so long without my meeting your family?"

Clay snorted.

"Geography?" he blew out a breath of frustration. "Why didn't she reach out?"

Mac didn't answer, letting the question play through his mind. It was obvious why, but he understood why it needed to be pointed out.

"She's like you," Mac continued, shaking his head. "She's your damned twin in every sense of the word. You'd do the same—take on the world, try to show how tough you are. Deal with everything yourself..."

"I know, but I wish..." Clay didn't finish, instead, looking out on the city.

"You realize, if you're going to help, you're going to need to be mindful that you're going to piss her off?"

Clay laughed then. "You realize we've been doing that to each other our entire life right?"

He sobered, his hands flat on the railings, his entire posture rigid, and Mac reined the anger back as he said.

"I need to talk to her. Figure out where her head is at. If I can do that, there may be a way she'll let us step in and help. I don't want to do it behind her back. But I will if I must."

Mac and Clay re-entered the bar some fifteen minutes later, and Mac's attention drew straight back to Savannah. For the first time in his life, he understood the concept of moth to a flame in humanistic terms. There was something about her, a beacon-like quality that called to him, and for whatever reason it was, he could not shut it off.

In that moment, she glanced his way, her smile shy, and the sensual way in which she dipped her head, almost side-eying him, created an inexplicable wave of something that slammed into him, stealing his breath.

Did she know just how sexy she was?

He winked in response, ignoring the wail of alarm bells in his mind, and made his way back to the table, frowning at a handful of furtive glances from her siblings.

He wanted to ask why but didn't.

Instead, reaching for a glass of water and necking it.

There were too many unspoken feelings at this table right now. There'd be time for discussions later.

For the rest of the evening, Mac observed Savannah revert to the professional and aloof persona he witnessed earlier. Effortlessly, she moved from table to table, engaging in laughter provoked by comments along the way. Yet, now, and then, when no one was watching, a subtle falter would occur.

A flicker of fear and uncertainty would resurface, rendering her much younger than her actual age. Then, with a swift blink and a straightening of her spine, she would switch back to her dazzling smile, resuming her role.

When the call for the last dance resonated through the room, Mac acted on instinct, taking her hand, and guiding her to the dance floor. Once there, he cradled her in his arms, a deep sigh escaping him as she rested her head on his shoulder, finding solace in the embrace.

"Thank you," her whispered words were barely audible, almost as if they were a figment of his imagination. "That was one blinding night."

Mac chuckled, the low sound blending with the fading music. "It sure was. But you nailed it."

There was a pause before she responded, and Mac held his breath, awaiting her next words. "I'll pay far more attention to the guest list next time—not to mention security."

"Oh, I reckon your ex showed his true colors in front of many people he shouldn't have."

"Which will rile him more."

Mac stopped, drawing back to hold her at arm's length as he studied her face. "You're serious?"

She shrugged, a nonchalant gesture that belied the weight of the situation. "We did more than hit target tonight—we've smashed it. You and my brothers made a fool of him in front of a lot of well-respected faces. He'll..."

Mac raised a finger, brushing it over her lips. She didn't flinch but furrowed her brow in bemusement.

"And tomorrow, he'll be looking like the biggest idiot in the city, just you watch. Tell me, would you want a lawyer who treated family the way he did you today? If you were a judge overseeing a case that saw him protect somebody who behaved the way he did, would you give him any serious consideration? Jeez, Clay said he'd considered running for office—can you imagine anyone taking a candidate who behaved like that?"

He shook his head, his expression solemn. "You need to get this guy out of yours and your babies' lives once and for all. And I'm not saying that from a controlling perspective. I'm saying that as someone who knows how much your family worries and cares about you. If he's prepared to do this, what comes next?"

Even as he said it, Mac couldn't shake the conviction that Clay was right. She needed to be free of Charles. She needed that carefree confidence to shine, and for the uncertainty and doubt to be erased from her life.

They danced once more until the music faded away, and Mac watched her step into the next phase of the evening, shaking hands, waving goodbye, engaging with potential clients, and navigating the extensive clean up.

Mac watched; an unavoidable respect grew for the woman who stole his breath. The frustrating part, however, was that he never wished to witness that fear or uncertainty in her eyes. He craved the smile, the confidence, and the passion-filled heat he glimpsed, rational or not.

Chapter Eight

SAVANNAH

Only a few blocks from the venue, in the heart of Manhattan, nestled amidst the expanse of Central Park West, the Dakota Building exuded an aura of refined luxury and old-world charm, with sweeping views of the iconic park and its lush greenery.

Clay's New York base was far from what most would expect of the self-made billionaire. Its elegant façade, adorned with intricate architecture, only hinted at the opulence within. For those who knew Clay, though, they understood just what it meant to have his home there.

Savannah smiled as she stepped into the lobby at a little after midnight, inhaling the rich scent of the polished wood, the soft glow of antique lamps giving it a sense of welcome and homeliness.

Every muscle ached, a slight post-party gloom hanging over her as she realized all the planning was now over. Not to mention the ramifications of Charles theatrics.

Yes, there would be ends to tie, bills to pay, calls to make, but the lead up to the Gala she and Felicity had worked at a frenetic pace, ensuring every I was dotted, every T crossed, and firefighting where issues arose.

Now, she realized, for the next two weeks she'd be alone to fall back into some semblance of normality. With the girls away, life would be lonely.

Earlier, she'd planned on returning to her Brooklyn apartment, but the prospect of her siblings all being in one place, after the highs of the evening, despite Charles' antics, she wanted to let her hair down and celebrate. And there was no-one she'd rather do it with than them.

Not to mention the fact the tousled-haired stranger with the intense eyes and sexy-as-all-hell smile would be there, and she was looking forward to getting to know him better.

Savannah had no idea of what it was about him, why she seemed to react to him the way she did, or why she'd thrown herself at him the way she had—but there were no regrets, and that went against every one of her core beliefs.

She let herself into the apartment with the key Clay gave her. The same one she used from time to time to check in and make sure all was well. His housekeeper did a great job, so it was unnecessary, but it kept her finger on the pulse, and helped her feel she was still a part of Clay's life, even when he was travelling.

Like outside, the interior exuded elegance, and while Clay added some of his own touches, the apartment maintained the same elegant sophistication as when he'd purchased it five years earlier. Intricate moldings adorned the ceilings, heavy velvet curtains hiding the large windows over-looking the park, and an opulent ivory rug on which the furniture was placed protecting the rich hardwood floor.

She stepped into the doorway, and leaned against the hardwood frame, smiling as she observed her siblings as they laughed and talked, as though they'd barely been apart more than a week or two.

That was the case with JD and Gray.

They still lived in Sweetheart Falls not a kilometer between their homes, but the others... Nick lived here in New York with Gwen, and Clay... well.

She blinked, dismissing the thought before it took hold. Even now, the thought of her twin living on the opposite side of the world permanently stung, but she wouldn't admit it. He was a grown adult with a life to live, not to mention a multi-million-dollar empire relying on him for leadership.

A small chuckle resonated inside as she realized how bizarre that was. In her eyes, he'd always be the pain in the ass brother she loved so much. That he'd built such a massive, successful organization was mind-blowing.

She focused back on the group, listening to them now. She loved the banter, the reminiscing, the chatter about tonight—this was what family was about—and oh, she'd missed it. During her marriage, Charles had done everything to keep her away from her siblings, and Sweetheart Falls, but she'd resisted at one time of year, and that was Christmas.

The saving grace that had kept her connected with her siblings, despite everything. She'd still struggled to relax though, Charles gaslighting keeping her just separate enough that she'd return home with him after.

If she had have only seen that then.

The pandemic had changed things, though. For the siblings unable to return to Sweetheart Falls, they'd remained close, but Clay, he'd wound up in lockdown in New Zealand, and opted to see the pandemic out there.

As a result, last year was the first year since... she winced, as the name played through her mind... Paul, that they'd been one short for the holidays.

The memory of the brother they'd lost remained strong. The pain had lessened with the passage of time, but not having him at Christmas, and other celebrations, never failed to bring memories of what life would be like had he still been with them.

A classic clown, she had the impression they'd all have been rolling around with laughter at his antics this evening.

She closed her eyes, sending a quiet message heavenward. "I know, I know, you're still with us, Pauly," she whispered. "Never forgotten."

She smiled softly, her gaze now shifting to Mac.

He oozed charisma, sharing the same playful spirit as her brothers. Not a clown like Paul, or but witty, with an additional quality, something deep, and she sensed this was the reason behind his close friendship with Clay. They were so alike, it was kind of scary, if she didn't know her brother so well.

She closed her eyes, allowing the memory of Mac's kiss to re-play, the rush of heat she'd experienced reigniting in a rush, the warmth seeping through her veins at a slow crawl creating a tingling in its wake. and, almost instantaneously, a slow burn lit. A burn that she knew had the capacity to become incendiary with his touch.

How had a simple kiss stirred such desire?

She brought her hand to her cheeks, acutely aware of the flush, her fingers gently brushing the line of her cheekbone, her mind anywhere but her with her family. Her thoughts inexplicably focused on a man she barely knew. The prospect of an encore a certainty.

Mac had remained close to her for the duration of the Gala, watchful, ready to step in when appropriate, and she'd been grateful.

Tongues wagged. The gossip-mill in full form. But he'd helped her dodge the questions.

He'd invited her to dance in the closing hour of the evening, and without a thought, she'd accepted. She stepped into his arms and swayed to the crooning voice of Chris de Burgh; aware the gossip-mill would give Charles more ammunition.

By then, though, she didn't care.

Get a grip. You don't know him.

She opened her eyes, glancing in his direction, meeting that warm green gaze, the instant shock of awareness rippling through her, and she shivered not from cold, but from an inherent sense of anticipation.

If a look had that effect, what would...

She blinked, and shook her head, attempting to shake the thought from her mind, and tore her gaze away, letting it settle on Felicity at the far side of the room.

The last thing she needed was to be hung up on a man— particularly Mac. It wasn't as though he had a life here or any investment.

A relationship would be impossible.

But—she frowned, her gaze flicking back to him. Nick asked a question, drawing his attention away, and she watched, fascinated by the play of emotions across his face, at the ease with which Mac had struck up a conversation with her older sibling.

Why would there even need to be a relationship?

She was single. Mac too. A little fun between consenting adults couldn't hurt—could it?

He laughed at that moment, throwing his head back with a hearty chuckle, and her stomach clenched, her heart giving the slightest flip at the flurry of emotions it awakened.

Dammit, Savannah, stop acting like some hormonal adolescent. Enough already.

He turned then, their eyes locking once again, and this time a ripple of warmth coursed through her, stealing her breath. The fluttering in her stomach fast becoming a sensation she liked, and she froze as her heartbeat that little bit harder, heat once again flooding her cheeks at the unspoken communication in his eyes.

She'd heard the term 'bedroom eyes' before, but now she stared right into them.

A frown creased her brow, but as he responded with that warm, genuine smile, her expression softened. His reciprocated smile triggering a rush of inward thoughts that went far beyond simple kisses, delving into dangerous, unchartered territory.

You need some distance. Not this, Savannah, she scolded herself. You're a grown woman and mother, not a sophomore with a crush.

This was not only uncharacteristic but also sheer madness—except... she groaned, eyeing Mac with unbidden curiosity.

What was the appeal?

This never-ending argument would drive her mad.

Despite the awareness that now was not the time to entertain anything so radical, an inexplicable force pulled her toward him on a level she couldn't comprehend, and she realized it scared the life out of her. But in the same breath, it excited her.

"It's time you moved on. Leave Charles where he belongs, honey. You deserve someone you can depend on."

She hadn't heard Felicity come up beside her, and her friend spoke in barely a whisper. "What Charles did this evening was beyond disgusting. He's on a road to self-destruct, and you need to put as much distance between you as possible before that happens."

Savannah nodded. She could hardly argue the point. She'd seen the madness in his eyes. The anger like nothing she had ever seen before.

You can't keep playing the nice guy. You don't deserve it, and nor do the girls."

Savannah raked her fingers through her hair, hating the stress headache pinching her forehead. Wishing she could wash Charles out of her mind once and for all.

As if reading her mind, Mac looked in her direction, the warmth in his eyes sending a flash off comfort through her. The awareness she'd experienced reawakening.

"Exactly" Felicity prodded, noting the unspoken communication. "Charles is part of your past, it's time to start looking to the future. And you can't judge all men by his standard." She sent an assessing gaze in Mac's direction, before adding. "There are some decent ones out there, Sav. You can't close your eyes to that fact."

Felicity chuckled, raising her brows. "Not to mention the fact he isn't half bad."

Savannah rolled her eyes.

Should she admit to her friend that was where her mind was at? Or deny it?

She'd once believed Charles was her everything, but reality shattered that illusion. Early on, she saw the signs, but blamed herself, falling into the trap of self-doubt he crafted. He had isolated her from her family, making her believe they wanted nothing to do with her, eroding her self-worth through gaslighting, and constant criticism became the norm as she struggled to meet his unrealistic expectations.

Every effort to please him failed until the day she discovered him in their marital bed with a new intern from his firm. In that moment, her eyes slammed wide open, and realizing the control he wielded over her, hit her like a sledgehammer. It was the wake-up call that spurred her to plot her escape. And she had.

Despite the fear lingering in the memories of his control, a deep rage emerged, fueling her determination to prove she was not the hollow shell he had reduced her to. Never again would she allow herself to be in such a position.

The scars remained, but they were badges of survival.

As she dipped her head, exhaustion set in, the weight of her past bearing down.

Too much, too soon. She murmured to herself. A voice inside her reminding. You're not ready, Sav. Focus on you.

Yet, warm, watchful, green eyes and a reassuring smile lingered in her mind.

A stranger.

And yet so, so familiar.

She glanced back at him, wondering if she were losing her mind, when an inexplicable sense of disappointment flooded her. His attention was again back to Nick.

He raised a tanned hand, raking his hands through his hair, oblivious to her, focused on their conversation.

Savannah smiled, just the smallest smile.

Felicity was right. This man was more than just interesting, he was an enigma, and whilst everything in her screamed to run, something else, deep inside her, was drawing her to him. Unprepared to ignore it.

Clay had offered her the use of a guest room, aware that she'd not want to make the trek back to Brooklyn in the small hours. It wasn't far, but heavy-eyed, exhaustion was settling over her limbs.

Sleep wouldn't be far.

"I need to call it a night," she whispered to Clay, not wanting to draw attention. She needed some distance, the chance to clear her addled mind and figure the mess that was her current headspace. "I'm beat."

"You're, okay?"

Savannah nodded, unashamed of the lie.

Anything but okay, brother.

She couldn't talk about it, not now.

He studied her—worried.

"It's been a massive day," Savannah said. "I just need to put my head down. We'll have plenty of time for catchups while you're in town." She cast him a quizzical look. "You're planning on staying for a while, right? It's not just a whistle stop?"

Clay wrinkled his nose in that familiar expression she'd known since childhood. "We're back for two weeks—everything on track in both New Zealand and Bora Bora, so I need to spend some time here. I've been more than a little absent of late."

Savannah snickered, the sound lacking any genuine amusement. She couldn't deny the ache of missing him. Their bond had been unbreakable, sharing every secret and triumph.

Charles had driven a wedge between them, and despite months of rebuilding their relationship, the thought of Clay considering a new life on the other side of the world felt like abandonment just when she needed her twin the most.

The hurt ran deep, and she couldn't shake the threatening sense of loss.

"Dinner tomorrow?" he asked, changing the subject with a speed that could cause whiplash.

Savannah nodded. "I've got a ton of wrapping up for tonight and a debrief with Felicity, but sure, sounds good."

She expected many meetings on the horizon with potential clients, but while Clay was here, she'd make the most of him.

For now, though, she bid her siblings goodnight, seeking the sanctuary of the guestroom, and much-needed sleep.

Chapter Nine

MAC

For more than an hour, Mac observed Savannah blend into the familial camaraderie, their laughter and banter filling the room as if the evening's turmoil was a distant memory.

Yet, amid the apparent normalcy, he couldn't ignore the subtle moments of introspection. Sometimes she pulled back, observing—that haunted expression flickering in her eyes once more. And he knew instinctively that the silent struggle against the internal demons continued to hold her captive, despite her outward denial.

In those moments, Mac found an echo of his own experiences. He too hailed from a large family, and it terrified him that this evening's scene mirrored what had happened to his cousin with disturbing familiarity.

Just the possibility scared him half to death.

The laughter, the animated conversations, the shared updates on life—all reminiscent of the warmth he associated with family, and just like his own kin, the Devereaux siblings reveled in each other's successes and milestones. And like his own, they rallied together in challenging times. They thought. Until something like tonight brought reality to light, as it had with Carla—only in her case, it had been too late.

What resonated most, was the reaffirmation that the essence of family remained a universal constant—a comforting familiarity. Well, Savannah would need this in the upcoming weeks and months. He knew how isolated she'd become. Clay had voiced his concerns, but to what, they clearly did not know.

A little while after, Savannah had bid them goodnight, and a somber atmosphere settled among the siblings, their faces etched with concern.

Mac exchanged glances with Clay. The understanding that despite Savannah's resilient exterior, the vitriolic intrusion of her ex-husband had left a profound impact on all of them. The realization that Charles still had his claws embedded in her, terrifying.

"You did good tonight," Clay's oldest brother JD said to Mac, angrily breaking the uncomfortable silence. "I believe if a single one of us had gotten our hands on him, we wouldn't be sitting here now."

Gray, the second youngest Devereaux, nodded. "Damned right. After what he did…" he closed his eyes, inhaling a deep breath, as though to balance himself, then stared at JD. "How does he even have a law license?"

"Good question?" Clay responded.

"Trust me, I considered dangling him from the roof by his ankles until he promised never to set eyes on her again," Mac retorted, his words complete truth. Laughter echoed through the room, but it lacked the genuine warmth and spontaneity that had accompanied their earlier conversations. Instead, it sounded strained and artificial. The tension was so thick it seemed palpable. Clay turned to Felicity, who sat beside Gray.

"Felicity, can you tell these guys what you told me earlier?"

Felicity baulked, glancing at the door, and Mac hated the discomfort she displayed, noting the moment Gray's hand brushed her leg, a reassuring gesture, but somehow intimate.

He frowned but said nothing. At several points during the evening, he'd noticed their little gestures, but he shrugged it off though, turning his attention back to the conversation at hand. Charles' capacity to pull this kind of stunt meant he'd try at anything. Not to mention the fact Savannah needed help, even if she had yet to ask for it.

"Listen," Mac said, swallowing back the expected wave of emotion. He glanced at Clay.

He'd been the one who drove Mac to the hospital when the call had come, and to this day, the demons still haunted him.

"This isn't something I discuss often, and the only reason I'll discuss it tonight is because it's relevant." Mac said, glancing around at the others. "You'll understand why I reacted the way I did this evening, and why—believe it or not, I'd like to have hurt him as much, if not more than any of you."

He inhaled what he'd hoped would be a deep, cleansing breath. It didn't work, and his fists clenched, the memories now so fresh, it might have happened just yesterday.

"My cousin, Carla, was a year older than me. We grew up within a mile of each other, went to school together, created mayhem during vacation time, went to university together. She was the only child of my aunt and uncle, and as near as dammit, a sister to me, not to mention my best friend growing up."

He caught Clay's eye and smiled the smallest smile at the nod of support his friend offered.

This wasn't a conversation he enjoyed, nor wanted. But he continued.

"A year after we graduated, she moved to Christchurch for work. She qualified as an architect, and when the rebuild following the Christchurch Quake ramped up, she took a job with a well-respected local property developer." He glanced across at Clay, who nodded, urging him to continue. Jeez, this was hard. "With the city only two hours from home, we all thought it was perfect."

Mac took his time, but he needed them all to understand where the parallels lay.

"Just three months after she arrived there, I received a text—correction—we received a blanket text, with a photograph of her and a man she'd met and fallen in love. They'd eloped to Fiji." He closed his eyes, remembering. "We were stunned. Our entire lives, we'd celebrated births, christenings, weddings, and graduations together. As my aunt and uncle's only daughter, they'd always envisioned a grand affair—the big fancy white wedding, party, etc. They only found out she'd married after the fact and cut a long story short. An argument erupted that left a rift we would never bridge. Just three years later, we mourned together at her funeral."

Gwen gasped, and Felicity's eyes widened in horror.

"What happened?"

Mac blew out a breath, fighting back the overwhelming wave of grief.

"Five years had passed, but to talk about it, cut deep—and the pain still cut bone deep. He fought to continue, wishing in that moment he could step outside into the Mackenzie night and breathe in the calm silence it brought. Of course he couldn't—it was a world away. If he'd not been so stubborn, had checked in on her, rather than letting her get on with her life—would things have been different?

He blinked, replaying that thought through his mind, the seed of an idea permeating the grief.

"As we discovered later, Peter, her husband, had handy fists, and not in a good way. A jealous, conniving, serial cheat, who treated her like an unpaid help. After the birth of her first child, she stopped working, and became a full-time mom. The birth of their second just eleven months later. We never met those babies until after the…"

This time, he had to stop. Close to choking, he pushed himself out of his seat and walked over to Clay's bar. He said nothing until he'd necked an ice-cold soda, using those long, precious seconds to compose himself. He thought he'd grieved, moved on, but in that moment, he knew the guilt was as present today as it had been five years ago.

When he spoke again, his back was still to them, the awareness that those six pairs of eyes focused on him. He stood motionless, allowing the words to come without turning. His back was a shield as he fought the complex wave of emotion.

Was what Savannah had gone through the same? He'd seen the similarities. But to what extent?

Had there been physical abuse? Or just mental? The sound of crushing metal filled the air, as he crunched the soda can in his fist. He lifted his hand, watching the small sliver of blood appeared on his forefinger, where sharp edge had cut.

He ignored it, turning to face them as he continued.

"She still had me as her emergency contact in her phone—God knows why—it had been years. I often wonder if she feared something would happen to her. That if her family were her point of contact, she'd be safe somehow." He swallowed, his Adam's apple bobbing as he forced back the vicious lump in his throat.

Keep going.

He leaned back against the cool mahogany of the bar, needing the support as he continued.

"When her friend found her unconscious at home, they called me. I had no clue about Peter's violent streak at that point. The police treated it as a home invasion, and only after the friend said she suspected abuse did the police question him. His defensive wounds identified on him gave him away. She put up the mother of all fights—too little, too late."

Mac took a deep breath, aware the words had come out in a rush. The realization coming quick on the heels, that the only person he'd talked about this with until now had been Clay, five years ago.

So long, yet it seemed like yesterday.

"Shit," Gray whistled. "I'm so sorry, Mac. If I'd had any..."

Mac cut him off. "Nobody could have done a thing. She'd decided and stood by it."

"She needed us to be present in her life, but we weren't, and that's something you all need to consider."

His steady gaze travelled across each, hoping he'd gotten his message across.

In the wake of Carla's death, the family had made it their business to raise awareness of domestic abuse. Statistics highlighted how widespread the issue had become on a global scale, too.

Perhaps driven by guilt, perhaps simply to ensure what had happened to their daughter, never happened to another family, his aunt and uncle had founded the #BehindClosedDoors foundation, which offered refuge to victims of domestic abuse who found themselves isolated from families.

"In New Zealand, there were more than one hundred and seventy-five thousand reports of family harm last year, with the suggestion that one in three women will experience physical or sexual violence during their lifetimes. It is scary statistics, and we find it too easy to play ostrich, pretending it doesn't exist."

He moved to the couch, and sat forward, elbows on knees, his hands clasped together.

"I don't know what the stats are here—but Savannah got out of it. It's clear Charles has a nasty streak, though, and she needs to get clear. Kids or not, contact or not, I've seen that kind of nastiness before. I'd hate to..."

He couldn't finish the sentence, his mind playing over all he'd said. The similarities, the concerns, the conclusions.

Was that why he'd reacted the way he had? Had he felt the instinctive need to protect Savannah because of Charles? Was it protectiveness and not attraction?

No.

He'd reacted from the very moment she'd entered the room before he even knew who she was. There was no question.

But...

A mental headshake.

"On many levels, I shouldn't get involved. This is a family thing, and she needs every one of you." He glanced down at his hands, swallowing back the overwhelming sense of apprehension. "If I'm honest after Carla, we closed ranks—all of us. The inquest, the court case, everything. You have the chance to help now, and if tonight was an escalation, which, it looks to have been, then you don't want to leave it too late."

He glanced across at Clay.

They'd not talked of what had happened from the moment they'd returned to the gala, but inside, anger burned, his friend had watched Savannah from a distance. Brooding, in a way that was uncharacteristic, and Mac understood. His friend was considering his move, contemplating how on earth he'd protect her. Now, and when he was back overseas.

Even with five other siblings, she was his twin, and that created an undeniable bond.

There'd be that same mix of anger, guilt, disbelief Mac had experienced. The difference was that they could still help Savannah—could still protect her.

"I imagined all the things I would have done differently after we lost Carla. The what-ifs, and buts, if only. Here, you're ahead of the game. The only problem is Savannah is trying to deal with it herself. And that is dangerous. I don't know if she sees that, but she needs to."

Gray glanced at Felicity. "Would she listen to you? If you pointed this out?"

Felicity shrugged. "Honestly, I don't know. She talks about things to a certain extent, but I know she holds others closer to her chest. Her life is about protecting the girls, and if she felt there was any risk of them being hurt, or exposed to Charles' current games, she'd clam up. That's what the court order was about."

"What about if we could persuade her to stay with mom and dad for a week, deal with Charles' ourselves?"

It was Nick who spoke, and Mac eyed the older of the Devereaux brothers with newfound interest. As a doctor, his life was about his work, but in that moment, the look exchanged between him, and Gwen spoke a thousand words.

There was a fierceness to his voice, and it was impossible not to see the flicker of anger in his eyes. "I've seen too many victims like your Carla in the ED. If there's any chance Savannah could ever be one of those statistics then I will do what it takes to prevent it—not just because I, despise Charles, for everything else he put Savannah and the girls through."

Gwen nodded her agreement, but Felicity cut in.

"I don't know that Savannah would want us to be talking about this without her," she said in a hushed voice. "She's so private, and she didn't tell you for a reason."

"And look where it got her," Clay cut in.

"She divorced him." Mac said, repeating Savannah's earlier words. "That's huge, and it took guts."

He glanced up at Felicity. "Savannah's an independent spirit, that's clear, and she's moving on with her life. But you're right. You need to speak to her." He looked at each of the brothers. "All of you. Let her know you're a united front. Charles isolated her. And now she's so visible—and making a success of this new chapter of her life. He's not happy about it, that's clear. For her, the divorce is over. She has her family, but does she know that she does—I mean, like before? That isolation will have taken its toll."

He felt as though he were preaching, but he'd heard the talks, read the books, seen the statistics. If there was one thing he understood besides his business, it was this. His personal investment running so deep it hurt.

"Savannah needs to understand now that the family is there for her no matter what—tonight, you had a united front—that's what she'll need."

"So, what next?"

"We deal with Charles, keep Savannah and the girls safe, and make sure they're kept as far away from his vile behavior as possible." Gwen said, aware of the growing undertone in the room.

"I'll find out where the court order stands, and whether there is a way to get action on the breach in the morning... if that's what Savannah wants," JD cut in.

"And I'll speak to mom about getting Savannah back to Sweetheart Falls for a week." Gray finished.

The conversation shifted from Charles to the success of the evening, and it was an hour later, the Devereaux family dispersed. Mac, having enjoyed his introduction to the full contingent of Devereaux siblings, bid them goodnight.

Jetlag gripped him, a heavy lethargy settling over him, demanding a few hours of shut eye. Yet, sleep proved elusive. It was more than that, though. Every time he closed his eyes, he saw Carla's face, heard the cries of Maia and Tegan, Carla's children, and then saw those beautiful blue eyes that were Savannah's.

He groaned.

Accustomed to the quiet of his home in the Mackenzie back in New Zealand, he lay in the darkness, unable to drown out the cacophony of city sounds—traffic on the streets, the distant hum of aircraft above the clouds, and the laughter of late-night revelers. Sirens and car horns added to the nocturnal symphony, a stark contrast to the serene nights back home. A deafening accompaniment to his thoughts.

"C'mon brain, shut down. Sleep," he urged himself, but the city's nocturnal orchestra persisted. Thumping the pillow and tugging at the blanket did little to remedy his restlessness.

More than the city's sounds, it was thoughts of the woman in the room next door that kept him awake. The proximity of her presence resonated in his awareness, memories of her lips and the feel of her in his arms echoing through his mind. Frustration built as his body responded, a groan escaping into the darkness.

"Surrender, Mac. Sleep isn't happening. Not tonight," he admitted to himself.

He threw off the sheets, and padded across the room, eased the door open, mindful not to disturb Clay or Savannah, and sought solace in the kitchen with a cup of coffee. An endless night awaited him.

He froze upon sensing movement in the kitchen, realizing he wasn't alone.

The familiar scent of coconut and vanilla permeated the air, and he identified the intruder. She was there in the darkness, silent and watchful.

"Sorry, I couldn't sleep. Hope I didn't wake you," Savannah's soft voice broke the silence.

"You didn't wake me. I couldn't sleep," he admitted, blaming it on jetlag. "It's shocking."

Savannah chuckled, and Mac could make out a porcelain cup in her hands. "Wish I could say my lack of sleep was jetlag."

"You always sit in the dark?" Mac asked, stepping into the kitchen.

"Figured if I put the lights on, I'd wake you both. Sometimes the dark is the best place to ponder on problems."

"Did you want hot chocolate?"

His eyes adjusted to the darkness. "I'm a coffee-fiend, I'm afraid. Hot chocolate just doesn't cut it," he confessed. "Too sweet."

Savannah hopped out of her seat, heading for the jug. Mac squinted as the under-cabinet light clicked on.

"Guess there's no point us both sitting in the dark," she grinned. "Take a pew, I'll do the coffee."

In the dim light, he hadn't seen her. But now, standing before him, her allure was undeniable.

Dammit, she's a temptress.

The mid-thigh t-shirt borrowed from Clay showed her long, slim legs, the soft fabric clinging to her curves. Mac fought the urge to close the distance and pull her into his arms again.

White-knuckled, he balled his fists.

"I liked it," Savannah's unexpected admission interrupted his turbulent thoughts.

"Sorry?" Mac responded, unsure if he heard her correctly.

"I liked it when you kissed me," she repeated, still facing the countertop.

Oh rats!

Mac braced himself for a different reaction but hope blossomed. Alarm bells rang in the back of his mind. This should be so wrong, yet there was also something so right.

"I did, too," he whispered, wishing he could gaze into those beautiful blue eyes.

"Would you like to try it again?" she asked, engrossed in busying herself with the coffeepot.

Mac said nothing.

"Speak to me," she said, turning to face him. "I'm asking if you'd like to kiss me again?"

Words eluded him. His stomach was in knots.

Speak, Mac. You're not a kid.

His tongue ran over dry lips, the internal battle strong. This was moving too fast.

He shouldn't... but as she closed the space between them, he set aside all doubt, brushing aside his uncertainty.

There'd be time for regrets later, as her breathy whisper sounded against his lips. "Show me."

Chapter Ten

SAVANNAH

The warm morning light seeped through the large, ornate windows, casting a soft glow on Savannah as she awoke, disoriented in the unfamiliar surroundings.

Sleep clung to her, and it took precious moments for her sleepy mind to piece together the events of the night before. Her gaze swept across the vintage peach wallpaper, high ceilings and heavy drapes she'd left open before she'd slid between the sheet, settling on the vintage chandelier hanging above the bed. Her mind muzzy.

Frowning, she closed her eyes, remembering why she was at Clay's. The events of the previous night tumbling into her mind.

The Gala.

Charles.

Mac...

Her gaze shot to the slumbering form beside her, surprised to find no regret. Mac lay bare-chested, the white cotton sheet draped over him, revealing a tanned, muscular torso that captivated her in the small hours, the lack of chest hair surprising her given the mass of curls on his head.

Instead of the expected self-reproach, a sense of fulfilment settled within her, and for the briefest moment, she had the urge to stretch like the proverbial cat with the cream.

She rolled onto her side. Savannah propped herself up on her elbow, a smile playing on her lips as she indulged in running her fingers through Mac's tousled curls. The night's passion turned his hair even more chaotic, and she smiled.

If his hair had been a wild canvas last night, the aftermath of unbridled passion and peaceful slumber transformed it into a tangled masterpiece. She wound one silky curl around her finger, then allowed it to bounce back into place, eliciting a groan and a lazy smile from Mac.

"Morning," he greeted with his eyes still closed, reaching out to pull her atop him in one fluid movement.

Savannah shrieked, giggling, as she swatted Mac's chest.

"Serious?"

She studied the smoky arousal in those sleepy green eyes.

Mac's moan conveyed an obvious message, and he wriggled, rubbing her against him.

"Most people call that morning glory," she teased.

"Most people don't wake up next to a sexy-as-hell blonde with a time limit."

Savannah responded with a deep, fiery kiss, transitioning from the night's intense passion to a slow, lazy exploration as morning unfolded.

Breathless and sated, Savannah lay beside Mac, contemplating the surreal turn of events more than an hour later.

"We ought to talk," she said, gaze fixed on the chandelier, reluctant to meet the eyes of the man who rocked her world. His presence was more than a little distracting.

Mac propped himself on his elbow, tracing fiery circles on her abdomen with his finger, sending tiny waves of awareness through her.

"You know, talking's overrated, right?" he replied, placing a feather-soft kiss against her throat.

The sensation sent shivers down her spine.

"I mean it," she insisted, pushing him away. "We need to figure out where this goes. I don't want..." She hesitated. "I don't want a relationship, Mac. The last years have been hard. But... I've missed the physical closeness."

Until his arms enveloped her, she hadn't realized how much she craved it.

"I understand," Mac said, his forefinger tracing the length of her cheekbone, creating another wave of pleasure. "You've just come through a divorce, have an ex who isn't making life easy for you, and I live on the opposite side of the world."

He counted each thing on his hand, now holding three fingers up. "Add to that the fact your brother is my business partner, and that's four things against this."

He rolled onto his back, staring up at the ceiling.

Savannah felt the undercurrent of regret, and for a moment she fell silent.

How was it? Even after the divorce, Charles still wormed his way into her life. All she wanted was a night of adult fun, to have a man's arms around her, to feel... sexy... needed again.

She blinked at how brazen that sounded, nuzzling closer to Mac once more.

She'd spent the single most steamy night of her life with the man beside her, discovering new sensations she'd not known existed.

Just a stroke of his fingers sent delicious shivers of awareness coursing through her, as though firebugs danced across her skin, leaving a trail of tingles all over. What he'd done with his mouth...

a violent shudder rippled through her, and she gasped at the sheer heat that followed.

No, she wasn't about to stop now.

Logic and rationality whispered that it was time to bring this — whatever it was — to an end.

Arching her brows, she turned to face him, unsurprised at the intensity of that green-eyed gaze.

"I know," she admitted, rueful. "But I think last night hit home."

With a playful tug, she wrapped one of his curls around her finger, planting a feather-light kiss against his furrowed brow.

"I'm over the complications Charles keeps throwing my way. The divorce was supposed to end this, but it didn't. Not only did he try to ruin last night, but he also breached the court order, and there were three court judges from the city who witnessed last night."

She released the curl, watching it spring back into place. "First thing I intend to do this morning is call my lawyer."

This wasn't the first time she'd reached this kind of breaking point, but guilt restrained her in the past. She hadn't wanted to cut Charles off from their daughters, striving to appear civil even in the face of his strong-arm tactics.

Any lingering guilt evaporated now. She no longer wished for her daughters to witness Charles' toxic behavior. They deserved a stable environment with trustworthy adults.

More importantly, Charles's actions were escalating, and she refused to become another statistic. If they were to have any semblance of a family life, this toxicity needed to be cut out once and for all.

She frowned, realizing the direction her thoughts had taken. Yes, it was time to move on. Not toward romance. She wasn't ready for that. It would be a long while before she of bringing someone new into her life romantically. However, a different proposition presented itself, and she eyed Mac.

"I was thinking," she said, on a deep inhale, uncertainty in her eyes.

Is this a good idea?

The temptation to backtrack tugged at her, but she fought against it. It can't hurt, Sav. You need downtime, and what's better downtime than this? With determination, she turned her head to meet his gaze. You can do it, c'mon.

"You're visiting New York. My girls are staying with my parents, and you've never seen the city..." She wrinkled her nose with worry. "I love showing people the Big Apple; it's got so many stories to tell. How about you take some time out for me to act as your tour guide?"

The words spilled out, and she grimaced as Mac burst into laughter, eyeing her as though she was mad.

"Don't look at me like that," she giggled, wide-eyed. "Last night, you made a massive donation to the foundation and also bid on an auction for my services as an event coordinator." She shrugged. "I can't provide that if you're flying out in two weeks, so let me introduce you to the city. Show you a little of how we do things on this side of the world."

She contemplated this idea last night. Mac mentioned he would be in town for a few weeks, and even with work commitments, exploring the city together would be fun— wouldn't it?

"You're looking at me as though I've gone mad. Speak, for goodness' sakes!"

Mac frowned. "You think Clay would be okay with that—me spending time with you?"

"Clay," Savannah said, "is my brother, not my keeper. He's also a teddy bear," she grinned. "Besides, what he doesn't know won't hurt him. If you're doing the work that needs to be done, who's he to stop you doing what you want while you're in the city?"

Mac chuckled. "I get the impression this is a conversation you've had before..."

"Let's just say, Clay never let a partner of mine slip by without a thorough investigation—be it firm talking to's in the schoolyard or my date to the school prom."

She smiled, a hint of shyness in her eyes, withholding the fact that the only long-term partner until now, was in fact was Charles.

"Clay also knows that right now I need a distraction, so I don't think he can complain!"

"I'm a distraction?" Mac asked.

Savannah, still amazed at the liberating experience, eyed him from beneath lowered lashes, nodding, her lips lifting in a catlike grin as she held up his phone to unlock the screen, then thumbed in her number. "I'm rather hoping you are a distraction in the best possible way!"

A little after ten, Savannah slipped into her dress pants and threw on a loose T-shirt, appreciative of the spare clothes she kept at Clay's place. She didn't stay over often, but over the years made sure she kept a handful of things.

In the kitchen, she popped some toast into the toaster, pouring her first coffee of the morning, and glanced at the clock. She needed to be back in Brooklyn by one to meet Felicity.

Getting out of bed had been more challenging than she'd expected, and she scolded herself. While Mac served as a great distraction, she discovered she enjoyed talking and laughing with him more than she bargained for. In fact, they'd talked for hours about his home and her business.

Deeper conversations would come, but for now, she relished the idea of conversing with another adult and the enjoyable contact they shared.

Her cell phone vibrated on the kitchen counter, and she grinned when she saw the name on the caller ID. "Hey, baby," she smiled, thankful for video call capability that allowed her to see her girls even when they were in Sweetheart Falls.

Jess, with her hair braided and a yellow ribbon at the end of each braid, grinned back. "Mom! Chloe said it would be too early to call. I told her it wouldn't!"

Savannah laughed. "As if! When do I ever get a sleep in?"

"Well, it was a late night, wasn't it?" Jess asked, eyeing her mother with an assessing gaze. "There's no way it would have been early—not with all of those guests."

"Oh, and how do you know?"

"The gossip columns are full of stuff this morning," Jess grinned.

Savannah frowned. "What do you mean?"

With a theatrical eye roll, Jess retorted, "Are you telling me you didn't check yet? What kind of business are you trying to run?"

"Jessica Cora-Lea Carlisle don't be rude," Savannah chided, recognizing that the full articulation of Jess's name served as a severe warning.

"Well, you need to check. There's so much news. You didn't tell me that Taylor Swift would be there. I'm so jealous. You know how much I love her music. And what about Brad Perry? We knew you were going to have a lot of celebrities, but A-listers?"

Savannah watched as Jess did a theatrical swoon at the potential of the guest list. "And what about those dresses? Did you see the Dior Charlotte Price was wearing? It was...." She swiped her brow, feigning another swoon, and what about the Gucci, Kate Andrews had on, that yellow..."

As Jess shared all the details, her excitement palpable down the phone, Savannah's head spun, trying to keep up. She loved her daughter and hoped that confidence would stay with her for life, but sometimes, a bit of slowing down would be nice.

Jess looked to her right, scowled, and shook her head. "Uh oh, looks like I must go. Gran says she needs help with her wardrobe." She blew an exaggerated kiss at the screen and handed the phone to Chloe.

For the second time in as many minutes, Savannah smiled and greeted, "Hey, baby," this time to the quieter of her girls. Despite being identical, Jess and Chloe differed in demeanor and personality. While Jess exuded sass, Chloe was quiet, preferring to stay in her twin's shadow. Astute and more observant, Chloe addressed her mother with a gentle smile, and Savannah saw the concern in her eyes.

"What's the matter?" Savannah asked, sensing Chloe's unease.

"I just wanted to be sure you were okay." Chloe hesitated. "I... I, uh, heard Gran and Pops talking this morning. They said..." She glanced behind her, as if checking to ensure privacy. "They said that Daddy was there last night."

Savannah's breath stilled, and shock rebounded through her. She hadn't thought to warn her parents about what happened; she'd been so wrapped up in the night. Guilt-ridden, she frowned at Chloe, wanting to reassure her it wasn't as bad as she thought—except Chloe would see through that lie. She'd witnessed too much for an eight-year-old.

"It's okay. I heard a little. Just that Daddy turned up and made a scene. Pops was on the phone to Uncle Nick, who told him."

Savannah closed her eyes.

"I'm sorry, Chloe. I would have told you. It's just... it's been pretty..."

"Did he hurt you?"

Of all the words Chloe could have uttered, it was those that cut deep, and Savannah fought back the threat of tears. A combination of guilt, anger and hopeless futility overwhelmed her.

"No, baby. He didn't," she replied in a fierce whisper. "There were so many people there; he couldn't—wouldn't dare."

"But he tried?"

"Sweetheart, we've been through so much. I'm okay—we're okay. I hate you getting caught up in this, but we need to find a way through it. I promise, Mom's going to do everything she can to put this right."

Savannah tried to shield the girls from Charles's actions, but it had been inevitable in the past year that they would see things. With Jess, it was easy enough to distract her from uncomfortable situations. However, Chloe absorbed atmospheres and information like a sponge, always aware, always alert, reading people, and it was rare for her to miss signals. She had an old head on young shoulders, and she knew Savannah better than most.

She forced a smile, reaching out to touch the screen where Chloe's cheek was.

"I wish you'd been there last night," she said with a faux brightness. "It was so exciting, and we doubled our target for Uncle Nick and Gwen's foundation. Next time, I promise you, you will both be able to come."

Chloe didn't look convinced, but Savannah persisted. "Ask Jess to show you the pictures of the dresses and the different people who were there. Honest, it was worth it."

Moments later, she ended the call, promising herself to call her mother later. For now, Savannah needed to get on with the day. That brief conversation pushed Mac to the back of her mind, but now he was there once more, and a flicker of sadness bit. She couldn't see him meeting her girls, especially not in the capacity of a love interest. Perhaps as Clay's friend, but she didn't want to delve into it. She got the impression he'd make an incredible father.

Chapter Eleven

MAC

A distracted Mac walked into Manhattan a while later. Freshly showered, he needed to work—to distract himself from the blonde bombshell who'd blown his mind.

He opted to walk, determined to give himself time to clear his thoughts, but it didn't work, and he walked oblivious to buildings towering overhead, casting their long shadows across the pavement, as he weaved his way through the throng of pedestrians.

Barely even hearing the cacophony of city sounds enveloped him—the honking of car horns, the chatter of passers-by, and the occasional screech of brakes, his thoughts focused on Savannah Devereaux.

If he'd had any sense, he'd have ended things this morning, kept it a one-night stand. She'd made it clear though, she wanted no-strings, no commitment, just fun, and he didn't have the strength to say no. Not with Savannah.

The impact she'd had on him from the first moment made saying no impossible. And now, as he contemplated the evening before, Charles, and the emotional rollercoaster of memories associated with Carla's death, man, he wished on multiple levels he'd held back—it was a conversation he'd avoided a long time, but he'd known last night was the right time.

Mac growled.

He'd become too invested, even in this brief space of time, and there was so much potential for things to get messy.

"Afternoon." Clay grinned as Mac entered the office. "Half day today, then?"

Mac glared.

"Like you don't do it often enough."

"Anyone would think you had a hangover."

Mac raised his eyebrows, not bothering to deny it.

"That was some night," Clay grimaced. "Did you get some sleep in the end?"

Mac walked across to the windows, staring at the city view.

"Any updates?" Mac asked, turning to look at his friend.

Aware that he wasn't talking about work, Clay replied. "JD spoke with the DA this morning. Charles breached the court order last night. Seems a lot more has happened than we were aware of, but confidentiality meant there were things they couldn't discuss."

A text alert sounded on his phone, and Clay responded before continuing.

"Savannah must report the breach, after which the police will pick him up. It's uncertain what will happen after that, but it's likely he'll have to appear before the judge again—determine whether they charge him, remand him, or perhaps an ankle tracker to deter him from going near her again. Either way, his work will be affected, not to mention his possibility of ideas about elections. Nobody is going to vote for someone charged with domestic abuse."

Mac blew out a breath of frustration. "That'll piss him off."

Clay laughed, but again, there was no humor. "Do you think any of us care about that? If he's held accountable, then he'll stay away and let Savannah and the girls move on without all his crap."

Mac nodded, turning back to the window.

The contrast between this dull grey and white concrete jungle and the lush greens and blues of the Mackenzie disoriented him, leaving him yearning for the crisp air and expansive landscapes of his home. He felt penned in, claustrophobic, and he hated it.

The disparity between the two places was almost surreal, as if caught between two worlds that would never coexist.

His mood deepened.

He shrugged his hands into his pockets, rocking back on his heels as he scowled down at the bustling street below. The sheer scale of the buildings was something he struggled to fathom, such a stark contrast to the modest structures in New Zealand, let alone the pristine beauty of the Mackenzie.

In his mind's eye, he envisioned the panoramic views from the chopper. The stunning scenery he'd seen his entire life from the peaks of Mount Cook. Known as Aoraki, its Maori name, meaning 'cloud piercer.' As New Zealand's highest peak, there was a breath-taking majesty that needed to be seen to be believed.

How ironic that anyone of the buildings around here could be called that, the concrete and steel buildings easily piercing through the cloud on a cloudy day. They weren't nearly as beautiful, though.

Although, he now wondered if anything, or anyone in the world could be as beautiful as... he groaned, closing his eyes as the image of Savannah's blue-eyes flashed in his mind.

Oh boy, you're in trouble, Mac Mackenzie.

The memory of her dazzling smile and beautiful blonde hair sparked an overwhelming desire to reach out and touch her, and he rolled his shoulders, attempting and failing to stretch out the tension that now held him in its grip.

What transpired between them in less than twenty-four hours left an indelible mark on his thoughts, and since awakening that morning, every conscious moment seemed to lead back to her, leaving him questioning his sanity.

The concept of home loomed large in his mind, and he grappled with the realization that Savannah could never integrate into the life he lived.

Her world existed amidst the chaos of New York, with her business, her friends, her family, and her girls.

He shook his head, attempting to dispel the persistent worry.

How on earth had she infiltrated his mind with such ease?

From the events of the night before, to the amazing sex in the early hours, she'd become emblazoned in his mind. The image of her laughing, close to tears, and of course climaxing around him.

That was how.

Just the image in his mind made him hard.

Jeeez, man, you're not some hormonal teenager. Pull yourself together, he cursed. All too aware of Clay close behind him. Here he was in the office with his best friend and business partner, with a threatening hard on caused by the memory of said friend's twin sister.

Appropriate—not!

"You look like death warmed up," Clay commented, and he heard something different in his tone. Wary, perhaps. "I'm taking it you didn't get a great sleep."

"Not a great deal," he muttered, shoulders slumped. He'd been so deep in thought; he'd not responded to Clay's comment. At any other time, he'd have asked Clay's advice, but he couldn't bring himself to even consider discussing this with him. To say the situation was awkward would be an understatement.

"She's beautiful, aye."

Clay moved up to stand beside Mac now, staring out at that same view that for him had been home for a long time. The change of subject so sudden, Mac felt as though he had whiplash.

"Sorry?"

"Savannah."

Mac frowned. "Mmmm." Did Clay suspect already?

"Take it slow," Clay continued. "She's fragile now. It wouldn't take much to hurt her."

"I don't know what..."

Mac began, but there was no way he could deny it.

He'd never lied to Clay. Nor did he want to. But at the same moment, he wanted to keep this private. To discover whatever, it was that was budding between them, at his own pace. This stayed in the holiday romance box.

"We all saw it last night," Clay interrupted. "She was different around you. None of us have seen her that way in a long time. As though, for the first time in forever, she let her guard down. It was...." He heaved his shoulders with an enormous sigh. "Such a relief to see."

Mac shook his head.

"I don't know that it's something we should discuss. But in the same breath, I need to be honest."

"Anyone else, I'd be concerned. But you — I trust you, and the others do too. You've been my friend for a long time. I don't want to see her hurt any more than she has been, but if she doesn't move forward, well, you're aware of how concerned we've been about Charles."

"Nothing can come of it though," Mac added. "Her life is here, mine is..." he glanced behind at the enormous canvas of Mount Cook, with the stunning turquoise waters of Lake Pukaki in the foreground, the deep green of pine trees lining its shores, and a smattering of white fluffy clouds against the vivid blue of the sky. The image that played through his mind moments earlier, gesturing with his head. "There."

Clay nodded.

He followed Mac's gaze, thoughtful for a moment.

"It can turn into a shit-show, but in the same breath, you never know what will play out. In my heart of hearts, I want to protect her, as do my family, and it's clear so do you. In another breath, though, we want to see her fly, to grow her independence, whether that be through the business, or through the steps she needs to move forward. The way she behaved with you... that was, without doubt, her first step."

"How was she?" Mac asked, referring to Clay's comment about last night. All too aware of the way she'd affected him, but unaware anyone else had noticed. That she responded the same way?

"Oh, come on, Mac. You must have noticed? We lost count of the number of times we saw the two of you looking at each other. I thought that kind of thing was for chick flicks, but trust me, there was something there. Even Gwen saw it, and she's no romantic!"

"Perhaps you're overthinking..."

"And what about outside?" Clay interrupted. "After that lowlife had gone? You will not tell me that the glazed expression on her face was about him? She was smitten—there's no doubt whatsoever."

"Smitten?" Mac snickered. "What the hell, did you swallow a Victorian romance thesaurus or something?"

If he'd ever considered there'd be a conversation like this with Clay, he'd have suspected the world was nuts, but then she was there in his mind, her arms around his shoulders as they slow-danced their steps and bodies in time, as though they fit together.

He'd contemplated it last night, then shrugged it off as insane. But Clay made a point. There had been something. Something, his frown deepened, magical.

He pinched the bridge of his nose, shaking his head. Whatever Clay was on was contagious.

Was this a mistake? The answer was simple. But he ignored it.

From the moment she'd swept into the room last night, she mesmerized him. Not knowing who she was, he'd watched, fascinated. She was stunning. Whether it was chemistry or something more potent, he wanted—no, he needed—to know Savannah Devereaux.

What made her tick? Made her smile? Made her laugh?

He wanted to hear her favorite music, see her favorite color, taste her favorite food. He wanted to discover every single way he could bring Savannah the utter satisfaction he'd seen last night, because in just one night, she'd reached him in ways no woman had before.

"I guess what I'm saying is take it slow, mate. The reality is you live in two different worlds. Have two different lives. But, if moving forward gives you the opportunity to enjoy each other's company—and jeez, I don't believe I'm saying this about my twin sister—then go with it. Just please, try not to hurt her."

A rap on the door sounded, and Mac fell silent as Lisa, Clay's PA, handed over a wad of brown folders with fluorescent yellow sticky notes attached. "Need signatures," she said, before ducking back out, clearly aware she had interrupted.   When the door clicked closed, he added.

"Leave Charles to me. JD and I are paying him a visit this afternoon. With Nick, Gray, JD, and I, we'll figure what happens next. In two weeks, we'll be back in New Zealand. I don't want to leave anything to chance. Savannah needs to worry about getting her life back, not that piece of scum."

Mac nodded, quite frankly, the further Savannah was from her ex, the better. And whilst a part of him wanted to step in and protect, Clay wanted to deal with things in his own way—and as Savannah's brother, he couldn't argue. He'd have done the same for Carla, had he known anything that had happened with her.

Besides, there'd be time enough to keep her distracted for the next two weeks. If Clay held Charles at bay during that time—then great.

Good luck to him.

He focused upon a small aircraft flying overhead, the sun peeking between two clouds, glinting off its wings, in the same way the lights glinted off the tiara Savannah wore last night—and she was there once more, smiling at him as though he were the only person in the world.

It might be too much, it might be too soon, it may lead to nothing, but they'd figure it out, and if it ended up just two weeks of fun between two consenting adults, then he'd head home richer for it. He hoped she would, too. And as for Charles—he was Clay's problem and for now, he had work to do.

Chapter Twelve

SAVANNAH

Savannah met Felicity at a little after one. Two hours had passed since she'd left Mac near the Central Park gates. A large part of her had wanted to kick back her heels and cancel work today. To forget the drama of last night and enjoy his company.

It'd be so easy to just carry on as though nothing had happened. But she'd put way too much into setting up her business, and she was damned if any man, a tall, dark, sexy-as-hell-Kiwi included, would come between her and the success she needed. Even as she'd thought it, doubts had flooded to the fore.

What had possessed her to be so brazen? To take such a risk? And with somebody who, regardless of how long it had taken to meet the wider family, was in fact one of them?

What he offered was dangerous. Lethal, if she was honest. She'd given nine
years to her relationship with Charles. Okay, so a handful had been good—if playing the doting housewife could be called that.

She'd enjoyed hosting dinner parties, overseeing the admin, and playing the role of wife to Charles. But it had gone off the rails hard and fast when they'd become parents, and she hated that. It was a time couples should come together; solidify the relationship to provide the support and love their babies needed. In their case, though, the opposite happened.

She blew out a breath.

Whatever this was with Mac, it would be fun and carefree. No strings. Something that for the next two weeks would give her an escape. An opportunity to be young and free, and if she were honest, single—in a way she hadn't her entire adult life.

No strings, just a lot of fun.

She heaved a sigh and grinned, glancing at the briefcase in her hand. Yes, she intended to have fun, but for now, work was a priority, and it was where her focus would lie.

There was no way on God's green earth she'd fail. She'd show Charles and everyone that Savannah Devereaux was a rising star on the New York business stage.

Striding through the park, Savannah reached for her phone and punched in the number for her lawyer. She intended to do it earlier, but waited until she was alone, aware of what came next. The last thing she needed was to drag Mac into that, too.

Quickening her pace, she grinned when she entered the Park Plaza Restaurant minutes later, where she spotted Felicity already seated. The air buzzed with excitement, and her friend greeted her with a smile and a wave.

"I ordered a double pumpkin spiced latte with oat milk but held off on food. Wasn't sure if you'd lean toward brunch or lunch, especially given it was such a late-night last night," Felicity quipped, a mischievous glint in her eyes.

"It was," she agreed, adding. "Looked as though you and Gray had a ball."

Felicity flushed, her hand coming to her cheeks, and she smiled. "He's sweet, isn't he?" she said in a small voice.

"Why don't you give it a shot?" Savannah asked. Felicity and Gray shared a kiss last Christmas, when she'd joined the family for the holidays in Sweetheart Falls.

It came to nothing when Felicity returned to New York with Savannah a few days later.

Felicity chuckled, but there was no humor in the sound, more sadness. "We live too far apart to even travel that route."

Savannah flinched. It was the self-same thing she'd said earlier, and yet the distance between here and Sweetheart Falls was less than New Zealand.

"Nonsense!" She snorted. "It's a few hours away."

Her friend shook her head, reaching for the file beside her seat. "Let's leave it," she said, an uncertain edge to her voice. "We've got too much to talk about today..." she eyed Savannah. "You were pretty cozy last night too, as I recall."

Savannah froze.

"Point taken."

She knew all about changing the subject, and she'd expected Felicity to come out firing questions about Mac. On many levels, it was a relief. "Well, I know things got a little out of hand, and to be honest, I was livid when I thought you'd hung me out to dry with the auction. But your little stunt pulled off."

Felicity frowned. "In what way?"

"Eleven voice messages with booking requests, and several emails which I didn't check yet — not to mention the fact the lots with the final auction last night sold for well over the forecast. I can't help but wonder if there was an element of sympathy." Savannah laughed. "It's ironic that Charles' stunt had such a positive effect—not to mention the extra hundred thousand donated by Mac."

Felicity's expression relaxed, and curiosity sparked in her gaze. "I was hoping the conversation would veer this way," she said, tilting her head. "I want to hear about that gorgeous, sexy, curly-haired Kiwi who rocked your world last night."

Savannah, lifting her latte to her lips, spluttered, and choked on the silky-smooth liquid, and it took her a few seconds and a downed glass of water to steady herself.

"Rocked my world? Where on earth did you get that term from?" It seemed ironic that her friend reiterated the word she'd thought this morning.

Felicity laughed, and Savannah was relieved to see the anxious expression that she'd worn earlier gone.

"Well, didn't he?" She inhaled the steam from her latte before taking a tentative sip. The foam coated her upper lip, and she licked it off, savoring it before speaking again. "The way you were looking at each other," she wolf-whistled, and picked up the menu, fanning herself. "That was some serious heat!"

Savannah's jaw dropped. "Did you have a drink last night?"

"A few! Well, two. One in the early evening, one at the end, so no—I wasn't drunk. I also wasn't the only one to see it."

She reached for her phone and swiped the screen, grinning when she turned the screen to face Savannah, whose eyes widened further.

"No. Oh-mi-God. What on earth? Who..." she stared at an image of her in Mac's arms, that last dance of the night, in the same moment she'd pulled back and stared into his face.

"That can be an image from the cover of a romance novel," Felicity snorted. "We all saw the chemistry, but whoever snapped this...wow. They nailed it."

Savannah cringed.

She scrolled to see the headline above.

'Who is he? Mystery Heart Throbs steals the heart of the Fundraiser of the Year's Very Own Cinderella.'

Ah, crap.

She scrolled down now, reading the text that accompanied the image, cringing with every word. How on earth had she been so obvious? This was a stranger, yet to look at them...

Heat rose in her cheeks, and she glanced up at Felicity, and back at the screen, playing over in her mind the events of the night.

"See what I mean now?" Felicity all but gloated, and Savannah's irritation flashed in her eyes.

She passed the phone back to her friend and reached into her bag for her notebook. Determined to pull herself together.

She'd consider the ramifications of whatever—she glared at the phone—that was later. Right now, there was business to discuss, but not before Felicity got in a last jab.

"You're young, single, and will be flirty thirty in a month. C'mon Sav, play a little. You don't think there'd be women out there who'd kill to have him look at them the way he did you last night?"

Savannah gave an exasperated sigh.

"I've known the guy for less than twenty-four hours. Do me a favor."

For the next hour they discussed the next steps for the fundraiser, focusing on organizing the check presentation, amongst other things. Then moved onto the potential bookings that had risen from the night.

Savannah busied herself cutting her Impossible Burger she'd ordered into four, realizing as she did, that it was what she'd done for the girls for so long, she'd not even noticed until it was done.

Eight-year-olds or not, the number of times they'd worn ketchup or other sauces down their tops, it became a common practice.

She grinned to herself as she ate it piece by piece.

"Senator Markham wants to present the check," Felicity commented while jabbing her fork into her Caesar salad. "It will be a great photo opportunity for the campaign—although he didn't say that in as many words."

Savannah rolled her eyes. Markham was one politician who'd voted to cut funding to medical facilities like the Access2Care clinics across the state, so on many levels it seemed a hypocrisy—in the same breath though, it would make great press fodder for the Primaries. Might even make him reconsider his position—given the post-pandemic situation.

"I take it you already reached out with his office, then?" She said, taking another bite of her burger.

Felicity shook her head. "No, they emailed this morning—I figured I'd call them this afternoon after we're wrapped up."

As it was, by some miracle, they'd broken the million-dollar mark a little after midnight last night. By fluke as much as anything. Charles had failed in his mission to destroy the evening, and for that, Savannah was grateful beyond words.

She smiled. On many levels, that wasn't all Charles had failed at. If things hadn't blown up the way they had, she got the feeling there'd have been no way she'd have found her way onto the balcony alone with Mac—let alone summoned the courage to demand that kiss—or what followed later.

Not for the first time, heat flooded into her cheeks, and she focused as hard as possible on the list in front of her, determined not to allow Mac any purchase in her mind. Not now. That would come later.

After wrapping up their debrief, the duo treated themselves to warm brownie sundaes—perhaps not the healthiest choice, but what the doctor ordered for a celebratory treat.

An hour and a half later, they strolled back to their neighboring apartments on the historic brownstone, tree-lined, Remsen Street, engaged in an animated conversation about the star-studded line-up of last night, and potential new clients.

Upon reaching the main entrance of their building, they encountered a tired-looking Gray, who leaned against the black metal railings, hands in pockets, observing the world around him.

Savannah greeted her brother with a grin, wrapping her arms around him in a warm embrace. As she pulled back, she noticed Gray's gaze fixed on Felicity. Raising her brows, she cast a knowing glance in her friend's direction.

"Great to see you, little bro," she said, giving Gray a one-armed hug and kissing him on the cheek. "I better leave you to it, though. I need to shower and change."

Gray frowned, then appeared to let out a breath of relief, nodding his thanks as Savannah left the two of them on the sidewalk and entered the building.

Felicity would growl later, but it looked as though the two of them needed all the help they'd get, and after last night, she owed Felicity one, anyway!

She stepped into the elevator and tugged the cage door closed. Thumping the button for the third floor, she blew out a breath and leaned back against the back wall.

As it ascended, she pulled out her phone, staring at the screen.

Felicity had said flirty thirty.

An idea came to mind, and she unlocked the screen, opening her contacts.

Could she?

She grinned to herself, then thumbed in a message to Mac, enjoying a devilish sense of mischief she'd not experienced in years.

"Hey kiwi, how about a little adventure? Meet me on Bridge Park Drive, outside Iris Cafe, 6.30pm. We'll grab coffee to go, then go for a walk around Brooklyn Heights. No pressure, just good company, and the best of fun. What do you say?"

Grinning at her flirty text, Savannah exited the lift and walked across the landing to her front door, grateful for the ability to send a message like it. She'd never have been able to say something so flirty face to face.

Her grin widened when Mac's response appeared in an instant.

"Sounds like a plan! Loving the introduction to the city. And Brooklyn Heights... looking forward to a fun date with great company. See you there!"

Savannah shoved open her apartment door and closed it behind her, then leaned against it with the anticipation of a giddy teenager. Tossing her keys in the basket and her bag on the hook, she kicked off her shoes and sprinted for the bathroom. Tonight, she felt fun awaited, and she couldn't wait.

Chapter Thirteen

SAVANNAH

The sun dipped beneath the iconic skyline of New York City, casting a warm glow across the bustling streets when Mac came into view on Bridge Park Drive.

Savannah smiled the moment she saw him, dressed in beige chinos, a dark shirt, and a cream jacket. It was a stark contrast to the tailored tux he'd worn last night, and she found herself unable to tear her gaze away as he approached.

"Hey," he grinned with a wink, and that boyish charm that had piqued her attention last night was there once more. He leaned in to peck her on the cheek, and she inhaled the already familiar scent of the sandalwood and spice that was his aftershave.

Woah, he smelled good.

"Hey, yourself," she beamed back.

The day had been productive, and while she'd fielded work calls, and calls from her lawyer, as well as the meeting with Felicity, she'd been hanging out for this moment all day.

"Ready for a little adventure?" she teased, a playful glint in her eyes.

Mac chuckled, pulling back, and taking hold of her hand, as though it were the most natural thing in the world.

"Absolutely, let's do this."

As they strolled through the vibrant streets of Brooklyn Heights, a sense of peace settled on her, and she wondered whether it was him, or whether it was because now was time to move on.

With each step, their shoulders brushed, sending tingles of awareness through her. They had nothing to do with the intimacy of last night, but everything to do with this unfolding chemistry he was truly, truly enjoying this.

As they walked, they talked, and laughed, shared anecdotes, and exchanged sometimes prolonged glances now and then. The warmth surpassing the casual banter of newfound companions, and she was surprised at how easy just being with him was.

It should be wrong. So wrong. But this was what she needed. And terrifyingly, what she wanted.

So, for the first time in a long time, she intended to be selfish and take what she wanted. The ramifications could come later.

"I figured we'll go for light, scenic and easy this evening. Then tomorrow you get the whistle-stop of the best sights." She explained, adding. "It's different from what you're used to—that's obvious."

They were walking along the promenade. The sun had set, and now the early evening sky held a warm lilac hue mingling with a gentle peach tone, a stark contrast to the sheer silhouette of Manhattan. The first stars peeked through above the city lights.

"There's something magic about a city at night, and I really want you to give it a chance."

Mac laughed. "You mean the noise? Or the lights?"

Savannah rolled her eyes.

"I mean the lights. The noise—that is the next level—I know, in Sweetheart Falls, the nights are so quiet. You can hear nature in every sense of the word, but not so loud that it drowns out your thoughts. Here, there's never a quiet moment." She gestured to the towering landscapes across the river. "The lights, though. They're magical. They show the sheer capability of what mankind can achieve when they dream."

"I agree to a point. When you see the immense height and scale of the buildings, not to mention the incredible architecture, it's hard not to experience a sense of awe. But..." he cast a rueful glance Savannah's way. "You can't beat the natural beauty of home."

"Tell me about it. Tell me about your home."

It was a statement, and Savannah pointed to a bench overlooking the water. Mac took the hint and smiled, gesturing for her to sit before sitting beside her.

Mac's eyes sparkled as he spoke, his tone reminiscent.

"If you imagine open plains as far as the eye can see, of lakes and canals the color of turquoise, with snow-capped mountains in the distance, you're getting close," he explained, finding a spot to sit beside Savannah.

His gaze turned skyward. "And at night—it's breath-taking. It has International Night Sky Reserve Status, which means restrictions on light pollution within its proximity. The result is a perfectly clear sky—it's all that's visible in the darkness. Particularly, when there's no moon."

He continued, his voice a gentle cadence on the evening breeze.

"I remember my grandad taking us on a camping trip as kids. We lay out under the night sky, and he described it as a celestial tapestry. I was too young to understand what he meant, but it was a phrase that's always stayed with me, and, in adulthood... Imagine the black velvet in a jeweler's, with tiny shimmering diamonds strewn across it, then multiply it by millions." He gazed upward, a whimsical look on his face.

He strained to look up at the night-sky above the New York skyline. "You can never believe just how many stars there are until you lie beneath the Mackenzie Sky and experience just what the universe looks like—it's magical."

Savannah, captivated by his words, smiled. "I remember Clay first telling us that. He said it was the first time in his life he saw just how insignificant we are in the scheme of things. Like, this insignificant planet amid a gigantic universe." She blew out a sigh. "One day I'd love to see for myself."

Mac, lost in his thoughts, replied, "You honestly have to see it to believe it, and if there weren't the need to keep visitor numbers to a minimum, I'd recommend everyone experience Mackenzie in their life—it's humbling, and puts priorities firmly into perspective."

His expression sobered, and he looked down on the reflection of the glittering cityscape on the river.

"Canals link the lakes in the Mackenzie," he continued, his voice taking on a reflective tone. "Each filter through a hydro-dam that powers a good percentage of the country's electricity each year—which is ironic given the restrictions on light. The sounds are distinct, though. The sound of the water, occasional aircraft, minimal traffic, minimal people, for that matter. Often, the only sounds are those made by nature. The rustling of the long grass, the wind in the trees, bird song, all things that belong with nature, if that makes sense at all."

They lapsed into a companionable silence, absorbing the lively scene around them.

Couples strolled hand in hand, dogs wagged their tails as they walked their owners, conversations and laughter filled the air, and teenagers set out for the evening. Still, the seagulls squawked in the growing darkness, and water lapped on the shores.

106

There was nothing stagnant or quiet; the city buzzed, vibrant and alive. In the background, the perpetual hum of traffic and the occasional rattle of the subway. underscored an urban rhythm Mac was unsure he'd ever grow accustomed to.

After a contemplative pause, Mac broke the silence.

"Do you often walk in the evening?"

Savannah let out a quiet sigh.

"Not really. Perhaps twice a week, Felicity and I will walk here just to blow away the cobwebs. More often than not, our exercise happens at the gym."

"You're missing out."

"I get it," Savannah admitted softly. "I escape to Sweetheart Falls as often as I can. It's a great place for healing," she smiled, a whimsical smile, continuing. "My mom always called the town medicine because our family has always returned there. Often to heal."

Her gaze drifted to two boats on the water filled with early evening revelers, the distant music adding to the vibrant atmosphere. There was nothing peaceful here.

"It's different, I understand that, but there's so much I want to show you. I want you to go home with a new perspective of New York. There's so much about it that's unique and celebrated. It's not all just an urban jungle. Will you trust me to show you?"

Mac nodded. "I'm here, aren't I?"

She squeezed Mac's hand. "All day I questioned the sanity of this. But the more I questioned, the more I knew it's what I need."

"I'm the same," Mac replied. "Clay and I talked today."

He shook his head when Savannah raised her eyebrows, eyes wide. "No, I didn't tell him everything. He gave me—us—his blessing, reckons this," he gestured between them and then towards the city, "is the perfect distraction." He rolled his eyes. "I'm not sure how I feel about being a distraction, by the way, but I think we can help each other. Heck, we're both adults; we can work it out ourselves."

Laughter gurgled out of Savannah. "Seems I need to have a word with my brother. Twenty-nine years old and still interfering!"

She rolled her eyes, a mixture of annoyance and amusement clear. As much as she appreciated her family's concern, she yearned for them to trust her judgment, even if it had faltered in the past.

Her expression turned thoughtful, and she glanced back at Mac.

"How did you meet Clay?" she asked. She knew the short version but was curious about the details. As twins, she and Clay had always been close, and he had shared many stories of their adventures in New Zealand, accompanied by a few photos. But the specifics of how Mac and Clay had come into each other's lives and forged their deep friendship was something she'd never known.

Mac chuckled.

"Would you believe sheep-shearing?"

Savannah blinked in surprise. "Sorry?"

"Seriously—sheep shearing."

"Why did I never know this?"

"Perhaps because it was one of the few things he sucked at?"

Savannah rolled her eyes, and Clay was naturally gifted. He always had been. Anything he turned his hand to. He'd succeeded, and often she'd been jealous.

It was how he'd turned the software programs and hotel chains he'd developed into a billion-dollar international organization.

"Okay, I want the entire story now. Let's find food and you can fill me in on all the—hopefully not-too-gory—details, poor sheep."

They were walking along Atlantic Avenue now, and she paused outside one of her favorite places in Brooklyn. "Do you like pizza?"

Mac nodded, following her gaze to the restaurant. Table 73, a local pizzeria, had a tidy facade with a contemporary black and highlights of gold, renowned as the home of the Coal Oven Pizza. Inside was cozier than the outside, that was enjoyed by everyone. Its family vibe had won Savannah over, and it had become a bi-weekly place for her and the girls to visit on Friday evenings. Bustling with energy, she loved it was never quiet, its seats always filled, and laughter and chatter in the air.

"How about dessert pizza?"

Mac tilted his head, his quizzical expression almost comical, and Savannah brought her hand to her mouth in mock horror.

"You've never tried dessert pizza—seriously? You haven't lived!" She held out her hand and dragged him toward the door, feeling ten years younger. "C'mon."

Chapter Fourteen

SAVANNAH

A silver-haired woman rushed around the counter when they entered, rosy-cheeked, with a beaming smile and twinkling eyes.

"Savannah! Where have you been?" she asked, sweeping Savannah into the hug a bear would be envious of.

"Hello Sylvie," Savannah smiled, winking at Mac over the older woman's shoulder.

"I've missed you—and the girls..."

Savannah pulled back, giving Sylvie a rueful grin. "We've missed you too—and your delicious food—afraid work got in the way," she shrugged. "But I'm here now."

"Oh, the Gala! Yes, I read about it! You've been hot goss' around here for a few days. And..." she stepped back to glance around Savannah at Mac. "The mystery Prince Charming! Are you going to introduce us?"

Savannah chuckled, a little flustered.

"Don't you buy into the hype," she said, cheeks now as red as Sylvie's. "This is Mac. He's my brother's business partner."

"And good friend by the looks of it," Sylvie stepped toward Mac, hand outstretched. Her smile reached her eyes, and he liked her instantly.

"Nice to meet you," Mac replied, and Sylvie's eyes widened. "Ohhh, not local—Australian?"

Mac laughed, and Savannah cut in. "New Zealand!"

"We get the same problem as you guys and the Canadian's get," Mac chuckled.

"That's dangerous talk right there," a booming voice sounded from behind the counter, and the three looked at a rotund man of perhaps the same age as Sylvie, adorning chef's whites, red-faced with a moustache and beaming face. "It's like telling the difference between maple syrup and Aunt Jemima's."

Puzzled, Mac flicked a glance Savannah's way, and she laughed. "It's ok, I'll explain while we eat. "Tony, you got any of that delicious soppresata pizza the girls love so much?"

Tony nodded. "I sure do, and your favorite Mediterranean Veggie," and he winked, allowing Sylvie to show them to a table beside the front window.

"You've got a looker there," the older woman said to Savannah in a hushed voice, as though Mac couldn't hear, and he grinned to himself as she gasped.

"He's not mine! He's visiting, so I'm showing him the sights."

"You tell yourself that, sweetheart, you tell yourself. Pictures can tell a thousand words, as can actions. Just you wait—you're made for each other."

Savannah shot him a look. Her eyes widened as she clearly knew he'd heard and fell silent as he pulled out her seat.

"M'lady," he grinned, winking at Sylvie.

Savannah sat, but not before she cut in. "Don't give her ammunition! She doesn't need any help with matchmaking, do you, Sylvie?"

Fifteen minutes later, they stared in mouth-watering awe at a tray with steaming slices of pizza on the table, along with a plate of bruschetta and a caprese salad.

"Wow, they don't go easy on the servings," Mac said. "This looks amazing."

"Wait until you try it!" Savannah reached for a slice of the Mediterranean pizza, eying it hungrily. "Be prepared for a slice of heaven," she warned, lifting her slice with eager anticipation.

Mac, however, didn't immediately dive into his meal. Instead, he observed Savannah savoring the first bite, her eyes closed in pure enjoyment. A sudden wave of warmth washed over him, catching him off guard.

"Enough, already," he chided himself, attempting to shift his focus to his own plate.

But the taste of the pizza couldn't distract him entirely. Throughout the afternoon, memories of conversations with her twin brother, Clay, had resurfaced. One discussion echoed in his mind; a conversation several months ago that revealed the heart-breaking betrayal Savannah had endured.

Clay had been in a foul mood that day, a rarity for him, and Mac sensed something was amiss. After some prodding, Clay reluctantly shared the painful truth about Savannah's marriage and the shocking betrayal by her husband, Charles Carlisle.

As Mac recounted the conversation, he couldn't help but feel a surge of anger towards the man who hurt Savannah. "She rolled up at Nick and Gwen's at eleven at night," Clay explained, his frustration clear. "Soaked by the rain, a single suitcase, and the twins drenched. What kind of father lets that happen?"

Mac's knowledge of Charles Carlisle wasn't based on personal interaction but gleaned from Clay over the years. The disdain he harbored for him growing as he learned more about the man's treatment of Savannah. He may never have met her at that point, but it was clear how much the family wanted her as far away from him as possible. Clay discussed it several times along with the possible interventions.

"She was alright though?" Mac questioned, an immediate flash of regret at the way he phrased it. "I mean, he hadn't hurt her in the physical sense—I mean?"

Clay shook his head. "No, at least Nick didn't think so. She caught him—in their bed with someone from the office."

"With the kids home?"

"Kids were in bed; Savannah was out at a school of parents and teachers meeting. Seems Charlie boy didn't think she'd be home until a lot later."

A heavy sigh escaped Mac's lips, and he shook his head in disbelief. The image of the betrayal vivid in his mind.

"So, she left? Just like that?"

Clay snickered, bitterness in his tone. "Yeah... I often wondered how long it would be for her to see him for the scumbag he is. I just hate..." He shrugged, frustration wrinkling his nose. "I just hate the fact that she, and the girls, hurt so bad."

Mac took a moment to absorb the weight of Clay's words.

"Sometimes it needs that though—it's a bit like ripping the band-aid off. You've said for ages she needed a shot of him. Perhaps this is the shock she needed," he replied.

Clay reached for a printout that had just finished printing and glanced at it before walking across to the windows overlooking the pristine turquoise waters of the lake. "Agree, I just—jeez man, she's my twin sister. I feel I should have been there for her, not prancing all over the world consumed with business."

"Soooo.... are you going to tell me?"

Mac blinked, realizing that Savannah was talking to him, and refocused on the beautiful woman before him.

"Sorry?" He asked.

"The sheep shearing, I want the whole story," she said, brows arched. "Sounds as though it's another perfect wind-up tool."

114

Mac grinned. "I'm not sure Clay will thank me!"

"I can't believe he did that," Savannah laughed. A natural storyteller, Mac told her the tale, embellishing it with words and actions so typical of Clay it had to be true. When he talked, he talked of Clay like a brother, and she liked that.

"He's never uttered a word," she said when he fell silent. "Would you?"

Another laugh, this time belly deep, and Savannah shook her head vehemently.

"Jeez no! In our family, even the slightest sign of weakness and they're all over you! It can take a long time to live down this kinda thing—he'd be mocked about it the rest of his days."

Mac closed his eyes.

"Uh-oh, so I've just given you the ammunition against my best friend..."

Savannah arched her brows and an evil glint twinkling in her eyes. "Oh yes, you did—and it's perfect."

She took another bite of her pizza before adding.

"I used to kick his ass at Donkey Kong. Oh boy, did he get upset?"

"Me too."

Savannah's jaw dropped.

"Sorry?"

"Yeah, you know what the winter months are like. There were a few times we wound up stuck inside, especially during the pandemic. Donkey Kong became a favorite go to — especially for me, because it was one thing I was better than him at."

She snorted. "No way! You're kidding me. Mr-Too-Grown-Up-To-Play-Computer-Games, big city entrepreneur, strait-laced Clay, still playing computer games."

She closed her hand over her mouth, stifling fitful giggles, her shoulders shaking as she laughed so hard.

"I can't believe he... you... oh boy," she raised her arm for the bill, barely giving Mac a head up what she was doing. "We got to go."

He wasn't sure what had just happened. One minute they were enjoying dinner and conversation, the next it appeared she couldn't get out of the restaurant quick enough. The Nutella and banana dessert pizza she'd raved about boxed to go.

It was still early. So, what on earth?

A few minutes later, they spilled out of the door and onto the sidewalk.

"We're going to see how good you are at Donkey Kong," she grinned, seizing his hand, and pulling him along Atlantic Ave.

"What..."

"You'll see. C'mon."

He trailed after her, unable to divert his gaze from the woman who had this uncanny ability to wreak havoc with his senses. Last night, in that silver gown, he thought she was beautiful, but tonight, watching her dart along the street, in a long, loose black skirt, and ankle boots, he questioned if he could ever tire of looking at her.

Even as the notion flickered through his mind, alarm bells rang, yet he pushed them aside. There'd be time enough to worry about that later. Right now, he wanted to savor every fleeting second with Savannah Devereaux. He understood that when this moment ended, they'd each find their separate paths, lead their separate lives, exist on opposite sides of the planet, and never to return to whatever this connection was.

The knot in his stomach tightened, unrelated to the food and everything to do with that last thought.

Back it up, Mac, his inner voice scolded. The last thing she needs is for you to get in too deep. She has enough of a mess on her hands.

Yet, he sensed it was too late. Savannah Devereaux had already well and truly infiltrated his head. Now he needed to ensure she didn't infiltrate his heart, too.

Chapter Fifteen

SAVANNAH

Savannah roused alone the next morning, the chirping of her phone disrupting the quiet. For a moment, she debated ignoring it, but the awareness of the probable callers compelled her to snatch up the phone.

"Hey baby."

Just like the morning before, Jess beamed back at her. "Hey mom!" A brief pause, and then Jess gasped. "You're still in bed?"

Savannah chuckled. "I'm not allowed a sleep-in when you're away?"

"It's a workday, though."

"Who made you my timekeeper, Jessica Cora-Lea Carlisle?"

Jess grinned. "Me! You don't have one, so you need one."

"You rascal!" Savannah sat up, swinging her legs to the floor, stealing a glance at her smartwatch. Seven-thirty. Though she was half an hour later than her usual waking time, Jess was all too aware that she didn't start work before eight thirty. Given she worked from home most days, there was no need to 'dress' for the office, but she also didn't stay in her pajamas!

"Gran says I'm just like you—so who's blaming?" Jess's retort came with a tart edge.

Savannah shook her head, unable to dispute that one. She was aware of how easily the backchat came to her childhood self.

"Are you enjoying yourself?"

Jess yipped. "I am! Especially since my mom started trending on social media!"

"Excuse me?"

"We knew you looked gorgeous in the dress, mom, but wow, the pictures online today are—wow!"

Savannah frowned. "What on earth are you talking about?"

"The pictures of the gala!"

Alarm bells screamed. She'd seen the pictures yesterday. Did that mean more?

"Why are you on social media? And what do you mean, trending?"

"Oh! We're not, Gran showed us. Mom, you looked amazing—but who... ouch! Chloe not funny!"

Savannah squeezed her eyes closed, forcing her breath to steady as her heart slammed in her chest, while the two girls exchanged words.

Seconds later, a wrestling match ensued over the phone. After last night, the last thing she needed... she froze, the memory of Mac on the steps leading to her apartment planting a chaste kiss on her cheek before excusing him.

A surge of embarrassment washed over her, the memory of Mac's polite refusal to come upstairs flooding back with startling clarity. The blood rush to her cheeks as she recalled her impulsive invitation, now regretting it in the harsh light of day.

With a deep breath, she tried to shrug off the lingering mortification, focusing on the matter at hand.

"Mom?"

Jess's voice cut through her swirling thoughts and Savannah blinked, her brow furrowed in confusion.

"Social media?" she echoed, her tone mingled with a mixture of frustration and apprehension. "Will one of you please explain what on earth you are talking about—or hand the phone to Gran?"

It took a few seconds, and the grappling and shrieks of protest continued until an out-of-breath Chloe appeared.

"Hey Mom." Savannah blinked in surprise. Her daughter brushed the hair that had escaped her ponytail away from her face and composed herself. The quieter twin seldom came out on top because Chloe made a habit of walking away from any conflict and letting Jess win.

"You want to explain what on earth Jess is talking about?" Chloe coughed.

"Um..." Her gaze darted to her right, where Savannah assumed Jess stood, then refocused, fidgeting in her seat. "The pictures of you at the Gala. Gran showed us them on her Facebook. You looked beautiful, but..." She searched for the right words. Another yelp — this time from Jessica. Savannah just glimpsed Chloe's arm as she pulled it back, her eyes darting to the side as she smirked at Jess before Jess shoved back.

"The guy..." Chloe said, breathless, moments later, as Jess sat thunderous eyed behind her, arms crossed.

Savannah's eyes slammed shut, and she flopped back onto the mattress, and for the briefest moment, fighting to hide the wave of emotion threatening to overwhelm.

This wasn't happening. What on earth?

She reached for the tablet and swiped the screen, aware that Chloe was still on her phone, but needing to see what on earth was being said now. She didn't have to look far, her social media feed was full, her message inbox even fuller, the headline 'Caption this: When you meet someone who makes your heart skip a beat. #LoveAtFirstSight.'

Jeez, how on earth did she find herself associated with headlines like that? Prince Charming was one thing, but this... there were far more important people at the event to focus on— why her? Why weren't they focusing on the good achieved they'd achieved with the fundraiser?

Insanity!

Savannah's heart pounded as she scrolled down the page, reading comment after comment. Her cheeks flushed. How on earth did this happen? Disbelief washed over her, and she had to fight not to bury her face in her hands.

"Mom?"

She blinked, realizing she still held her phone in her hand, the camera now face down on the bed.

She'd not mentioned the pictures, hoping they'd go away.

They hadn't.

She lifted the phone, forcing a smile as she stared once again into Chloe's face.

"Hey, baby, they're..." Savannah swallowed back the golf ball style lump in her throat, she tossed the tablet ono the bed beside her. She didn't want to see it right now. "Total garbage. I taught you better than to believe everything you see online. Or at least Gran should."

As she said it, she glanced back at the image on the tablet screen.

What would Mac think?

Ha, she wouldn't blame him if he booked the next flight back to New Zealand if he saw this. He hadn't been able to get away quick enough last night, and yet... boy, she'd enjoyed it so much... perhaps too much.

"He looked nice," Chloe commented. "Gran says he's Uncle Clay's friend. Is that right?"

Savannah blinked. The comment was so normal. So... Chloe...

"That's right, baby. He comes from New Zealand. But you... we've all wondered what he's like before."

"Do you like him?"

She didn't reply, wondering how best to frame her words, then said.

"Of course I do. He's Uncle Clay's best friend. It's hard not to."

Like it mattered.

"No—I mean, do you like him?"

She emphasized the 'like' with air-quotes. It was uncharacteristic for Chloe to be so persistent, and Savannah frowned.

"Sweetheart, I only just met him. He's here working with Uncle Clay for a few weeks. So, I'll see him a little while he's here, but that's all."

Okay, so that was a lie. But a little white lie wouldn't hurt—would it?

There was no point in worrying the twins about it. They'd be home soon enough, by which time Mac would wing his way back down under.

Savannah could almost hear the cogs ticking in Chloe's mind as silence resonated. She wasn't stupid, but there was no reason she'd consider anything more. A few pictures made for nothing more than a friendship—particularly to an eight-year-old.

"Mom."

Chloe's spoke in almost a whisper, and Savannah answered. "Yes, baby?"

"You know it's okay to meet someone else, right?"

Savannah froze, the unexpectedness of Chloe's words catching her for the second time in as many minutes, and for a moment she questioned whether she'd heard Chloe correctly.

It took several times of replaying the words over in her mind for her to register that she had.

"Chloe, I'm not ready for anything or anyone yet. There's way too much going on in our lives. Don't worry. I have no intention of..."

"I know, Mom," Chloe interrupted. "We just need you to know that we might only be eight and three quarters, but we love you, and it makes us sad to see you sad. If making new friends makes you happy, then we want you to make lots of new friends."

"And go smoochie, smoochie, smoochie, with Prince Charming," Jess's voice piped up in the background, her face appearing on the screen with her lips pursed as she blew kisses.

Savannah growled.

"I think I need to speak with Gran," she told Chloe, still struggling to comprehend how on earth this conversation had veered off course.

"I'll get her, and Mom..." Chloe hopped from the chair she'd sat on and walked through the familiar doors into her mother's kitchen. "We love you. You really, really, really looked beautiful in that dress."

After pizza, she'd taken him to Barcade, a local hotspot and oh, they'd had fun. The combative streak in both creating chaos as they'd challenged each other at first the vintage Donkey Kong, then Mario, Tetris, and last of all, Pacman.

She couldn't remember the last time she'd laughed so hard, realizing it was the easy camaraderie that made it so effortless. She'd known him just three days now, and yet, she felt as though she could be herself, no pretense, no effort, just be.

As a family, they'd always been boisterous, so fiercely competitive that they'd play for hours. Should she be nervous at how easy to be with Mac was, deny she'd enjoyed every single minute?

The sting of rejection lingered, leaving her bewildered and unsettled.

She shouldn't be worried. They'd agreed, no strings. Work, with a little, or perhaps a lot, of play.

She scowled, the worry of her conversation with the girls, her mother's smart remark about how good she and Mac had looked together, and how she ought to spend the long weekend in Sweetheart Falls. The fact Clay was home, the family would have the chance to meet Mac, and her girls were there, serendipitous in her mother's eyes.

Grumbling, she hauled herself out of bed, wishing for all the world that she didn't feel as though a thundercloud hovered above her head.

When she stepped out of the shower and into the warmth of her bathrobe, her phone chirped again, this time with a text.

"Hey there, princess. Last night was great! Sorry I had to run. How about you and I play hooky today, though? The thought of exploring more of New York with you is too tempting to resist. What do you say?"

Savannah snorted. She ought to throw the phone back onto the bed and ignore it. Give him a taste of the rejection she'd experienced. But, in the same breath, she loved the fact that Mac had followed the same tone she had yesterday.

Flirty, fun, and in the moment.

Had she over-thought about his response last night? Had he even seen the socials?

Still, that little voice bothered. The doubt triggered by his leaving her last night. An incredible evening somehow tainted.

She glanced at her watch. There were a handful of things still needing wrapping up following the debrief, and several follow-up bookings, but the next event was a week away. There weren't a lot of things Felicity couldn't handle if she wanted some time. And there was no way Felicity would mind. In fact, she'd been pushing Savannah to do this for months. It wasn't the way she planned to run the business, but as her family had pointed out, she needed her time, too.

This wasn't about jumping from one overwhelming commitment into another. She had to find a work/life balance that worked for her and her girls.

She sighed.

Who was are you kidding? You want this.

She punched in a response, fighting back a grin.

Two could play at this game.

"Hooky, huh? Well, Kiwi, you might need to work harder for that privilege. Skipping a night doesn't earn you a day of fun. Maybe I'll consider it if you bring a pumpkin chai latte with a sprinkle of cinnamon and a convincing apology."

A minute later came the response.

"Challenge accepted! Coffee and a heartfelt apology on the way. Prepare for the charm offensive, princess."

Chapter Sixteen

SAVANNAH

Dressed in casual blue jeans, a white tee, and a blue blazer, her hair scraped into a neat ponytail, Savannah swung the door open an hour and a half later, to find Mac with a coffee tray in one hand, and two folded brown paper bags in the other.

"I come bearing gifts," he said, holding out the brown bags to her.

She took them, eying him with curious eyes, then unfurled the first.

"Cinnamon Snail?" she asked, eyes widening when she saw the label. Her favorite place in the world for "Cinnamon Buns! My fav..." she said, head tilted to one side. "How did...Clay!

Of course, he'd found out what her favorites were. She wouldn't expect anything less.

"She turned to walk back to the kitchen, hearing the front door click closed behind him, and he followed.

"Pumpkin spiced latte, with a sprinkle of cinnamon," he said, placing the tray on the countertop. "Server suggested I try Apple Crisp Macchiato—so I hope it's good!"

He leaned back, tucking one hand into his jeans pocket, and for the first time since he'd arrives, allowed her gaze to drop, taking in his clothing. Like her, he'd opted for jeans today. Dark navy denim with a brown belt that matched his shoes, an open-necked white shirt that displayed that sprinkle of dark hair that fascinated her so much that first night together, and a black jacket.

Savannah swallowed. How did he do that? No matter what he wore, he looked good enough to eat.

"Just the apology to go," Mac smiled when her gaze lifted to meet his. In his hand, he'd retrieved another bag, which he now held out to her, and she took it, retrieving a small blue bag from within.

"Oh!" she gasped, lifting it out and reading the label. "Colombia La Familia Guarnizo, how... Clay! He remembered?"

It had been her favorite spot to buy coffee beans for a long time. The flavor combination of bitter with sweet, just perfect for the morning hit she needed.

She placed it on the counter beside the other bags and turned to Mac, who watched her with earnest eyes.

"I need to apologize," he said, reaching to take her hand. "Last night was... incredible. No. It was more than incredible. I can't remember having that kind of fun in years."

Savannah nodded, nervous.

Why? She'd wanted the apology, hadn't she?

"Why..." she started, but Mac shook his head.

"Let me explain, please."

He swallowed, his Adam's apple bobbing as he continued.

"I had calls to make. That was true. We're on a very different time to New Zealand, but it wasn't the only reason." This time he lifted a hand to her cheek, brushing it with a tenderness that stole her breath. "The fact is, I understand you were hurt. I promised Clay, I wouldn't hurt you. That I'd do everything it took to protect you. But..." Another gulp, and he inhaled a deep breath, his eyes searching hers. "I'm not sure I can settle for..." he waved his arms between them. "This—the fun and games were a great idea, but I... I want more—I don't know how, or if it's even possible. Or, if I'm honest, you'll even consider it."

Savannah's eyes widened, her breath caught in her throat.

"I... Mac..." she dropped his hand, moving away, desperate to put some distance between them. "I can't, it's... it's too soon... too," she turned, hating the understanding in his eyes, panic permeating every inch of her body.

She closed her eyes, forcing herself to take control.

Breathe Savannah, for God's sakes, pull yourself together.

This was wrong on so many levels.

Too much. Too soon. But he persisted.

"I get it, and it scares the bejeebers out of me. I've known you what—three days? It's insanity, but I want to know you. Not only the Savannah who wants to show me the city she calls home and to spend time with. I want to know the Savannah who kicked Charles' ass when he tried to humiliate you, who made a success with something that should have been so difficult in this city. I want to see the real you, the feisty, confident, fun-loving Savannah who is kicking ass and forging a new life for her family."

For long seconds then, he fell silent, allowing his words to sink in, playing each potential response over and over in her mind and shutting down each conclusion as ridiculous. Aware that Mac watched her, in that same way he'd watched her before, as though he read every expression, and every thought.

"Mac..." she stared up at him, eyes shifting from one eye to the other, trying to read his, but all she could see was.... Fear?"

She lifted her hand to his cheek, so close now his breath brushed her cheek.

"Last night... it hurt. Having you brush me off as though I didn't matter... yes, yes, I... you say you had work, but we'd had so much fun, it was like—I was unimportant. Like..." she saw the tick in his jaw as he tensed, the regret in eyes so clear she didn't want to continue. But she needed to. If she didn't, there'd be a lot of regret for her too. "Like none of this is real."

She emphasized the real with air quotes, blowing out a breath of relief at having gotten those words out.

With every passing minute, she understood him that little more. Liked him a little more. And she liked the thought that perhaps—just perhaps this could work. In the same breath, though, it was the last thing in the world she needed.

Was it selfish to enjoy this so much? When she needed to devote so much time to the girls, to the business, to just learning how to be just her. A part of her didn't want to contemplate this. If she did, she'd run at high speed in the opposite direction.

"Mac," she loved the sound of his name on her lips. "I can't commit to anything yet. I want to—trust me. If you'd told me this time last week, I'd be tumbling into bed with someone and considering something more than a one-night stand. I'd have laughed in your face. Yet here I am, enjoying every moment I get with you. But I can't... I can't commit to anything more than what we have here."

She couldn't lie to herself; she wanted it. But not at the cost of her kids, and this new life—of her independence. It meant too much to be risked.

"I get it, I do. I just need to be honest with you. You deserve that much."

Savannah's smile was small, her eyes sad. "Is it selfish, though?"

"To whom?"

"To you? Denying what had the potential to be good because I'm scared?"

She fell silent, a persistent voice worrying her mind. What would happen if it didn't work? Would it be messy, an inward laugh? Of course it would. He was her brother's best friend. What if she ended up hurt all over again? If she risked giving her heart, only to have it broken?

Could she risk giving her heart? She frowned, a thought crossing her mind. Had Charles ever had her heart at all?

She'd so often considered what it might be like to move on with someone new—someone who wasn't Charles, or anything like him. But she'd shrugged it off as ridiculous. Mac was nothing like Charles. He had values, and morals, two things she found more important than anything else.

She stared into those deep, green eyes, and she knew that she'd experienced nothing like this... whatever it was.

Mac chuckled.

"It's what makes you, you, Savannah." His head tilted to one side as he studied her face, looking for something she didn't know what, before adding. "How about we continue to take it one day at a time? Stick to the fun and games. If it becomes something more, great, if it doesn't, then we've both had an incredible time, and will part ways with a lot of happy memories?"

This time Savannah laughed a hearty chuckle, and she relaxed.

He pulled her close, wrapping his arms around her waist, his head rested against hers.

"I'm sorry," he whispered, his breath teasing her ear, the atmosphere charging. "Last night I had work to do, but tonight," he pulled back to study her face. "I missed what we shared the night before." He grinned, eyes twinkling with mischief. "Fancy a redo?"

The laugh that gurgled out of Savannah surprised even her, their faces so close that the whisper of his breath brushed her neck, sending a shiver right through her.

She liked this.

She liked this a whole hell of a lot.

"Me too," she whispered, cheeks flushed, eyes sparkling with anticipation, but she still added. "I... I thought perhaps you'd had second thoughts. That perhaps...we, we had so much fun last night."

"You mean getting your ass kicked at Tetris?" Mac's sly grin sparked another bark of laughter.

"You mean you getting yours kicked at Mario?"

"Would you settle on a draw?"

"No."

Mac's laugh was belly-deep, and he pulled back, studying her. "Damn, you're as competitive as Clay, aren't you? Your poor family—having to deal with two of you."

"They're all as bad," Savannah quipped. The atmosphere lightened, despite the underlying tension. Mac winced, playing along.

"That would make for some tense vacations," he retorted.

"Or hilarious, depending on which way you look at it."

Mac's eyes dropped to her lips, and her breath stilled, her heart quickening at the intensity of his gaze.

Did he have any idea how hot he was?

Her tongue flicked out to moisten dry lips.

Kiss me. The words played through her mind, and she didn't realize she'd vocalized them until the brush of Mac's thumb across them across them, stole her breath, his featherlight touch, sending ripples through her, her heart pounding the inside of her chest like a rhythmic drum. Each beat the sound of an ancient, potent song only the two of them could hear.

"Mac," she whispered, but she said no more when his mouth closed over hers, his hands coming up to cup her arms, the contact sending ripples of pleasure fluttering through her.

Her moan echoed into his mouth, reciprocated by his, his hands slid up from her wrists to her elbows and upper arms, repeating the movement down, and sending small shivers of pleasure, as the gentle tease of his tongue played across her lips, enticing her to open to his kiss, welcoming him into her mouth and unlocking something else, something that scared the life out of her.

Her arms closed around her neck, allowing his to encircle her waist once more, so that her frame pressed tight against him, pulling her closer, and for long minutes she allowed herself to indulge, enjoying every taste, every nibble, and every breath they shared.

When he pulled back moments later, it took long seconds for her to react. Her eyes fluttered open, meeting the heat of his, wanting to lose herself in them the way she had two nights earlier.

"We have to stop," he said, breathless. "If we don't, we don't leave your apartment today."

Savannah couldn't think of anything she'd like more right now.

"I want to get to know you. Yes, this is about fun, no strings. But I want more than just…" A fleeting look of confusion crossed his face. "Sex."

She blinked.

Sex. It seemed such a basic word. And when he spoke, it sounded nothing like what they'd shared. They'd explored, teased, challenged, and indulged in ways she'd not known possible. Was it because she'd been so starved for attention? Or was it because there was something different? Should she be running full tilt for the hills? Or should she embrace it—enjoy it for what it was?

The alarm bells should be screaming, but they were now silent, as though something in her mind had clicked into place. She just didn't know what.

"It was more than that," she whispered, unable to hide her own confusion. "But you're right. I want to explore this."

She stepped back out of his arms, hating the chill that settled over her. She wanted to stay there, warm, safe, in his arms. To melt into the strength, he offered. Enjoy that sense of security, however damned mad it was. No matter how illogical it was.

She straightened her shoulders, and reached up to re-secure her ponytail, remembering how moments earlier, Mac's fingers had raked through her hair.

Enough.

"Coffee, buns, and we head out. We've got a lot to cram into today, so we'd better get started."

Mac's eyes warmed, his smile deepening, and he reached for the two takeout cups.

"First things first," he said, offering hers and raising his own. "Here's to a busy day on the town."

"And an even busier night on the sheets," Savannah winked as they both laughed. The comment liberating in how flirtatious she'd been.

There was no question of his not staying tonight. Savannah had every intention of exploring every inch of him after they'd explored the city.

"Why did you stay in New York?" Mac asked several hours later.

They stood in front of the Statue of Liberty, gazing out over the Upper New York Bay. Last night, they'd looked over at it from Brooklyn. Now the position was reversed, and Savannah stared at the areas she called home with fresh eyes.

"Because it's the girl's home. They were born here, go to school here." Her gaze travelled the width of the bay, taking in the Brooklyn Bridge, Skyline, and Manhattan Overpass.

"You never thought about raising them closer to your parents?"

"I did," she admitted.

How many times had she considered packing up and going? She'd lost count. The idea of small-town country life for the girls had sounded like a piece of heaven. Only, she'd admitted to herself that it was guilt that had stopped her. The way she'd shut out her family during her marriage had left a gulf that had taken a long time to heal, and while on many levels they were a family again, the guilt still ate at her. She was unsure if she could live so close to her family with that gnawing away at her.

"The girl's life is here, though. They have their friends here, their dance classes, sports teams—their dad...."

The word hung in the air like an unspoken curse, and Mac grimaced.

"How did the lawyer go?"

"Police picked him up yesterday," she replied. She leaned against the cold metal railings, closing her eyes, and allowing the cool sea breeze to brush her cheeks, breathe the salty scent of the sea and the smokiness of hotdogs.

"My lawyer will keep me updated; he says even though this is the first breach, there will be ramifications. What those ramifications are, nobody knows."

She threw up her arms in a gesture of hopeless frustration.

"I'm hoping it's enough to scare him from doing anything again, but in truth..." A shrug. "He's been impossible for months, and if I'm honest, he's escalated."

"His behavior was vile—and given he's a lawyer, he knew what he was doing in violating it—especially with the audience there. If he's escalating, do you feel safe?"

Savannah winced, she hated this line of discussion. She'd had it with Felicity earlier, and Clay before that. Then with her mom, dad, and other brothers, even, and she hated to admit there might be a risk he could get worse. Even her girls had expressed their worry that their father seemed to get angrier.

Being here with Mac drew her away from that world, even for a few hours, and she wanted to embrace that. Immerse herself in something fresh and untainted.

To enjoy not having the worry or the fear, and just be herself—Savannah Devereaux.

Not Savannah Carlisle, ex-wife. Not mom. Or a daughter. Sister. Friend. Just her. Savannah Devereaux.

"Can we change the topic?" she asked, hoping he didn't take offense.

She pushed herself away from the railing and reached for his hand, tugging him into a gentle walk. Closing her eyes, she inhaled the fresh breeze blowing in off the bay, and shuddered, allowing it to permeate her lungs and balance her, relief coursing through her when Mac replied.

"Sure. Honestly, I'd like to talk about anything but him."

He pulled her to face him, stalling.

"In saying that, though, you need to be honest with me. If there is anything you need to talk about, you don't have to hold anything back. I'm here, and I'll listen. No strings attached, like we promised."

She met his gaze. Not for the first-time homing in on those small gold flecks, his expression sincere. With a hint of.... She frowned.... Desperation?

Jeez, why did he have to be so honorable? The way he'd pulled her to face him might have triggered her; she didn't want to answer to anyone, and particularly not a man. With Mac, though, she sensed he cared and concerned for her.

Was it wrong that every time he spoke that way, she found herself that little more connected? Was it wise? Savannah didn't want to consider that now. She wanted to enjoy every moment she had with this sexy kiwi, and Charles Carlisle had nothing to do with any part of it.

She frowned. Not wanting to respond to Mac's comment, and for long seconds held his gaze.

Closing her eyes, she fixed a smile on her face and, bright eyed, said. "Right, so that's Battery Park and the Statue of Liberty. Next,

Ellis Island, and after we're heading downtown. I want you to see the High Line. Sound good?

It was false bravado, but it would do for now.

This was right. Too right. And the more right it felt, the more she questioned it. But right now, that didn't matter. She wanted to enjoy whatever this was, however, temporary it was.

They climbed aboard the ferry and Mac purchased their tickets, sitting close beside her as they continued their tour of the Big Apple.

Chapter Seventeen

SAVANNAH

"I'm sorry, I'm doing it again?" Savannah said a few hours later, her cheeks reddening.

Mac grinned, enjoying Savannah's animated storytelling.

"Doing what again?" he teased.

"Rambling on like a history professor. I can't help it. I get carried away," she admitted, a playful glint in her eyes.

"Well, Professor Devereaux, I'm all ears," Mac said, gesturing for her to continue.

As they strolled through Central Park, Mac's fingers found Savannah's, intertwining effortlessly, as though it were the most natural thing in the world.

He didn't hesitate, didn't question the gesture. It was right, a natural progression of that growing companionship and with their hands clasped, they wandered, taking in the sights and sounds of the park.

All the while, Savannah's voice filled with enthusiasm, narrated the history of the Bethesda Terrace and Fountain. Her words weaving a captivating story of the park's evolution.

Each step they took, the fall leaves rustled beneath their feet, the occasional breeze whipping them into the air before settling them again, carrying with it an earthy, woody aroma, not so different from home.

"I have to say, this is one impressive park. And you make it even more interesting with your stories," Mac remarked, appreciating the moments of quiet intimacy they found amidst this bustling city.

Savannah smiled, her eyes reflecting the glow of the setting sun.

"You're not just saying that, are you?"

"Cross my heart," Mac replied, bringing a hand to his chest in a mock-sincere gesture.

They continued their leisurely walk, enjoying the tranquil haven away from the city's relentless energy, and Mac understood just why the park was so significant to the city's residents. It was like an oasis, a place you could just stop and breath after a frenetic day.

He found himself entranced by Savannah, unable to do anything but admire the way Savannah's eyes lit up when she spoke about the places that held significance for her.

"You know," he said, breaking the comfortable silence, "I've been to a fair share of cities, but this one has a vibe of its own. And you, my dear tour guide, add an extra layer of magic to it."

Savannah chuckled.

"Magic, huh? I like the sound of that."

As they reached Bow Bridge, Savannah leaned against the railing overlooking the water. The city skyline painted a stunning backdrop against the evening sky. Mac joined her, captivated not only by the view but by the woman beside him.

"Sometimes, I think people miss out on the magic in their everyday surroundings. They get caught up in the routine and forget to acknowledge what is right in front of their faces," Mac mused.

Savannah turned to him, her eyes searching his face. "That's why I love showing people around. It's not just about the history; it's about making magic of the things they might have overlooked."

"Well, consider me enchanted," Mac said with a smile, and in that moment, beneath the glow of the city lights, the connection between them deepened, the magic of New York.

Savannah blinked, surprised at moment of introspection. She'd enjoyed how chatty he was, and how open. How, if she asked a question, he had a response. No contemplation, no cover. Just talk.

This is what she needed, and she was enjoying it. More than she possibly should.

Why now? With a man who belonged in a whole other world. A world Clay now called his own. She swallowed, hating the wave of emotion that hit in that moment. She'd been devastated at the new life Clay intended to build, even with the distance between them. The sense of abandonment, even as an adult, bugged her.

"It's okay to feel you know," Mac nudged, watching her closely.

"I know," Savannah replied, but it didn't help.

Was she strong enough to take this on? On top of everything else.

Could she juggle a relationship with the business and the twins, the battle she knew would come with Charles, and simply being able to live?

In that moment she didn't feel strong at all.

Jeez, it would be good to have someone to lean on. Not only to share the struggle, and the load. But to laugh and cry with. To simply be with.

Savannah's eyes welled, and she blinked to keep them at bay, but Mac reached up, using his thumb to rub them away.

"I... I don't always feel strong," she admitted, her voice a bare whisper. "Sometimes, it's like I'm just navigating through the wreckage, trying to keep everything together."

Mac's thumb moved down to brush a gentle stroke over her cheek, a soothing gesture that sent warmth coursing through her. Not the heat she'd become accustomed to, but a comfortable warmth that wrapped around her like a blanket safe.

"That's the thing, Savannah. Strength isn't about being strong all the time. It's about facing the storms, even when you feel you might break. And you, princess, have weathered far more storms than most."

She managed a small, appreciative smile, grateful for his words. His understanding went beyond the surface, connecting with the resilience she had to summon daily. It wasn't just about her past, but acknowledging the scars that lingered, and the nightmares that continued to haunt.

"Strength isn't always loud and assertive. Sometimes, it's the quiet determination to rebuild and create a better life," Mac continued, his gaze unwavering. "You've done that. You're doing that and you have an incredible support network of people around you, if you just open your eyes."

Savannah nodded, taking a deep breath as she absorbed his words. "Thank you, Mac. It's been a long journey, and sometimes it's hard to see the progress when in the midst of it."

"I get that," he replied, his tone soft. "But remember, you're not alone on this journey. You've got people who care about you, people who see the strength in you even when you might not yourself."

As they stood there, a sense of understanding and vulnerability hung in the air. The bustling city around them seemed to fade into the background, leaving just the two of them in a moment of shared connection. Mac leaned in, pressing a gentle kiss on her forehead, a silent reassurance of his presence.

"Ready to continue our adventure through the city?" he asked, breaking the quiet moment with a warm smile.

Savannah frowned, a newfound strength in her gaze. "Great! Let's make more memories."

Mac fought the urge to reach for Savannah's hand as they turned the corner. They were in the West Village now, and the pace of the city seemed to shift to a more leisurely rhythm. The cobblestone streets and historic brownstones added a charm that contrasted with the skyscrapers of Midtown.

Savannah led him toward a quaint cafe with a cozy outdoor seating area. The aroma of freshly brewed coffee wafted through the air, mixing with the sounds of casual conversation and laughter. Mac couldn't help but smile at the inviting ambiance.

As they settled into a table, Savannah grinned, her eyes sparkling with a mischievous glint. "Welcome to one of my favorite spots in the Village. This place has the best cappuccino in town, and their pastries are to die for."

Mac chuckled, appreciating her enthusiasm.

"You're the expert, so I'll trust your recommendation. Cappuccino it is—your life seems to revolve around coffee shops and pastries!"

Savannah laughed, raising her hand to gesture to a nearby server, and placed their order.

"Savannah," Mac said, breaking the comfortable silence, catching her gaze. "I never expected today to turn into such an adventure. I thought I'd be stuck in some generic tourist spots, but you've shown me," he shrugged, glancing around at the surrounding tables, and the window looking out onto the vibrant street. "The real New York—it's fascinating."

Savannah's eyes softened.

"I wanted you to recognize the city through my eyes, Mac. I love it here. There's so much hustle and bustle. The energy, it's alive and so much more than just landmarks. Like..." she contemplated her next words before continuing. "It's a collection of memories. Stories. It's the heartbeat of the people who call it home."

Mac nodded, captivated by her words.

"You've brought it alive for me. It's like I'm discovering a whole new world."

She chuckled, a melodic sound that echoed through the cozy cafe.

"Well, the day's not over yet. We still have a few more stops, so are you ready for the next chapter of our adventure?"

Mac grinned, his eyes locking onto hers.

"Absolutely, Princess. Lead the way."

Mac found himself swept up in the rush hour chaos of the subway to Brooklyn and Savannah's tight grip of his hand. The crowded platform vibrated with the energy of commuters eager to reach home. Despite the throng of people, Savannah navigated her way through the crowd with the deftness of one who fit in the city well, one hand maneuvering her phone as she thumbed a text. The pang of uncertainty pinched Mac, and he had to force the momentary uncertainty.

Mac trailed close behind, his eyes scanning the crowd for a sign of their train's arrival. So much noise–a cacophony of announcements, and the occasional screech of brakes as trains pulled into the station.

Squeezing into the packed subway car, Savannah found a sliver of space near the door, her phone still clutched in her hand, tongue clamped between her teeth, as she focused.

Mac smiled with a mixture of admiration and amusement, marveling at her ability to multitask amid such chaos.

"Why do I get the impression you're up to something?" he asked when she slid her phone into her pocket.

"Moi?"

"Yes, you... you've had a mischievous expression since I asked what is next."

She laughed, her head tilted to one side as she eyed him with what he could only describe as an expression of sweet innocence, but which he found as sexy as hell.

"You'll find out," she said after a long moment.

The train rattled across the East River and into Brooklyn and squealed to a stop at the Court Street station.

"Okay, one stop before we get to the apartment," she grinned as they bustled off the train and into the chaos of the next station and Mac was relieved when they rolled out onto the street, and away from the noise and chaos below ground.

The one stop was Felicity's apartment, which, given it was opposite Savannah's, took Mac by surprise, and his curiosity spiked when Felicity opened the door with a dress bag in her hand, which she passed to Savannah.

She winked at Mac, and he frowned, becoming more confused by the moment.

"Are you going to let me in on this little mystery at some point?" he asked.

But both shrugged, innocent eyed.

He'd seen that expression before when his sisters were plotting.

The elevator chimed as it opened, and Mac turned in time to see Clay step out, also carrying a dress bag.

What the hell?

His eyes widened, and he turned back to Savannah, who was now grinning like the proverbial Cheshire cat.

"Not you too," he groaned when Clay grinned at Savannah, the conspiratorial glint in his eye clear for all to see.

Clay shrugged his shoulders.

"Don't shoot the messenger," he gestured at Mac, before passing the bag to Savannah. "I did as asked."

He winked at Felicity, who smirked back, then stepped back into her apartment.

"Things to do, people to see," she quipped as she closed the door, adding. "Have fun, peeps."

Clay also backed off, giving Savannah the thumbs up, and Mac an innocent shrug before sliding back into the elevator before Mac could say another word.

If this was how the Devereux twins conspired, he was in trouble, and woah, did he know it?

He shook his head as the elevator doors closed, promising himself he'd deal with Clay tomorrow. He watched Savannah slide her key into the door and push it open with the words. "We have an hour to change, and another hour to get into the city. You think we can do that?"

Chapter Eighteen

SAVANNAH

Organizing dinner had proven to be more than a little fun,
Savannah thought as she slid into the little 1920's style black Coco
Chanel dress she'd loaned Felicity last year.

She hadn't imagined she'd need it soon, so had given it to
Felicity on long-term loan. Her friend loved anything twenties and
had a habit of organizing twenties nights in her apartment.

Now, Savannah stood before the dress mirror in her girls'
room, having offered Mac her space to change. She wanted to
surprise him and had been a little apprehensive about what his
reaction would be to her plans, so had opted to use the girls' room
to change.

Savannah twirled, grinning to herself as the tassels at her knees
swayed with each movement, adding an element of play to the
sophisticated cut of the black silk of the twenty's flapper style
dress. The fabric hugged her curves, felt so... she blinked as the
word played through her mind... sexy! She giggled, realizing how
Felicity, or her mother, would have reacted to that. She ran her

hands down her sides, wiggling as she hunched her shoulders, struggling to contain the ripple of excitement and anticipation.

This was fun. Oh, she hoped Mac would enjoy it too.

She reached for her hairbrush, tucking her hair into a tight roll at the base of her skull, and used pins to fasten it, then added the jeweled black flapper band to finish the look. She marveled at how good it was to feel attractive, excited, and even sexy again.

How long had it been?

She didn't even want to consider it. This week was proving to be one of the single best weeks of her life.

She froze when she heard the rap on the bedroom door, anticipation now reaching fever pitch.

"Yes?" she answered in a coy voice.

A low growl emitted through the closed door, and she chuckled.

"Come in!"

The door clicked open, and her breath stilled in her throat, her heart ramping up as she stared wide-eyed and open-mouthed. "Wow," she breathed.

"Keep looking at me like that, and we're going nowhere tonight, lady," he said. husky voiced, he breathed out a low wolf-whistle, adding. "Wow, you scrub up good, Savannah Devereaux."

Savannah chuckled.

"Why thank you, kind sir," she replied in her finest flapper voice, adding. "After the lengths I've gone to tonight—we're going out, buddy..." she eyed him hungrily. "Although, I can honestly say I'm not so sure I want to share tonight."

It was Mac's turn to laugh, and he held out his hands to the side, showing off his new look.

Also in twenty's style, he wore a single-breasted black dinner jacket with satin lapels that fit to perfection, matching pants with the classic twenties' satin strips down the side seam, a white dress shirt and bowtie. But rather than the Oxford's Clay had worn with the outfit, he wore the trainers he'd worn today.

Savannah snickered. "I don't know that they were fashionable in the twenty's" she pointed at his shoes. She exploded into fits of giggles and Mac laughed, closing the distance between them.

"Have I told you how much I love it when you laugh?" he asked, pulling her into his arms.

"No," Savannah replied. "But you can tell me while we walk. We've got a date at a Speakeasy."

She gasped as the word slipped out, her hand coming to her mouth, and she reached for his hand, dragging him from the room before he could ask questions. Rather than argue, Mac went with it, grinning like a demented sophomore with a crush on the lead cheerleader.

"Show me the way," he said, as they left the apartment and onto the street, headed toward Manhattan. Mac's love of books meant he was familiar with the concept of a Speakeasy, but nothing prepared him for the clandestine charm of The Bootleg Bar.

Nestled inconspicuously amid the bustling city streets, its entrance concealed inside a tailor's shop behind a row of fashionable suits. As invisible as it was possible to be.

Savannah muttered the password, Prohibition Punch, and the tailor's assistant pressed the button to open the automatic door, adding to Savannah's conspiratorial tone earlier. Mac squinted into the darkness beyond, his eyes taking a moment to adjust. They descended the steep staircase, so narrow his shoulders brushed the brick wall with each step.

Exposed lightbulbs hung from wires from the ceiling, illuminated with wire pull cords. The doors opened into a world long past. The roaring twenties brought to life with the dimly lit interior that bathed in the warm glow of candlelight and low wattage bulbs. Framed photographs and memorabilia adorned the walls and shelves, and you'd be forgiven if you thought you'd literally travelled back one hundred years to the prohibition.

149

"Wow," Mac breathed as they stepped inside, the surprise within rendering him speechless. Plush velvet curtains draped the windows, muffling out the sound of the city outside, while the air thrummed to the rhythm of a live jazz band, on a stage in a corner. Dark wood tables and chairs, sofas, and armchairs, with low coffee tables, and dark wood bar stools all added to the ambience, the art deco ambience clear in the bar's design and the mirrors behind it.

A magical underground world, underground.

"Wow, indeed," Savannah said, taking his hand and leading him to the bar. "Welcome to the world of ye-olde New York," she grinned. "You've seen the modern city. Now enjoy an insight into the past."

"This is what I always wanted," Savannah said when they'd ordered their drinks.

"What? A bar?"

"No," she laughed. "The ability to go out on a date and have fun. To laugh. To experience the..." she shrugged, embarrassment heating her cheeks. "Romance."

Mac smiled. "I get what you mean. This place is," he shrugged. "Magical?"

"I don't mean just here; I mean, to go out and enjoy myself. Not to have to include business in it, or worry about who is looking at who, having an affair with whom, or whatever. The world I lived in with..." she hesitated before she spoke his name. "Charles... it was different. Cutthroat, class driven, ugly... not nice. If that makes any sense."

Mac did.

Even in New Zealand, while it boasted no social classes, there were clear divides between the middle and higher income, and often seen in the very events that Savannah had organized.

His own family had long sat in the high income but had sustained their standing in their community by not flaunting their wealth. Instead, they worked side by side with everybody. Whether it was on the PTA board at school, or volunteering at a town fair, it didn't matter. They all waded in with their shirt sleeves up ready to get into the thick of it. The Devereaux's were the same. It was why he and Clay were friends and had been so long.

The barman passed Savannah the Gin Fiz she'd ordered, followed by Mac's Whisky Sour, and he eyed them with speculative eyes. "Not the same strength as moonshine, right?"

Savannah laughed. "Not a chance—although there are a few under the counter options if you're game."

"Thanks, but I'd like to stay sober tonight—the idea of rolling home drunk doesn't cut it."

"Good, because I have more than a few plans for later."

"Tell me about you," Savannah said as they sipped their drinks. "I know about where you're from, but what about your family?"

It seemed ironic that she asked that when he'd only considered them moments earlier.

"What do you want to know?

Savannah shrugged. "Your home, not just Mackenzie. I get how magical that is. Tell me about your family home, your mom and dad, your... sisters, is it?"

Mac smiled.

"Yup, two sisters, an older and a younger. Maggie is the older sister, Maria is the younger."

"Are you close?"

"Yup–Maggie and her husband live on the farm with mum and dad."

"Mum, that sounds funny—I'm so used to hearing mom."

Mac chuckled. "It's kinda weird hearing mom too, although I've heard it enough from Clay now that it doesn't jar the way it used to."

"What do they do?"

"You mean job wise?"

Savannah nodded.

"My parents live on the farm that has been in the family for more than one hundred and fifty years."

Savannah snorted. "Ha, sounds like our place."

"It is kinda," Mac replied. "Although I've never seen Heaven Sent—such a random name for a house."

The name of the family home rolled off Mac's tongue as though he'd known it for a lifetime, and Savannah found herself homesick. The name of the old house always resonated.

"Did Clay ever explain where the name originated?" she asked.

Mac nodded. "He did, but in truth, I don't remember the ins and outs—Clay said your ancestor built it and named it for his wife. Is that right?"

Savannah nodded. "Yup, Jacques Devereaux, my great times eleven grandfather built it. He escaped the Revolution in France at the end of the eighteen century and made a life here in the new world. His fiancée, Charlotta, left six months before him, but stayed in New York, or" she shrugged. "It was called New Amsterdam in those days—while Jacques attained land and built their home."

She took a long drink of the icy cocktail before continuing.

"The French monarchy granted him land pre-Revolution but hadn't planned on travelling until he married. Unfortunately, the Revolution brought that forward. "

"It's incredible that you have such clear insight into the story. Two hundred years is a long time," Mac commented, sipping his own drink, and Savannah laughed.

"I suppose the joy of still living in the family home all these generations down the line, is that you are surrounded by its history, whether it's in the portraits hanging in the main entrance, or the archives that have been well preserved over the centuries. We have fascinating collections of diaries, including Carlotta's. That mean even today we understand at least their personal experiences of the day." She frowned. "How did we get back on to my family? I was asking about yours!"

Mac grinned. "I can't help being fascinated by you."

"Excuses! C'mon," Savannah eye rolled.

"Okay, okay," Mac held his hands up in a gesture of surrender, the twinkle in his eyes still there. "In the old days, it was Mount Cook Farm, but my grandparents renamed in the sixties, as Starry Summit. Predominantly because of the rolling hills that led into the Southern Alps, and the incredible skies. I've told you before, only how incredible it is, and our family was lucky enough to have farmland across the plains and into the mountains." He reached for his phone and swiping the screen. He tapped a few more times before turning the screen in her direction. "Here, this is the farm. I'm surprised Clay never showed you a picture before."

Savannah glanced at it and nodded. "He has. I never placed the significance until now though—it's beautiful."

Unlike the stately splendor of Heaven Sent, the farmhouse was a sprawling white homestead, with a white veranda, and steps leading to a front yard filled with roses and other flowers. The vista behind was breath-taking.

"Is that your mom?" Savannah asked, pointing to a round, silver-haired lady with her hair secured into a bun, dressed in a long floral dress, and pink cardigan.

Mac nodded. "That's mum, and that," he pointed to a rotund man with the same chaos of curls as Mac's, leaning against the veranda railings with a pipe in his mouth. "That's dad."

"I see where you got your hair from," Savannah laughed.

"They're good folks," Mac said, a fondness in his eyes that caused Savannah's stomach to flutter. "They've worked hard their entire life. Not just on the farm, but with our other businesses. We have a few vineyards in Mackenzie, Otago and the Marlborough region, and a handful of small hotels—and Airbnb's, so life is never dull. Although, my sisters- and brother-in-law now play a big part in overseeing the business side of things—we've been trying for a few years now to get dad to slow down. Unsuccessfully, I hasten to add."

Savannah laughed, "Sounds like our dad," she eyed him with thoughtful eyes. "I'm taking it the hotel connection is where the Mackenzie project fits in?"

"It was something I dreamed of for a long while, so when Clay decided it was time to bite the bullet," he shrugged. "We've not stopped since."

Savannah laughed. "The typical Clay whirlwind—no chill, huh!"

They talked for hours, savoring drinks and dinner, before Mac reached across the table to take Savannah's hand. The touch sending shivers of awareness through him and with a gentle smile, he tugged her to her feet, his eyes twinkling as he said. "You know, I reckon that's more than enough talk. It's been over an hour since I laid my hands on you."

The jazz band's tempo had slowed, and now played a slow, sultry melody, and without hesitation, Savannah rose from her seat.

Mac led her to the makeshift dance floor, pulling her into his arms and, as they swayed to the music, he fell deeper as he held her in his arms.

Even on a light, easy-going date, he couldn't get enough of her. He'd talked, and she'd listened, but the entire evening he'd hung out for those breathless laughs, the moments when she held his gaze, so that the prospect of looking into any other eyes than those baby blues, was unthinkable. Watching the way her expression changed when she played thoughts and questions through her mind, the way her lashes lowered when she flushed or twinkled when she considered doing something out of the ordinary. Like this.

She was perfect in every sense of the word. But was that enough?

He tensed, hating that he'd even thought about it.

Casual fun.

Who're you kidding, Mac? You're head over heels.

Only...

Savannah pulled back, blue eyes homing in on his, clearly sensing his tension, her brows furrowed in that too-familiar frown.

"What's the matter?"

"Nothing," he lied, hating himself.

"Mac?"

"Serious, princess, it's nothing."

Savannah's heart sank as she felt the growing distance between them, a chasm widening with each moment. She couldn't shake off the unease gnawing at her insides. A nagging feeling that something was amiss, but she couldn't put her finger on it.

Her gaze locked with Mac's searching for the warmth and reassurance she craved, but. instead found a barrier, a wall her had erected between them.

The realization stabbed at her, the sharp pang of disappointment and confusion followed fast in its wake.

"Why are you lying?" she blurted out, her voice trembling with a mix of vulnerability and frustration.

She needed answers, clarification.

The evening had been perfect up until this point. What happened?

A suffocating silence followed, heavy with unspoken words, the steady beat of the band lost. Savannah watched as Mac's fingers twitched, a fleeting gesture that betrayed his obvious turmoil.

She longed to reach out, to bridge the gap that had emerged, but she held back, uncertainty holding her in a vice-like grip.

When he finally spoke, his words hung in the air, hesitant, with a profound sadness.

"Sav..."

"No, Mac," she cut him off, her voice firm despite the tremor of uncertainty beneath the surface. "This..." she gestured between them, "whatever it is between us—it can't survive on half-truths and hidden feelings. I need honesty. If you can't give me that, then..." she trailed off, her voice faltering as she struggled to find the words to convey the depth of her emotion.

For a moment she fought back the threat of tears, the waves of anger and disappointment.

"You were right," she finished, on a hoarse whisper. "Fun and games don't work. I was a fool to think they could."

And with that, she walked to their table, collected their coats, and swept out of the bar, without a backward glance.

Chapter Nineteen

SAVANNAH

Savannah stepped out onto the sidewalk and stood momentarily to inhale a deep breath, trying, and failing, to find some semblance of balance. Things had gone so well—and yet, in the blink of an eye, here she was again—alone.

"Savannah."

Okay, so not totally alone.

"Leave me alone, Mac," she murmured, not wanting to get into any form of discussion with him. Right now, she wasn't sure if she was angry, or plain devastated. She needed to put as much distance between herself and Mac as was humanly possible.

She stepped to the edge of the sidewalk as she saw a yellow cab approach and smiled a weak smile at the driver when he pulled alongside her.

"Remsen Street," she said, pulling the door open and sliding into the seat. At the same time Mac climbed in on the other side.

She muttered an expletive, but nothing else.

Damn him.

Even when he was an asshole, he had to act chivalrous.

The cab pulled out, the air inside thick with tension, and she forced her gaze straight ahead, not trusting herself to maintain her control.

It wasn't until the cab pulled alongside her building, and Mac insisted on paying the bill, that she finally broke the silence.

"You didn't need to see me home, and you sure as hell didn't need to pay the bill," she snapped, as she fished in her bag for her security tag.

"I damned well did, and I'm not having you pay the bill because you're packing some kind of snot."

What?" Savannah turned and gaped at him. "Snot? Is that what you think this is?"

She knew all too well what a snot was. The twins had thought the New Zealand term for a tantrum was hilarious.

Mac shook his head.

"I don't know what this is—all I know is that we were having a great evening, and then" he shrugged, as though he were confused. "This."

Non-perturbed, Savannah snapped. "I was married to a liar for nearly nine-years. If you can't tell me the truth when something is clearly bothering you, we've got nothing."

"Is that what you think?" Mac bit back, taking her by surprise. "That because I don't share how I feel. I'm lying to you?"

"Are you?"

"Does it matter? Because I can also tell you're lying?" There was no anger in him, only a sense of resignation, and Savannah's jaw dropped. Every muscle in her body tensed as she stared at him goggle-eyed.

"What?"

"You heard me, princess. Don't tell me you don't feel it." He wasn't shouting, his voice a deadly calm. "If you'd told me on the weekend, I'd have fallen head over heels for Savannah Devereaux,

I'd have laughed in your face. But hey, here I am, on a Brooklyn sidewalk, acting like a complete prick, because I promised you fun, no strings, and guess what—I can't give you that!"

He blinked, clearly surprised at what he'd said. Checking himself, he closed his mouth, shaking his head.

"The fact is Savannah; we have the potential to have something good. I've told you that, and I told you where my hang ups are. But I can't keep lying to myself. If we can navigate the crap that comes with it, this can be something great—something fantastic. The question is, are you game enough to try, or will you continue lying to yourself and go back to the sham you're living?"

She frowned, dropping her gaze to the step, as though avoiding any chance of meeting him. She hadn't expected to have so much fun, but that's what this was, and was enjoying it too much.

"You're doing it again."

She glanced up, unable to resist the warmth of his gaze, the concern clear in the dip of his brow.

"What?" she snapped, defensively.

"Overthinking. Whenever your eyes drop that way, your face tells a thousand tales of why this can't—or won't work."

Savannah blanched.

"That's not..."

"Go on, deny it," Mac cut in.

She couldn't. This was the legacy she carried from her marriage, it was obvious, and she was powerless to change it.

Mac stepped forward, cupping her chin, so close, the whisper of his breath on her lips, and she had to fight the urge not to melt against him, anticipating him close the distance between them. Only this time, he didn't.

Her breath suspended, his hurt gaze holding hers firm.

"What?" she murmured.

He stepped back, leaving her alone, and she froze, cold permeating every inch of her.

"Is this so wrong?"

The unexpectedness of his question knocked her off guard, and she blinked when he continued. "Listen, I understand this is crazy. Correction, its insanity, but the fact is you're in my head, Savannah. From the moment I wake to the moment I sleep. When I'm working, you're," he tapped his head, "In here when I'm sleeping too. I don't understand, I don't pretend to. But there's a reason, and I want to explore it. But, if need be, I'll wait. For however long it takes."

He raked a hand through his hair, frustration clear in his stance. "One thing I will tell you, though, and it's a promise. I'll never, ever lie to you—from hereon in, it's honesty all the way."

Savannah's eyes widened. Surprised when he voiced the very thing she'd played through her mind moments earlier.

Was she still hung up on the past?

She couldn't deny that last night she'd wondered at the possibility of moving on. Of leaving Charles in the past. Not just for the girls, but because she was all-too aware that Mac was the somebody else, she'd unconsciously been looking for.

The thought of being able to curl up in a man's—not just any man—Mac's arms at night, to share conversation about their day, to walk and talk, and laugh. But she'd shrugged it away as a ridiculous dream.

She believed right down to the core that Mac was the person she would be happy with—but was she ready? No, not yet.

She had too much catching up to do. Not to mention too much living.

"That's not what..." Savannah cut in, but Mac stopped her.

"Savannah, perhaps I need to give you some space, what this is..." he gestured between them, hesitating before he continued.

"Whatever this is, it has the potential to be good. But only when you're ready for it."

Savannah gulped, all-too aware of the golf ball sized lump in her throat, wanting to argue, but unable to find words.

How had they gotten to this point? Tonight, had been so good—last night and the night before, too. How was it only three days?

"I need to go," Mac said, his voice toneless, and the sound ripped something deep inside Savannah wide open.

Savannah couldn't find the words to respond, and she squeezed her eyes closed when Mac reached into place, a chaste kiss on her lips before backing away. She felt herself crack. The pain was so deep she wanted to curl up there and then and will the world away. His closing words cut even deeper, and he took her security tag from her, and opened the front door, before passing it back to her and gesturing for her to enter, his eyes burning into her back as she made her way through the lobby and into the elevator.

She'd known this would end in tears. The question she asked herself over and over, though, was whether she wanted it to end.

Alone in the apartment, Savannah glanced around at the space, loneliness permeating bone deep.

What happened? They'd had such fun. Not playing stupid games, but walking, talking, laughing. It had been so right.

She shrugged off her jacket and threw it at the coat hanger, ignoring it when it missed and fell to the floor. She kicked off her shoes and walked across to the small kitchenette. Wishing it wasn't so late.

Her fingers traced absent-minded patterns on the countertop. Right now, she'd do anything to sound out what had happened with Felicity, only she knew she wouldn't like what she said. Felicity had a way of saying it as it was, and plenty of times Savannah had wished she'd not asked.

Turning toward the window, she gazed down at the street below, a faint hope flickering that she might glimpse Mac before he vanished. But there was nothing. A pang of disappointment gripped Savannah.

With a heavy sigh, she retreated to the bathroom, the hot water of the shower offering a temporary respite from her emotions, and as she stripped away the layers of the day and stepped beneath the steaming jets, the tears fell. A silent release of emotion that was a vulnerability she seldom allowed herself to indulge in, yet, in that moment, it was the only thing she could do.

She took her time washing her hair and face, finding no relief in the usually comforting action of massaging shampoo into her scalp. Instead, she turned to stand with her face facing into the steady stream of steaming water, wishing it would wash away the disappointment and hurt.

Still, the tears fell, and it took long moments for the sound of knocking to penetrate her foggy mind, the noise gradually building to a frenetic pace that seemed to reverberate through the apartment walls.

"What the..." she muttered to herself, hastily turning off the shower and wrapping herself in the plush white towel robe.

"Mac?" she whispered hopefully, her pulse quickening at the prospect of seeing him again.

Who else would knock at this time? Had he had second thoughts? How on earth had he gotten into the building? Was she capable of being honest about her own feelings? Giving Mac hope where she'd not dared?

Somewhere deep inside, a little hope sparked. Perhaps he'd reconsidered walking away? Perhaps, just perhaps...

Any hope dashed as she swung open the door.

"Charles..." she trailed off, her voice faltering as she found herself face to face with her ex-husband, his expression twisted with fury. "What..."

"Slut."

The word hung in the air like a venomous serpent, its sting slicing through Savannah's defenses with brutal force, and she recoiled. Memories of their marriage now flooding back with chilling clarity.

"You can't..."

He grabbed for her hair, knotting it in his fist and driving her backward into the apartment, kicking the door closed behind him, the fury in his eyes almost madness. "Did you really think I'd let go so easily? And for..." he searched for the words, but finding nothing, spat. "You're mine... who the hell do you think you are calling the police?"

"You're..."

Still, he didn't let her continue. "You're my wife, and you have my daughters, and you have the gall to put yourself on your back for a stranger?"

Desperation clawed as she struggled against his hold. He had her against the wall now, fisting her hair so tight it hurt. "Charles, please, stop..."

But he didn't. His other hand cupping her chin, not gently the way Mac had earlier, but with fierce, unforgiving fingers that she knew instinctively would bruise. She pushed at him, but he didn't shift, his hold only tightening, as he spat the next words. "They're threatening to disbar me, because you couldn't keep your mouth shut... or was it your brothers'?"

He tilted his head to one side, his face so close to her the stench of stale scent of alcohol lingering on his breath.

"Charles, stop, please, en..."

"You think that your theatrics will stop me running for office?"

Savannah wriggled harder, kicking out at his shin. She missed, and instead, Charles used the move to pin her closer to the wall, his knee between her legs so that she had even less leverage.

"You did that yourself," she gasped desperately, her hands now coming up to claw at his shoulders.

"No—you did it, you spread your legs. Thought you could just brush me off like I didn't matter—hashtag love at first sight. Do you have any idea of how pathetic you look?"

Savannah's gasp brought with it a small shriek of disbelief, and she stared back at him.

"Me? I couldn't keep my legs shut. Who was the adulterer? You don't know the meaning of fidelity. And as for hashtag—Mac's twice the man you ever were."

Charles shifted, grabbing at her wrists, and lifting them above her head, pinning them to the wall. The other arm folded so that his forearm pinned her by the throat, restricting her airway.

"I can't br..." she gasped, twisting to free herself, to breathe in much needed oxygen, but as darkness consumed her, a sound shattered the suffocating darkness.

She didn't finish the word. A thundering crash resounding through the small space, followed by a strong, sure arm hooked around Charles' throat, wrenching him away with a forced that left Savannah gasping for breath.

"Get off," Charles roared, his attempts to break free thwarted by his unseen assailant. "She's my wi..."

"She is not your wife, nor will she ever be," came the furious response, the familiarity of the voice sending goosebumps rippling through her. She'd never experienced that level of anger in his voice, the warmth and fun of his voice gone and replaced by something she hoped she'd never hear.

"Mac," she breathed in barely a whisper, but he was too far gone.

"You ever, ever come near her again and I'll make sure you never walk again. No, correction, I'll make sure you never breathe again—you got that?"

"You can't threaten me, I'll sue…"

A click, and the door of the apartment opposite opened, cutting Charles off mid-sentence.

"What…oh my God," Felicity's gasped.

What happened next happened so fast, she barely had time to process it.

Charles, using Felicity's interruption, ducked out of Mac's grip, running at Savannah with a roar, snatching her by the hair and dragging her further into the apartment.

Savannah screamed.

The sound of a fist making contact so loud it echoed, and Charles propelled backwards for the second time, this time against the kitchen counter.

"You don't learn, do you, Carlisle," he roared. "Felicity, get the cops now, and Carlisle. You…" he glared at Charles. "Don't move, you got me?"

"Don't give me orders," Charles spat. His body language changed. Suddenly the rat in the trap, not the aggressor, but Savannah recognized it for the mask it was. Her eyes blank, as Mac walked to her, lifting her from the floor into his arms and in that moment, she was safe.

"Mac…" she murmured, but he shook his head.

"Not now. Hush. We'll talk later."

He carried her across to the armchair and set her down, and somewhere in the distance she Felicity's voice spoke to the police. "You're safe," Mac said, brushing her wet hair away from her forehead, and for the first time she realized what she was wearing.

He reached for the belt and tightened it, never for a moment shifting his gaze from hers, instinctively protecting her in the way she'd known he would. The concern in his eyes, so deep it reached into her very core, but there was no way of acknowledging it.

Not now.

She heard movement, and Mac shifted, shaking his head.

"He's gone." He stroked her tangled hair, tucking it behind her ears, his voice gentle as he said. "Don't worry, the cops will catch up with him. You're safe, princess. He'll never do this again."

Savannah nodded. As for the second time tonight, the tears fell, and this time she didn't stop them, giving way to the fear, the shock, and the overwhelming emotion of the night.

Chapter Twenty

MAC

Mac wasn't sure he'd ever experienced anger at the level he had at that moment. The sight of Savannah pinned against the wall; a sight he knew would haunt him for the rest of his days. If he thought Carla's death had affected him. Witnessing the attack on Savannah took it to a whole new level, and he knew instinctively he'd take Charles down before he ever let him near her again.

If there had been any question that Charles was violent before, it had been reinforced now. White-hot rage consumed him. The night of the gala angered him, but this... this was not only an escalation of dangerous proportions. Charles posed a real present threat to Savannah.

He glanced down to where Savannah sat. Her face drained of any color; every muscle was taut.

"Savannah," he murmured, but she shook her head, unable to talk. "Sweetheart, the police are going to be here, we need to get you..."

Another, more violent shake of the head, and he noticed it wasn't only her head, her entire body racked with shivers. Her skin was pale and clammy, her breath shallow. A whimper tore from her, a feral, desolate sound, and she was still.

"Sav? I'm here, sweetheart, you're safe." He leaned forward, studying her face, noting the blank look in her eyes. "She's going into shock."

Once more, he took her into his arms, hating that she'd withdrawn so much he couldn't reach her. Angry bruises were already forming in her throat, and Mac's murderous rage grew.

"I'll call Nick. She won't want an ambulance," Felicity replied.

She walked into the kitchenette and switched on the kettle, barely taking her eyes from him or Savannah.

A sound by the door caused them both to look up in the same moment Clay stormed through. Mac had broken it when he kicked it open, and they'd been unable to secure it. Instead, placing a seat in front to alert them if anyone entered.

"What the f..." he didn't finish the sentence, his gaze settling on his sister, all blood running from his face.

He stalked across the room.

"Sav..." he knelt in front of her, brushing her hair from her face, the rush of emotions so like what Mac had experienced moments earlier playing across his own. His furious gaze met Mac's; the question was simple.

"How did he get in?"

Mac explained what had happened, missing nothing as Clay's expression blackened with thunderous intent.

"Why aren't they doing something about it? He needs locking up. I want to..." he bit off what he wanted to say, when Felicity coughed, nodding to Savannah, who, Mac still held wrapped in his arms. "Savannah and the girls need a really long holiday down under. Give the authorities time to deal with Carlisle."

"They'll lock him up," Mac retorted. "He hurt her, physically this time, and we witnessed it. There's no way they can ignore it."

Clay wasn't assuaged.

His fingers brushed across the bruises on Savannah's neck, and for the first time, she flinched, her gaze lifting to meet her brothers, eyes red and swollen.

"I'm... I'm sorry," she murmured, as tears continued to fall.

Clay stood, and Mac released his grips, allowing his friend to lift her into his arms. He followed, as Clay carried her across to the bedroom, where he pulled back the duvet, and placed Savannah on the bed, wrapping the soft cotton blanket around her, helpless as once again the shivers took hold.

Felicity drew the curtains, and came across to climb onto the bed, wrapping herself around her friend, and Mac watched enviously, wishing he could be the one to offer her the support, but knowing in that moment she didn't need him. She needed friends and family—those closest to her.

The night stretched on endlessly as Mac and Felicity recounted the events to the police, Nick and Gwen took turns attending to Savannah, and Clay fielded calls from concerned family members. Amid the chaos, Mac stood by the window, hands buried in his pockets, staring out into the darkness below.

Guilt held him in its grip, and a futile sense of impotence. He wanted to look after her, to protect her, but how could he, when she had all this going on in her life?

Clay joined him, his expression mirroring Mac's mixture of frustration and worry.

"She, okay?" Mac asked quietly, his voice heavy with concern.

His friend let out a heavy sigh, his gaze still fixed on the street below.

"Yea, Nick says she's physically fine," he replied, his words punctuated by a sense of helplessness. "But the emotional toll..."

Mac nodded grimly; his jaw clenched. "I can't believe that bastard had the nerve to show up here," he muttered, his fists balling at his sides. "I saw him—no, I saw someone—I thought it might be him, and then questioned myself. Damn, I'm glad I came back—if I hadn't..."

"Don't... you can't beat yourself up for something that already happened. Jeez, we had people watching him this week. Somehow, he slipped them. There'll be room for questions—a lot of questions—later. Right now, let's just worry about her."

Mac's jaw tightened.

"He won't get away with this," he vowed, his voice low, but determined.

Clay nodded agreement.

Just then, Felicity emerged from the bedroom, her expression weary, but resolute. "She's resting now," she reported, her voice tinged with concern. "She's gonna need all the support we can give her, though."

Mac nodded, his gaze softening as he turned to face her. "We'll be there for her," he promised, his words carrying a quiet resolve, and he wondered if Savannah would even accept his support after this.

As the first light of dawn crept through the window, Mac wondered if he'd ever experience a sunrise without it reminding him of this night again.

"We have meetings with the New Zealand Tourism Board today. I don't want to leave..." Clay said at a little after seven.

Mac nodded, his mind already racing through the tasks that awaited the day. "You're good, Clay. I'll take it. I also have the compliance sign off for the spa, and the last sign off for the Paradise Under the Stars campaign today, so it's a full one."

A grateful smile spread across Clay's face.

"You're a good man, mate," he said, sincerely, the weight of the situation clear in his voice. "I really want to stay here. Everything's so..." he grappled to find the right word. "Uncertain," he finally settled on.

A pang of empathy coursed through Mac as he nodded in agreement. "I understand, Clay," he replied, his voice tinged with sympathy. "It's a tough situation for you all."

Clay frowned, holding Mac's gaze, as realization dawned.

"You're in love with her, aren't you?" He said in barely a whisper.

"Not the time, mate," Mac murmured.

"Come on, I've known you too long. You've never..."

But Mac didn't want to discuss it. Not now. He, too, was raw. The guilt of the disagreement, of walking away the way he did. What did mum always say? Never go to sleep on an argument.

Okay, so they weren't a couple per se, but he'd done the one thing he'd known never to do. He'd walked away from the woman he loved and left her exposed to...He couldn't shake the sense that if he handled things differently, he might have prevented all this.

He'd been walking away when he'd spotted Charles lurking on the corner. At first, he'd not been sure it was him, and he'd continued. As he'd walked, he'd questioned himself. Felicity said Charles lurked outside of Savannah's apartment building. Was it possible?

He'd turned and stalked toward Savannah's street, noting when he arrived Charles was not there and for a moment, he'd been relieved. Fortunately, though, worry gnawed at him.

He'd glanced up at the windows of Savannah's apartment.

If it had been Charles? If he'd seen her with Mac? Seen their disagreement?

Christ, had he been watching them the whole time—why hadn't he been more aware?

He knew the answer.

When he was with Savannah, she was all he could see or think about. Jeez when he wasn't with her, she was all he could think about. This was a mess on every level.

Even as the thoughts played through his mind, he remembered the moment he'd known something was wrong. He'd slipped through the door behind a couple focused entirely on each other. He ignored them, his steps fueled by the strengthening sense of foreboding, bounding up the staircase with single-minded determination.

He arrived at Savannah's floor, an eerie silence greeting him that only heightened his sense of dread. The air was heavy, and he sensed tension, a silent precursor to the storm that awaited behind Savannah's door.

The muffled sound from within reinforced it, a small scream followed by the sound of a struggle, and without hesitation, Mac threw his full weight behind him, his foot connecting with the solid wood with a solid crash.

The door yielded under the blow, swinging open to reveal a scene straight out of his worst nightmare. Seared into his mind like a brand, he roared as he lunged toward Charles, aware that this image would haunt him for a long time. A moment frozen in time and etched with chilling clarity. Another reminder of Carla, but now also, the woman he loved, Savannah.

"Maybe you need to put your head down for a bit," Clay asked, and Mac blinked, realizing he'd been so consumed with memories, he'd not heard his friend speaking.

"Sorry?"

"It's been a long night. Get a couple of hours shut eye before the meeting?" Clay repeated.

Mac knew he needed to, but he wasn't sure he'd be able to shut his mind off.

He wanted—no—he needed to be here, to be close. But in the same breath, he knew, the meetings would give him a welcome distraction.

The last thing Savannah would need was him hovering over her. Not when her family was so close.

The next few days, possibly even weeks, were going to be hectic. What she'd gone through tonight was an escalation beyond what any of them expected. And yet...

You should have known, Mac. You saw it with Carla. Why didn't you keep your eyes open? Stay alert? Wasn't that your promise?

With an inward groan, he met Clay's concerned gaze.

"You're right, mate. I'll go back to the apartment, change, and grab a couple of hours shut eye on the cot in the office," he raked his hand through his hair, ruffling it irritably, before adding. "You'll contact me if anything changes, if she needs..." he didn't add *me*, he'd no right to. If he hadn't put her in the position he had, it was doubtful they'd even be here.

Mac reached for the dinner jacket he'd worn last night, his fingers brushing against the fabric, as for the first time he noted the torn lapel, the stark reminder of the chaos Charles had unleashed.

His heart sunk, the laughter and camaraderie of the speakeasy, a faded memory against the wreckage that followed.

"Sorry 'bout this," he grimaced, holding it up to Clay.

"You're good, Charles will get the repair bill—don't worry about it."

Mac nodded. "Ok, I'm outta here," he glanced toward Savannah's bedroom door, and then back at Clay. "I know I don't need to say this—but look after her, right."

"We've got her, you're good."

The expression in Clay's eyes told him what he needed to hear, and Mac turned to the door.

Savannah needed time, space, and the chance to heal. He'd give her that, and then perhaps—damn it he hoped there would, be the potential of a future for them.

As he reached the front door, Clay spoke. again "It's a mess, I know, but don't give up on her mate. It's clear whatever you have is good. Give us a couple of days, okay."

Mac hadn't said anything about what happened before Charles turned up, and he knew he should, but that was for Savannah to say. Until then, he'd wait.

Chapter Twenty-One

SAVANNAH

"Darling," Cora-Lea Devereaux swept down the steps, not giving Savannah the chance to finish climbing out of the car before she swept her into a worried hug. "We've been so worried."

Savannah offered a small smile.

"I'm good, mom. Excited about this weekend."

She tried and failed to reflect any excitement, though.

The past four days had been a whirl of activity, and not the kind she enjoyed.

Lawyers, police reports, and a new therapist, at Clay's insistence, had kept her busy from the moment she opened her eyes, until the moment she fell into bed exhausted. A reflection of those days of her marriage—and just as negative.

"It will be so good to have you all under one roof again," her mom said, unable to hide her enthusiasm. "It's been too long."

"Mama!" Savannah glanced over her shoulder as Chloe launched through the front door, down the stone steps, throwing herself into her arms, and propelling her back against her small blue sedan.

"Oomph," Savannah laughed, wrapping her arms around her daughter, one hand around her waist, the other stroking her silky blonde hair, and kissing the top of her head. "Hey baby," she murmured against her ear. "I missed you so much."

A second missile hit as Jess wrapped herself around her waist.

"Gosh, I'll let you stay with gran more often if this is the welcome I get when I come collect you." She said, smiling a real smile for the first time in days.

Jess stepped back, eying Savannah with shrewd eyes.

"You realize if you'd flown up with Uncle Clay, you'd have been here *hours* ago?"

Savannah laughed. "And if I'd come with Uncle Clay, we'd have not been able to enjoy a road trip going home."

Truth beknown, she'd not wanted to fly. Given Nick, Gwen, JD, and Felicity were with Clay. She'd not wanted to make bright, enthusiastic conversation when all she wanted was to work through the mess that was her life.

Add into that the questions about Mac, and driving alone was without doubt the most preferential option.

She closed her eyes, her heart clenching when the image of those green eyes played over in her mind. The memory of the night of the speakeasy was still so fresh in her mind it hurt.

"I've fallen for you."

Damn, why did he have to ruin things? It was good until that point—except...

She swallowed. Now wasn't the time for this. Only he was all she seemed able to think of. Even when dealing with lawyers, police, work, Mac was there, his chaos of curls, his smiling eyes, the Kiwi charm that seemed to win over everyone, playing over and over in her mind.

But he'd been absent, and that stung.

She knew instinctively why, but it didn't lessen the fact she missed seeing that smile, hearing the witty responses to things that were said, and lightening the overwhelming weight of her situation.

In the same breath though, she was grateful.

She needed space. To work through the mess Charles had created, and to consider how she moved forward.

It was too soon for anything serious, and yet, she couldn't imagine moving forward without Mac there. In what form, she had no clue. But it was something she wanted she thought.

"We could have flown back in Uncle Clay's jet luxury style, instead of stopping at gas stations," Jess said, and Savannah glanced down at her, shaking her head,

"And not be able to stop at Eagle Mountain on the way home?"

Jess and Chloe's favorite stop between Sweetheart Falls and New York was a lifelong favorite for them, and they loved to stop there. With a cafe on the slopes, designed like a giant bird hide, they'd watch the bird life for hours. There was something so majestic in the way the eagles soared.

While Savannah had worried that as they got older, they'd lose interest, it remained a favorite. Helped by the fact they'd adopted an egret for the girls for their fifth birthday, that they continued to monitor in the wild through a tracking app.

Chloe glared at Jess. "Don't you think moms got enough to worry about without you moaning about how you'd get home?"

"It's distraction—remember? We said we'd distract her when she got here, so she doesn't have time to worry."

"I'm here," Savannah reminded the two, as Cora-Lea laughed, the affection ringing out loud and clear.

"How about we show mom the dresses we bought for the party?"

Savannah closed her eyes. She'd momentarily forgotten about the party, and now, she was dreading it. She'd come home earlier for her parents, but it didn't stop the gnaw of apprehension at being surrounded by the entire Devereaux clan, and their extended family. In the same breath though, she loved how supportive that network was. It had been a long time she'd allowed herself to be embraced by it.

"You've not been shopping again?" she asked, fighting to keep focus. Jeez, it felt good to see them.

The shock of Charles' attack had taken a toll this time, and she'd found her attention span a nightmare for the last few days. One minute focused on what she was doing, the next replaying his vicious assault. Between him and her growing awareness of Mac, she was a basket case.

When she closed her eyes to sleep, she'd awaken to a sheen of sweat on her brow, the terrifying image of Charles in a manic state of anger etched on her mind. The sound of fists hammering on the door, playing through her mind, and she found it impossible to distinguish real from imagined. When she opened her door to go out, nerves took hold, and she'd nervously peer around the door frame before trusting herself to open it wide. Even when she used the peephole, she half expected to see his face glaring back.

Her brothers had ensured she was never alone, and between them had taken shifts, despite her protests to accompany her to appointments. Even at night, Clay had taken to sleeping in the girls' room.

It drove her mad. On others, she was grateful, the sense of belonging growing with each day, somehow strengthening her, her resolve to move beyond Charles and into this new life stronger than at any time up until now. It was like the wall between herself, and the family had never existed. Awareness that that wall had been in her mind, created by Charles, and not something real.

As for Mac...

Jess and Chloe took her hands, leading her up the steps, and she realized once again they'd spoken. Willing herself to get a grip, she forced the smile onto her face, and focused.

An hour later, she left the room that had been hers during her childhood. Jess had turned it into a fashion runway, and between her and Chloe, they'd shown off the outfits their grandparents had bought them. Dresses, shoes, accessories, they'd not hold back, and Savannah had laughed as Jess, with her usual exuberance, pouted and posed, while Chloe showed hers.

An overwhelming sense of love overwhelmed Savannah. It was them that kept her strong. Even when she was at her most insecure, she only had to look at them to know that every decision, every moment of her life, now revolved around them.

It wasn't only the girls, it was the house and family that changed things. The sense of coming home was medicine for the soul, and while she was aware this would be a short weekend, for the first time in too long, she was where she needed to be.

"Sweetheart," she turned to find her mother had followed her from the bedroom, and now closed the door with a quiet click, as she eyed Savannah with worried blue eyes so like her own. "You're safe here, you know that. You can relax."

Savannah nodded. Of course she did, but she also knew every muscle in her was taut, and even the sense of safety wasn't enough for her to relax.

"What Charles did was unforgivable," the anger in her mother's voice was palpable, the rare sight of fury in her eyes an unexpected comfort, and Savannah clamped her teeth over her bottom lip as she fought the urge to speak.

She'd promised herself she'd not to think about him, or even talk about him this weekend, but she needed to. She needed to clear the air. To tell them everything. Not just the snippets she'd fed them over the years.

"You need to understand that all of us, every one of us, are here for you. Life's going to be that little harder for a while, but you'll come through the other side stronger for it."

Savannah nodded, finding the words she needed. "It's okay, mom, and I'm sorry—sorry for everything I've put you through. I..."

Her mother laughed. "Sweetheart, you put us through nothing that any other family doesn't deal with. It's what Charles did that takes it to the next level. You're free of him now, to move on. Live your life."

Savannah frowned. She knew where this was going, and that her mom understood it was too soon. Irrespective, she'd hold her off at the pass.

"Mom, please. No matchmaking. It's all too raw."

Cora-Lea smiled, brushing a hand over Savannah's cheek.

"It's okay sweetheart, when the time's right, it will be right. Until then, let's enjoy the weekend, hey?"

Her mother wasn't wrong. The next few hours were a whirl of activity, and Savannah found herself thrown into the mix as the dust sheets from the grand hall stripped and shaken off, the tables polished, and the floor cleaned to within an inch of its life.

They all weighed in, helping the team of staff hired for the weekend to transform it into what Savannah knew was its former glory.

She loved the old house. With its grand pillars at the entrance reaching from ground to roof, the statue of Hera, wife of Zeus in the center of the grand marble fountain in front, shipped from the original home of the Devereaux's in Paris during the early nineteenth century.

The entrance with its portraits of her ancestors, right through to her grandfather, lining the walls of the dark wood staircases that led from the first floor and curved around the walls of the front hall.

How many times throughout her life she'd found herself looking for the genetic traits that followed down the lines, the

Devereaux nose, square chin, blue eyes, and twinkle of mischief, even in those most austere of portraits.

Whilst the men in the hallways symbolized the house's history, other portraits scattered throughout the house, featuring the various families across the generations, of the women of the house. As though even years since their lives were extinguished, they were still fundamentally a part of the fabric of the home. Their stories whispered in every room.

It still bore the historic charm of its early origins, but as the years had passed, each generation had modernized it, and today, it held the old-world charm with modern tweaks, keeping its authenticity.

The grand hall was at the back of the house and was seldom used because of its sheer scale. With twenty circular tables, and enough seating for two hundred people, there'd been suggestions they use it for events. They used it for family celebrations, or the occasional local fundraiser, though.

"Don't you love when a plan comes together," Cora-Lea flushed, when she swept in a little after four. She'd disappeared into town for a hair appointment and a makeover.

Savannah's breath caught in her throat at the sight of her mother.

"Mom, you look incredible."

Her hair, always worn in a simple plait, was now styled into a chic bob, framing her face with soft layers that highlighted her delicate features. The silver-blonde strands shimmered under the light. Her makeup, a palette of soft pinks that complemented her fair complexion to perfection.

A wolf whistle from the corner of the room, followed by "Wow, who's the gorgeous chick who just arrived, Nick?" from Gray.

Cora-Lea laughed, fanning herself.

She twirled, showing off her hair, then posed. "Will I do?"

"Darling woman, you've done for forty years."

Savannah grinned as her mom spun round to find her dad, Jack, stood on the steps behind her, eying her with open approval. "Now come give me a kiss. I missed you."

Cora-Lea gasped, as her husband swept her into his arms and placing a firm kiss on her lips.

"Ew, can you save the mushy stuff for later?" Jess called from a table she and Chloe were dressing.

"Ah, come on now, pickle! When you're old and in love like us, you won't be able to resist stealing a smooch or two in public."

Jess pretended to gag.

"I'd rather eat my veggies!"

Savannah's father laughed, smiling at Jess with open affection. "Well, just you wait. One day you'll find someone who makes your heart flutter like a butterfly in the garden, and you'll understand."

Unable to find a response to that, Jess fell silent, and Cora-Lea spoke.

"Savannah, sweetheart, I need a hand. Can you come help?

Savannah frowned, turning to the girls, and Clay cut in. "I'll keep trouble one and trouble two occupied. You go."

He used the term the family had used for him and Savannah as children, and she grinned, and for the first time in days like she could relaxed.

"All yours, brother, all yours," she said, as she left them to finish the set up.

Two hours later, Savannah perched on the end of her mom and dad's beautiful old four poster, smiling as her mom stepped into the dress she'd bought for tonight.

It amazed Savannah just how excited her mom was, as she slid it up and over her shoulders, then turned her back for Savannah to fasten the zipper.

When it was done, she stepped away, glancing at herself in the mirror, and Savannah saw a momentary sense of apprehension, before she ran her hands down over her stomach and hips, twisting one way, and then the other, to check each side, and then twirling.

"My goodness, I never thought I'd feel like this again," she gasped, allowing the flowing skirt to twirl around as she did. "I feel like..." she glanced down at her left hand, eying the simple gold wedding band on the second finger. "Like I did on my wedding day."

She beamed at Savannah, and as she did, her expression faltered.

"Oh gosh, I'm so sorry, I didn't... oh blast! Savannah, I didn't mean..."

Savannah came to stand beside her mom, turning her to face the mirror once more.

"It's okay, mom, I'm fine. Honest. It's so good to see you so happy and excited. I'm happy for you."

Cora-Lea raised a hand to rake her fingers through her hair, but Savannah stopped her.

"Don't ruin your hair, mom. You look amazing."

Her mom sighed.

"I wish things had worked out for you, sweetheart; I do. If we'd have thought in a million-years Charles was capable of what he did, we'd have stepped in so much quicker."

"It wasn't your place to though, mom. It was a journey I had to take."

"Still—you should never have walked it alone."

Her mom walked across to where Savannah had sat moments earlier and sat patting the mattress beside her.

"C'mon, let's talk."

"Not today mom, today's your day, we can talk after."

"Nonsense, there's never a better time to talk than when family are around."

She took Savannah's hand and pulled her down beside her.

"You know, when I met your father, I was running," she said, when Savannah was beside her. "I mean, running. You know my mom and dad died when I was sixteen." Savannah nodded. She knew it had been one of the go to's when they'd learned to drive. 'Driving is a privilege not a right. There are a lot of idiots on the road. You can be the best driver in the world, but it takes one idiot for your entire world to come crashing down. My mom and dad learned that the hard way.'

She'd heard those words so many times over the years.

"What I don't talk about is what happened after," her mom continued.

Savannah frowned, unsure of where this was going, and she shifted to face her mom.

"The thing is, I was young enough that I had to have a guardian, but in the same breath at that transitional stage that was close enough to be without a guardian. Except...I'm not making any sense am I."

This time it was her mom who shifted her hands, and rested them on her knees now kneading them, as though trying to soothe, and Savannah placed a hand over one.

"Go on, mom," she urged, unsure of what to expect, but knowing that if her mom were showing such significant outward stress, it had to be something bad.

"After they died, I went to stay with a great-uncle. He was my grandfather's brother. My inheritance was placed in trust until I turned twenty-five, and my great-uncle was given the power to manage it—all of it."

She closed her eyes, inhaling a deep breath as her mind took her back in time before she continued. "He wasn't a nice person. The only way I could gain any control over it, was to be married. Only he didn't tell me that."

Savannah wasn't sure where this was going, but she listened intent, hating the uncharacteristic nervous twinge to her mom's voice.

"Thing is, he was an alcoholic with a gambling problem and a nasty streak. Which, when I didn't argue, wasn't a problem, but if I stood up for myself, or answered back," a nervous chuckle, "If I looked at him the wrong way, it soon became one."

"Mom," Savannah murmured, wrapping an arm around her mom's shoulders, and leaning in to rest her head on her shoulder. "I had no..."

"Let me finish, sweetheart, this is something only your dad is aware of, but I need you to understand—I've seen what you've been through."

Savannah swallowed and sat back, forcing herself to listen to the story her mom relayed.

"The day I turned seventeen, a gentleman came knocking," her mom's hand came to her mouth, her face pale, so that even with the makeup, she'd turned a ghostly white. "Listen to me, talking like the southern gal I used to be," she smiled, but there was a sadness in her eyes. "I didn't realize that it was my great uncle's intention to marry me off. You don't hear of that kind of thing anymore, but... well, let's just say, there was no thought for my well-being."

Savannah cringed. "How on earth is that even..."

"Shh, I'm getting to it." She heaved a sigh, entwining the fingers of each hand, her thumbs rubbing against each other in endless circles. "I didn't catch on. I was young, naïve, the world without my parents was... My goodness, I'd not even had a boyfriend until that point."

"What happened?"

"I overheard a conversation. Not a nice one. But discovered he planned to marry me within the year—sounds like something out of another age, doesn't it?" she commented, rolling her eyes, but the sadness was still there. "Which was crazy. I wasn't ready for anything like it. My gosh, I had all kinds of dreams of travelling, becoming independent, doing all the things my mom and dad would be proud of. And instead, here I was in a decrepit old house, with a creepy great uncle who wanted me for my money and nothing else."

Savannah wondered if she were dreaming, the surreal conversation nothing like what she'd expected on such an important day in her mom's life.

"Anyway, I'll cut a long story short. I confronted my uncle, and it turned nasty. It turned out the," she air-quoted, "Gentleman, was someone he owed money too. My trust fund would have cleared his debt. Which made it a win, win. Except he was thirty years older than me, and a letch." She swallowed, her hand closing over her wedding ring, twisting it round and round, as though grounding herself, and a few seconds passed before she continued. "It was the last time that man, or any man, lay a hand on me in anger." Her mom's voice cracked, a single tear rolling down one cheek, and Savannah reached out to rub it away. "I swore no man would ever touch a child of mine in anger."

A sob ripped from her, and she turned to stare into Savannah's eyes, swallowing hard as she said. "I let you down, Savannah, baby. I'm so sorry, I let you down."

"Mom! You didn't! How could you even think that? You weren't to know what Charles was capable of. My goodness, even I wasn't. How could any of us have..."

"But if I'd told you of my background, perhaps, just perhaps, you'd have been a little more wary."

"I was young, reckless, and in love with the idea of love. There was nothing you could have done to change that. Don't beat yourself up. I was an adult, and the decisions I made were down to me—no one else. Besides, things worked out for you in the end. They'll work out for me too, I'm sure of it."

Her mom smiled.

"You're a good girl, Savannah, or should I say, young woman," she said, brushing away another tear.

"And so are you, Cora-Lea." Both looked up to see her father near the door.

He'd entered, not wanting to interrupt, and Savannah had no idea of how long he'd been there.

"Are you not going to tell her the rest of the story, my love?" he asked, and Savannah frowned.

"You guys need to get ready; people are arriving downstairs." Her dad in no way placated.

"Your mom ran away, packed her back and got the hell out of dodge, she was a tough-assed cookie even back then." He smiled, the fondness in his eyes telling of a lifetime of memories. "She'd learned of relatives over the border in the Toronto, only she didn't make it that far, did you, sweetheart?"

Her mom chuckled, and Savannah understood why. Heaven Sent and the town of Sweetheart Falls were so close to the border. The place her parents had met was legendary, and the story had been told so many times over the years. Just another love story interwoven into the fabric of Sweetheart Falls history.

"She ran into Jack Devereaux Snr, fell in love and lived happily ever after," she quipped, and both parents laughed as her mom grabbed her hands once more, staring into her eyes with that same sincerity she'd always remembered.

"There's a moral to the story," she said, with so much love in her eyes, it stole Savannah's breath. "Even in the darkest times, and you know how hard it was when we lost Paul," Cora-Lea paused, the sadness in her eyes almost palpable, and the all-too-familiar lump appeared in her throat.

Seventeen years had passed since they lost Paul, the youngest of the Devereaux siblings, and while they didn't talk about him as often as they once had, he was always there.

Photographs of him were scattered through the house, and on his anniversary, they always ensured they called their parents, aware that he was still intrinsically a part of them.

The sense that one was missing at times though, overwhelming.

She glanced at her husband, who gave a small nod.

"It's okay to remember him, remember sweetheart." He thumped his chest, with a belt of passion, adding. "He's here, with us all the time, and he's still, and always will be one of ours."

Cora-Lea nodded back, and blinked, a single tear rolling down over her cheek, and she took a moment, fighting to shake off the momentary morose. The sadness still there, and a sense of something else.

Hope?

She reached out to brush her hand across Savannah's cheek, then stroked her hair. Eyes sparkling with more unshed tears, so close, as though she could see right into her soul.

"When all hope seems lost, there is always hope for a brighter tomorrow. When you left, Charles and I left Great Uncle Grant, we left behind those toxic relationships and opened the door to find genuine love and happiness."

She sighed as her husband walked across and took her hand, pulling her to her feet and wrapping his arms around her, bringing her in for a hug.

"I found mine," she said, with a moan of happy satisfaction. "Now it's time to find yours. I promise you darling, love has a way of finding you when you least expect it. Don't close your heart to

Chapter Twenty-Two

MAC

Mac felt like a fish out of water. He'd wrapped up as much as he could from this end of the world and needed to get back to New Zealand, but something held him, and he knew damned well what it was.

He hadn't been able to get her out of his mind. The worries constant.

The image of Charles pinning her to the wall by the throat, the shell-shocked expression when he'd picked her up and carried her to the couch, the visible shaking over-riding the images of the beautiful, sexy, smiling blonde he'd fallen in love with.

Every part of him screamed protect, and he wanted to be there with her—for her, but she'd allowed Clay and the rest of the family to close ranks, do what needed to be done.

She needed space. Only space hurt. Space ripped his insides out and stamped on them with relentless cruelty and he paced Clay's apartment like a cage animal.

He'd walked the streets of New York, but everywhere he looked, she was there. Just a cup of coffee sent his mind reeling, and he wondered if he wasn't going mad.

Was this what love did to a person?

Clay's call late Friday had left him in a quandary. His parents' anniversary party had come out of nowhere, and he understood it was down to Cora-Lea Devereaux, wanting to have all her kids in one place. It would also be a good time to meet the friend of Clay's who'd enticed him to the opposite side of the world.

He'd laughed when he heard Cora-Lea say, "I want to meet the man who handles hog-tying my Clay and keeping him on the other side of the ocean." Like anyone could hog-tie him.

Truth was, he was the guy who'd fallen head over heels with another of her children, but he said nothing.

As he steered the rental through the gates leading to Clay's family estate, a cascade of doubts surged through Mac's mind. Was this the right decision? Would Savannah even want to see him?

The crunch of gravel beneath the tires seemed to echo his uncertainty.

The driveway meandered through a canopy of trees, ablaze with autumnal brilliant, casting dappled shadows that danced across the path. The landscapes a canvas of vibrant hues of orange, yellow, russet, and brown, evoking a sense of enchantment, and his stomach clenched with anticipation.

The end of the drive opened into a vast turning circle, and Mac's breath caught in his throat at the sight that greeted him.

The imposing silhouette of the family mansion against the setting sun, like nothing he'd ever seen.

Four towering white stone columns soared skyward, exuding an air of regal elegance bathed in the gentle glow of up-lights, standing like sentinels guarding the grandeur within. The white stone façade like the kind of thing you saw in movies.

A sweeping stone staircase, flanked by two imposing stone lions, led to a wide, red front door. A fountain in front sparkling with a kaleidoscope of colors, its waters shimmering in the shifting light, casting prismatic reflections that danced like miniature rainbows.

"Heaven Sent," he murmured, swinging the vehicle around the turning circle to the side of the house as Clay had directed. All these years, he'd wondered, and finally he knew what the old house looked like.

Clay came out to greet him, wearing a tuxedo, and grinning from ear to ear.

"Welcome to Heaven Sent," he grinned, gesturing to the house behind.

"When you told me it was big, you didn't say palatial size," Mac replied, letting out a breath of disbelief. "It's stunning."

"Thanks, we kinda like her," Clay shrugged, reaching into the trunk for Mac's bags. "Mate, I'm glad you came. Mom's dying to meet you."

Mac nodded.

He was dying to meet her too, but there was someone he needed to see more, and Clay shook his head, aware of where Mac's thoughts had headed.

"She's here, and she's doing better," he confirmed, and Mac wrinkled his nose.

"That obvious, huh?"

Clay laughed.

"Any more obvious and you'd have a flashing beacon on your head," he grinned.

"Any news on the Charles front?"

Clay nodded.

"They arrested him for assault this time. With witnesses, he couldn't deny it. The fact he breached the order twice meant they fitted an electronic device, so there's little chance he'll risk coming near her again—at least for the interim. It's certain now he'll lose his law license, too. So, karma is biting him hard right now."

Mac grunted.

"Shame it didn't sooner."

"Enough talk about him, c'mon, let's get inside. You brought the tux, right?"

Mac rolled his eyes. And opened the back passenger door, reaching in to withdraw a suit bag. "Don't worry, I brought everything."

Clay slapped him on the shoulder, and the two climbed the steps to the front door.

Inside, he stopped and stared, his gaze sweeping the elegant front hall. The curved staircase, lined with austere oil canvases of the men of the Devereaux line. Both Clay and Savannah had mentioned them before, but to see them in full glory. Wow!

An enormous chandelier suspended from the ceiling glittered with crystals, casting rainbows on the wide-open space, while two giant palms in terracotta pots framed the far corners.

"This is like something from Downton Abbey," he murmured, earning a chuckle from Clay.

"S'ok, we don't have an upstairs, downstairs household. A lot of the house isn't even used these days. We all kept our childhood bedrooms, but we pretty much keep to the family rooms down here. The rest gets closed off, except for..." His words trailed off, as the deep southern accent he knew was Cora-Lea's interrupted.

"Clay is this..." Mac turned to see the woman sweeping through a side door. "Oh, it is!" she fanned herself with her purse as she walked toward the, a plump ginger cat draped over her am, looking to all intents and purposes like Garfield. She came to a stop in front of Mac peering curiously at him. "The socials didn't do you justice. Look at you," she held out her hand. "Prince Charming as I live and breathe."

A cough from behind, and Cora-Lea chuckled without turning to see who it was, as Jack Devereaux stepped through the doorway. "It's okay darling, there's only one Prince Charming for me, and I married him," she laughed.

She placed the cat at her feet, and Mac realized for the first time it had only three legs.

Before he could say anything, Cora-Lea stood, holding out a hand for Mac to shake, her eyes alight with warmth and mischief.

"So, you're the one who made our Savannah smile again."

Mac smiled.

"I hope so," he replied., unexpectedly nervous.

"And the one who enticed our Clay to the other side of the world."

This time, Mac laughed as Clay rolled his eyes.

"Guilty as charged, ma'am," he replied, holding up his hands in surrender.

Mac glanced down as the cat wrapped itself awkwardly around his ankles, letting out a small miaow as it did.

"Hmmmm, I was looking forward to meeting you, and I now know why."

Mac frowned.

"You do?

"Mmmhmm, you're a keeper," she declared.

"And you know this from one interaction?"

Cora-Lea's laugh filled the wide-open space, her eyes twinkling.

"Precisely, young man. You hold your own, but you protect too. That's just what our Savannah needs. It looks as though Em agrees too." She glanced down at the cat, which now sat by Mac's ankles staring up at him, with huge cat-eyes.

Mac had heard so many stories of the cat, that to finally see the ginger cat brought a grin to his face.

Em had been christened M&M, or double M short for the major mayhem he habitually caused, and by the looks of the attitude the cat had, it was well-earned, and Mac chuckled when the three-legged critter stood and awkwardly wrapped itself around his ankles, now purring.

Cora-Lea laughed delightedly, in the same moment her husband rolled his eyes. "Ah damn, we have two of them at it now?"

"Oh Lord,' Clay groaned, theatrically smacking himself upside the head. "She's kicked into matchmaker-mom-mode."

Mac closed his eyes and shook his head, before casting Cora-Lea a stern stare. "Give Savannah the time and space she needs. She's not ready."

"Oh, trust me, young man, she's ready. She just needs a little shove in the right direction. You'll see."

And with that, she swept him into a big hug, then turned back to Jack.

"We've a surprise to finish organizing. Are you ready, darling?"

She left with the cat following close behind, as she reached the door, she turned to look back at Mac with teasing eyes.

"Oh, and I hear she whooped your backside at computer games. You might want to try board games next time, she's awful at them! Unless she's cheating."

She winked at Mac this time, before sauntering through the door, ignoring both Mac's and Clay's audible groans.

When they were alone, Mac shook his head, bemused.

"Well, I see where you all get it from," he chuckled, following Clay to the bedroom he'd been allocated.

"Get changed, and meet me downstairs in thirty," he said, with a chuckle. "And beware, you've met the siblings—tonight you get to meet the wider family—if you thought we were mad, then you're in for some fun!"

Chapter Twenty-Three

SAVANNAH

"Jess, for heavens' sakes, we're waiting," Savannah growled, gesturing to her daughter.

"Just leave her, she can catch up," Chloe argued, but Savannah held firm.

"We go down together," she chided Chloe, adding a tired sigh. "Jess! Now!"

Jess swept from the bedroom and pushed past, heading for the stairs, and Savannah rolled her eyes with a groan.

"Funny—now wait!" Sometimes it felt as though she were still dealing with a toddler.

They made their way to her parents' room, where her dad stood by the door, beaming.

"Well, look at my girls," he grinned, holding out his arms as Chloe rushed into them for a hug. "Anyone would think you were going to a party."

"We are, pops." Jess rolled her eyes. "It's so exciting."

Savannah watched as her dad broke free, wondering if she'd ever seen him so happy.

Would she ever have the magic her parents shared? To have a man smile over her the way he did her mom.

She closed her eyes, shutting out the too familiar image that played over in her mind. Hurt following fast on its heels.

God, she missed him. She'd not known how much until that moment. But this was the reality, and she needed to deal with it.

Except...

Not now. She growled, fists clenched at her sides as she forced the image from her mind. There'd be time. But not tonight. Not now.

She opened her eyes to see her dad bend down to retrieve a box from behind him, and when he turned to face her, his eyes sparkled.

"Fact is girls," he said, glancing from one to the other of the girls, and then up at her. "It's not a party tonight, it's a wedding."

Savannah's eyes widened, and the girls shrieked with excitement as he retrieved two small baskets of mulberry-colored rose petals, and a small bouquet of roses, carefully arranged with a mixture of the same deep shade of mulberry and soft cream. Sprigs of baby's breath and delicate fern added texture and depth to the arrangement, while a satin ribbon in creamy hues tied it together. He passed the bouquet to Savannah. "Well, more of a renewal," he grinned.

"You and mom?" Savannah asked, realizing how stupid the question was.

"Who else?" her father deadpanned.

"Oooh, that's so exciting," Chloe gushed, as Jess froze, eying her grandfather with serious eyes.

"This means more PDAs doesn't?" she sighed, direct as ever.

"It sure does, honey. So, you'll be wanting to go hide in the bedroom to avoid the fun."

Jess's eyes widened. "And miss the party—no way!"

She took one basket from him, then passed the other to Chloe. "Guess we get to look cute tonight," she grinned, as Chloe pulled the same eye roll her mom had moments earlier.

Savannah slipped into the bedroom, where her mom sat at her dresser, fastening her earrings.

"Daddy told you then?" she grinned at Savannah's refection in the mirror, eying the bouquet in Savannah's hand.

"He did! Why didn't you tell me?"

"Because until yesterday this was just an anniversary party," her mom replied, holding up the string of shining pearls, she remembered her mom telling her they were a sweet sixteen gift from her own mother. "Can you?"

Savannah laughed.

"Full circle? Just a week ago, you were doing this for me."

Cora-Lea shifted in her seat so Savannah could reach around with the necklace, then held still while she fastened it, never for a moment taking her gaze from her daughter.

"You're so beautiful, mom. You'll knock dad's socks off."

Cora-Lea laughed.

"Bit late for that," she quipped, and her expression softened. "A small part of me was concerned it would be too soon for you," she said, eying Savannah with concerned eyes. "That perhaps doing this was a little insensitive."

"It's okay, mom, you don't have to tread on eggshells around me. What happened, happened. But I need to move on—need to keep building this new life. Eventually, Charles will be gone from my life, whether it is as punishment for what he did, or he gets bored and moves on. Either way, our lives are now ours to do with what we may."

"And Mac?"

Savannah gasped.

"Mom, no!"

Cora-Lea laughed. "He's a lovely man," she said, a soft note in her voice. "You could do worse."

"When I'm ready—not before," her voice took on a no-nonsense tone, and in that moment, she longed to be honest, to tell her mom everything, to tell her she'd... she frowned. Don't be ridiculous. But in that moment, something clicked, a realization that she'd harbored too long. Whether it was love, or something close to, she wasn't sure, but what she knew was that she wanted Mac to look at her the way her father looked at her mother. To have him hold her with that same gentle hold, watching the seasons change, their children grow, their... squeezing her eyes closed, she fought back the image playing over in her mind of a toddler, with a mass of dark curls, big green eyes.

"He's the one, sweetheart. It's obvious. When the time is right, you'll know it. Just you wait and see—now, what says you go down and sort your girls out, and I'll follow in a minute. I need a tick."

Savannah moved back, smiling at her mom's reflection, then bent down to wrap her arms around her mom's neck in a hug.

"I love you, mom, you know that right?"

Cora-Lea smiled back, tears shimmering. "I do, sweetheart, and I love you right back. Now go, before you make me ruin my make up!"

Stepping into the hall, Savannah's breath caught in wonder. Where earlier the space had been bare and utilitarian, now it was transformed into a scene of enchantment. Her mother's touch was clear in every detail. Tables dressed in ivory-colored tablecloths adorned the room, each topped with flower arrangements mirroring her bouquet. The delicate blooms exuded an air of elegance and sophistication, their subtle fragrance mingling with scented candles.

Candelabras adorned with teardrop crystals stood at the center of each table, their facets catching the light and casting shimmering rainbows across the room.

Savannah couldn't help but smile as she observed the gathering of familiar faces, a mix of family, friends and neighbors who had come together to celebrate.

"Wow," she whispered, eyes alight, watching as Jess and Chloe rushed to the front of the room where Nick and Clay stood talking.

"Don't just stand there, sweetheart," her father said from behind her. "Tonight's about celebration, and rather than organizing it, you're here to enjoy."

He hugged her, then walked across to Clay and Nick, who now talked with Father Andrews. For a moment she watched, soaking in the ambience of home. Of family.

This was where she belonged, and in that moment, she felt that familiar pang of homesickness as she remembered how far away their life was. Of how far Mac's... even as his name played through her mind, she baulked.

What on earth?

With a shake of her head, she dismissed it, following the path her father had taken moments earlier, greeting and chatting to cousins, friends, her uncle and aunt, and a handful of other acquaintances.

She missed him so much it hurt, but in the same breath, she understood why he'd given her the space he had. She needed it. Had so much to deal with, and yet, his declaration had scared the life of her.

She wasn't ready, was she?

Oh, for him to be here. To see the way their family was together. To understand, on an instinctive level, that he fit—which he did. She fought to push him from her mind, and launched forward, aware of the gentle sounds of the pianist on the grand piano in the corner.

It was as she came to a stand beside her father that the music's tempo changed, and her father spoke.

"Time to get this show on the road," he beamed, rubbing his hands together, his face transforming as he glanced toward the door. His expression for the second time today taking Savannah's breath away.

She turned to follow his gaze, her jaw dropping at the sight.

"Mom," she gasped, as her mother walked into the room, all heads turning to watch as Cora-Lea entered, the Mulberry A-line pleated chiffon flowing down to her ankles, a bracelet around her wrist that matched the pearls at her neck, her smile radiant.

Cora-Lea walked toward them, her eyes focused on her husband, her smile so filled with love, Savannah's heart squeezed, and she reached for Chloe's hand, fighting back the tears that pricked her eyes.

In the hour that had passed since their conversation, she'd seen her mom in a whole new light, and she wondered how she'd managed to keep such a significant life event to herself for so long. She'd come through the kind of trauma that was unimaginable, but to look at her now, she was so happy.

"Beautiful," she mouthed, to her mom as she came to stand beside her husband, beaming at each of her children, and reaching to hug her two granddaughters. Jack rolled his eyes in the same way both she and her daughters did.

"As ever, second place to the kids," he growled, with a self-sacrificing sigh.

Cora-Lea turned to him, placing a finger over his lips.

"We've survived forty years because you know when to, and when not to speak, right?"

The room erupted into laughter, and Father Andrews stepped in. The same moment Savannah turned to the table at which Gwen, Felicity and… she froze, her breath stilling in her throat, her heart thundering within her chest.

Mac?

She closed her eyes, terrified that when she'd open them, he'd be gone, but when she did, he was still there, his focus so intent she wanted to run to him.

Mac.

How familiar was that name now? How familiar was he? Just looking at him, she could feel the weight of his gaze, the gentle stroke of his fingers across her abdomen when he woke her, the brush of his lips against hers, as though he were physically in front of her. Heart in her throat, she opened her eyes, holding that beautiful gaze. Loving that he was here, but in the same breath wondering just what in the name of goodness she was thinking.

Fighting to focus on her mom and dad, she tore her gaze away, shifting it back to where Father Andrews continued to talk about the magic of marriage, of the obstacle's life puts in the way for couples, of how through everything Jack and Cora-Lea had been through, they'd reached their forty-year milestone together, and still in love as the day they'd met.

Savannah blinked.

The day they'd met.

"Cora-Lea, you crashed into my life with all the grace of a Billy goat," Jack now said, holding Cora-Lea's hands, his eyes focused on his wife, "and I mean that in the best possible way."

A ripple of laughter sounded through the room, as Nick piped up, "Nothing changed then."

"Hush," Cora-Lea scolded. "Your father's being romantic! That doesn't happen often, so let's make the most of it, hey?" She winked at her eldest and turned back to Jack. "Now, where were we?"

Another sigh, but Jack continued, a twinkle of mischief in his eye.

"From the moment I laid eyes on you, I knew you were something special. You brought a vitality and energy into my world I didn't even know was missing... Jess." he growled, side-eying his granddaughter who now pretended to stick her fingers down her throat. "My God, even our grand-kids are like you," he dead panned Cora-Lea.

Cora-Lea frowned at Jess and then Nick.

"Can we please do this without the interruption? Otherwise, by the time we get through this, it'll be tomorrow. You want to wait that long for cake?"

Jess mimed the action of zipping her mouth closed, then padlocking it and tossing the key away with a yelp as Chloe elbowed her.

"Right," her father cut in. "I've been practicing this all day. The next person who interrupts gets put out into the stable block for the night—got it?"

The room fell silent, and at last he continued.

Savannah, struggled to focus on her parents, and instead found herself unable to stop herself glancing at Mac. She felt the growing realization that there was something so much more to what they'd experienced, and to what they had the potential to share. It wasn't anything new, she'd known, she'd simply denied it. Forcing any chance of feeling too much as far down as was possible, for far, of exposing her heart.

She shook her head, frustrated at her inability to stay focused, those green eyes holding her trapped. Not in a sinister way, but in a way that made her want to jump in with both feet and experience the true liberation of loving, without a cost.

"When we took that leap, people thought we were mad. I must confess, when I look back, I think I'd have a coronary if any of our kids did it that quick—unless" he glanced at Savannah, and she caught his gaze, frowning as her own flickered back to Mac.

"Unless I believed, of course, they'd found what I did the day the day I met you." Jack winked, and Cora-Lea squeezed his hands. "I can honestly say, Cora, I knew in my heart it was the right decision, and I've never regretted it for a single moment."

A tear rolled down Cora-Lea's cheek, and a chorus of 'aww's' sounded from her off-spring, earning another glare, followed by her brushing it away.

"Quit spoiling the moment," she growled.

Savannah listened as her dad finished his vows, the last words resonating as he added. "You were heaven sent just for me, Cora-Lea, and if our babies find anywhere close to what we've shared the past forty years," he paused momentarily, a sadness clear in his eye, as he and his wife shared a moment. Adding, "I know sweetheart, Paul too," his Adams Apple bobbed at the memory of their youngest son, and it took long seconds for him to compose himself. "And the next forty," he squeezed his wife's hands, eliciting a small squeak out of her, finally continued. "I'll die a happy, happy, man."

The silence continued, neither speaking, and Savannah knew that moment was for the brother they'd lost nearly eighteen years earlier.

When Jack broke it moments later, he smiled tenderly at Cora-Lea before, side-eying Jess. "You ought to avert your eyes, lady, because there's going to be a very public display of affection."

Jess gasped and turned around, but not before her grandmother cut in.

"I don't get my say?"

A bark of laughter gurgled out of Jack, as he said.

"I might've known you'd have to get the last word!"

Chapter Twenty-Four

SAVANNAH

Thirty minutes later, and with the vow renewal over, the party started, the music ramping up, and guests mingling. Savannah found herself watching her parents, loving the sense of companionship they emanated. They'd always been close, but her isolation had closed her eyes to it, and now, as she watched the way Cora-Lea looked up into Jack's eyes, a lump formed in her throat.

It's what I want?

But is it even possible?

Still, Savannah hadn't spoken to Mac. That didn't mean that she'd not watched him, aware of his every move. As though... she blinked back the next thought, frustrated at how overwhelmed she felt.

She glanced over, a tinge of envy prickling at the ease when he talked to her siblings and cousins, curiosity when Chloe and Jess pulled him aside and grill him with questions, and abject adoration when he turned those green eyes on her.

With every passing moment, the feelings grew, and while she had no clue of how, or what the turning point had been, she couldn't switch them off.

"Hey," she said, when he finally approached her. His stance was uncertain, despite the hope in his eyes.

"I'm sorry. I wasn't sure if they'd told you I was coming. Your mom..."

"I get it," Savannah interrupted, and not you were coming, but it all adds up," she added with a smiled. "Mom got it in her head that we'd be good together, and she's been like a dog with a bone since."

Mac laughed. "I wondered."

"Oh?"

He smiled. "She grilled me when I arrived this evening. Not for long, but I got the impression she had an agenda."

Savannah groaned inwardly and darted a look Cora-Lea's way.

On any other day she'd have been annoyed, but in that moment, she understood why.

There was something different. Something special about this, and she while she had no clue what it was, it was ingrained so deep she didn't know that it could simply be shaken off.

How? In this short period of time had he become so important to her?

It should be impossible, and yet, in her mind she knew that anything was possible. Especially where Mac Mackenzie was concerned.

"You want to take a walk?" she asked, wanting beyond all else to get away from watchful eyes. Having a big family was great until you wanted privacy.

Mac nodded, still holding back, as though he weren't sure what to do or say, and Savannah grabbed his hand.

"C'mon, I've the perfect place," she said, tugging on his arm as she led him from the room, ignoring her mother's, "Don't do anything I wouldn't do," remark as she passed. Mac snorted and Savannah slapped his arm playfully. "Don't encourage her. She doesn't need it. She's incorrigible," Savannah grumbled.

They stepped into the quiet of the corridor beyond and walked through the large family rooms to a cavernous solarium at the side of the house. The views from which looked out over the silver-tinged hills of the Estate. So different from that first night in New York, the only lights sparkling from the sky, rather than the skyscrapers.

"We won't be interrupted here," she said in a small voice."

Mac nodded, following her through to where a bench was placed between giant palms and other bushy shrubs.

The area here, was dark, with only small lanterns, and the moon overhead created pockets of light.

"This is beautiful," he said, as he sat, patting the seat beside him.

Savannah didn't sit, though.

Instead, stepping to where the windows offered a view over those extensive grounds, and rolling hills of the estate, her hair shimmering like spun silver in the silver moonlight.

"I need to apologize..." she started, and Mac held up his hand, shaking his head.

"No, you don't," he cut in, but Savannah persisted.

"I do. I knew how much I enjoyed your company, and that I was developing feelings, but I wasn't prepared to take the risk of committing. If I hadn't reacted the way I did the night of the Speakeasy, I wouldn't have been alone when Charles arrived, and I wouldn't have let my guard down."

"And if I hadn't left you, you'd have not been alone," Mac cut in.

"I knew the risk Charles posed. I was stupid, ignorant, and..." she shrugged, "complacent. I never will again."

"That's ridiculous," Mac interrupted, on a low growl.

"But true." She tilted her head upward, focusing on the brilliant light of the moon. "The fact is, Mac, I knew before tonight that I had feelings for you, but it took hearing my parents, and seeing the way they are together tonight..." she waved a hand, shaking her head. "Part of me screams that it's way too soon. But another, far deeper part, knows that I want those things—with you."

She glanced down at Mac, smiling when his jaw dropped, the surprise in his eyes sending a ripple of warmth through her.

"I want companionship, and love, fun-filled memories, and perhaps one day, more kids. But above all, I want it with you," she chuckled, and the sound tinkled in the quiet of the solarium. She shrugged. "And that makes absolutely no sense at all—but I'm learning that sense doesn't come into it where you're concerned."

Mac said nothing. Just watching her, the expression in her eyes filling her with a level of hope she'd not known she needed, and she shook her head, gesturing to him.

"Say something!"

He didn't, not immediately. Instead, he rose from the bench in one fluid movement, and pulled her to him, his hands cupping her face as he stared down into her eyes, as though trying to reassure himself that what he saw was real.

"You mean it?" he said in barely a whisper.

"Every single word," Savannah replied. "It won't be easy, but I want to work on it with you. And whether that's in New York, Sweetheart Falls, or Mackenzie, I don't care. I want it all. The love, the life, the stars, the sky, every single part of your life and mine."

Mac took her hands in his, silent for long moments, still staring, as though still not sure whether to believe this was real. She laughed, tilting her head to one side as she scrutinized him back.

"The moment I saw you at the Gala, you stole my breath," he said matter-of-factly. "It was as though the universe ceased to exist, except for you and I. Tonight, it happened all over again. I willed you to look at me, and then you did." He glanced down, an uncharacteristic tick of uncertainty in his jaw. "And it was just you and I all over."

208

Savannah laughed.

"You were the last person I expected to see."

"Really? You didn't suspect your mom would have something up her sleeve?"

Savannah deadpanned him. "She didn't even hint!"

"Well, I'm glad. I was worried once you saw me, you'd hightail for the hills."

She reached up to brush her hands over his cheek, enjoying the sensation of his beard beneath her fingers, lost in the intensity of his gaze.

"I couldn't even if I wanted. Everywhere I looked in New York there were reminders, and even here, somewhere you'd never been, there were the reminders in Clay, or a type of cake, or a coffee—I mean hell, if I can't even get a coffee without thinking of you, I was screwed anyway, wasn't I."

"I'm glad."

"What, that I can't even enjoy a cinnamon scroll without being reminded of you?"

"Truth be known, princess, after what I witnessed with Charles, I was worried I'd not be able to see beyond it." He winced. "I'm sorry. It's not something you'll want to hear, but I need to say it."

Savannah nodded, just the smallest nod, her eyes wary as Mac continued.

"I wanted to hurt him. Another time, I'll tell you the story of my cousin Carla." He shrugged. "Seeing Charles unleash on you; I was so close to throttling the life out of him."

Savannah placed a finger over his lips, shaking her head.

"Shh, no. I'm glad you didn't. He's the one needs locking up—not you. I couldn't forgive myself if you'd ended up in prison because of..." anger flashed in her eyes, venom in her voice as she hissed, "Him."

It was Mac's turn to hush her now, and he smiled.

"The important thing is, he's out of your life. From here on in, you get to move forward without his crap, and focus on what's important—I understand if you need to take baby steps. The girls are your priority. But you need to understand that I'll wait—if you need me to."

Savannah's laugh was almost incredulous.

"Slow, perhaps, but if you think you're getting away now, after everything—you're in for a shock, Mac Mackenzie. With the girls—yes, but with me, no way. Clay asked if I wanted to see New Zealand, so I'm thinking it's time we considered an extended vacation. Felicity already told me she'd step up if I needed a time out—it's much earlier than I expected, but hey, needs must." She tilted her head to one side, eying him shrewdly. "Plus, you may need an event coordinator with the resort launches."

Mac laughed, and it was the best thing Savannah had heard all day.

"You have it all worked out, don't you?"

"No," Savannah replied, in a tart voice, "I'm thinking on the fly. None of this was planned ten minutes ago. You make me think outside of the box, not to mention make irrational decisions."

"Is that right?"

It was impossible not to see the message in his eyes, the suggestion in his voice loud and clear.

"What says we make irrational decisions together and the hell with the world?"

"I'm game," Savannah smiled, melting against him as his lips covered hers, the world falling away, as two became one.

Long seconds later, she pulled back, lost in the depths of his eyes, as she said in a voice barely a whisper.

"With Charles, I think I was young enough to believe I was in love, because I loved the idea of being in love. This is different, though. I love the idea of being in love with a man who loves me back, and respects me for who I am, warts and all. But... " she eyed

Mac with a heavy sense of apprehension. "But there's something else... the thing is, you're in here," she held a hand over her heart, "and you're in here," she tapped her head. "I can't think of anything but you, even when I'm dealing with the other," she shook her head, "crap."

For long moments she fell silent, unsure of how else to articulate what she needed to say.

"The next few months are going to be rocky, and I want to protect the girls from it as much as I possibly can. I don't want life to take over though. Clay made a few suggestions, and I want to run them past you—and then the girls. Not to mention follow up on legal ramifications. Can you work with me to get beyond that."

Mac nodded his head profusely, never for a moment taking his eyes from her, a twinkle of mischief manifesting as his lips curved at one side.

"I can, princess," he raised his brows, that smile deepening as he added. "I have a question though..."

Savannah frowned. "Go on..."

"If you have warts, can I rethink?" Mac grinned, the twinkle of mischief in his eye so evident, Savannah laughed out loud.

This is what I need.

She loved that expression.

Fun, and the ability to simply be *me*.

She side-eyed him.

"Like I'm going to admit it. You'll have to investigate—see what you find."

She loved the laughter in her voice.

The sound one that had been missing too long.

"I like the sound of that," Mac replied, his expression becoming serious when she spoke again.

"Mom said something tonight that really resonated. I didn't get it at first, but here now, I do—I totally get it."

"What was it?" Mac asked.

"She said that sometimes, love finds you when you least expect it, you don't have to be looking for it, you don't necessarily even have to need it, but it sneaks up on you when you least expect it." she said, her eyes searching, "I wasn't expecting *this*..." a shrug. "*You*. But I need you to know. Last time I got it wrong and found Mr. Wrong. I wasn't looking for it when you walked into my life. But I know, this time I want to be right. I need you to be my Mr. Right. Can you? For me?"

Mac's response brought a wail of consternation from the corner, as he said, "How about I spend a lifetime showing you?" as Jess responded from a hidden vantage near the door.

"No," a resounding slap upside the head reverberated through the quiet, followed by.

"Not more PDAs per-lease," whilst Chloe giggled behind.

THE END

A Note from the Author

Savannah's experiences not just physically, but emotionally, reflect the experiences of not only women, but men too, the world over. Just as Savannah found support from Mac, and her family, it's vital for anyone experiencing abuse to know that help is available. Whether you're a victim, or someone who knows someone in need, don't hesitate to reach out to local organizations and support networks.

Together, it is possible to create a world where everyone feels safe, supported, and emotionally empowered to break free from the cycle of abuse.

Don't suffer in silence.

Don't stand back in silence.

Be the person who helps break the cycle what in many circumstances spans generations.

About the Author

Born in the UK, and now a Kiwi, Emmy-Lou James loves romance. So much so, she writes it. A wife, mom of six, grandmother, and cat-mom, to the most mischievous tabby, Cass, she spends life travelling between New Zealand, Australia, and Canada.

When she's not adventuring with her adult children and her grand-daughter, Rosella, she enjoys reading romances, cozy mysteries, and memoirs, keeping up to date with international politics and cooking!

1Vedder River Walk, 2024

To stay up to date with Emmy-Lou's upcoming publications and travel news, visit her Facebook at
https://www.facebook.com/EmmyLouJamesAuthor
    Or email at: emmyloujamesauthor@gmail.com

Coming Soon from Emmy-Lou James

Finding Mr. Rekindled

Sweetheart Falls Book 2
(Grayson & Felicity's story)
Release Date: June 30th, 2024.

"Every cupcake you bake, brings me one step closer to wanting a taste of something sweeter—us."

Fate has a funny way of bringing people together, just when they least expect it—or at least when two meddling relatives decide it's time to intervene.

For Gray and Felicity, a shared task to organize his sister's wedding in the idyllic small US town of Sweetheart Falls, rekindles the sparks of a past romance. But, with Felicity set to start a new life on the opposite side of the country, and Gray tied to the Sweetheart Falls family business, they must navigate a whirlwind of emotions, unexpected storms, and near catastrophes to discover if their love can truly find a way forward.

Amid wedding chaos and life-altering decisions, can they overcome distance and rekindle what they once had, or will this second chance prove too fragile to hold on it?
Mr. Rekindled is a heartwarming tale of love, destiny, and the power of second chances.

Finding Mr. Forever

Sweetheart Falls Book 3
(Jack & Miranda's story)
Release Date: October 22nd, 2024.

In the picturesque town of Sweetheart Falls, Miranda Rivers leads a quiet life running her quaint bookstore. For years she's nursed a secret crush on the town's lawyer, JD Devereaux. But when tragedy strikes, and Miranda becomes the prime suspect in a local murder investigation, she turns to JD for help.

As they work together to unravel the mystery, Miranda and JD discover that their friendship may be blossoming into something more. But with danger lurking in the shadows, and a secret buried deep within the town's history, they must race against time to clear Miranda's name.

In a heart-warming tale of love, loyalty and small-town charm, Miranda and JD navigate the twists and turns of both romance and mystery, finding solace in each other's arms amidst the cozy backdrop of Sweetheart Falls. Will their newfound bond withstand the challenges that lie ahead, or will the secrets of the past tear them apart?

Finding Mr. Christmas

Sweetheart Falls Book 4
(Nick & Maddie's story)
Release Date: December 5th, 2024.

Maddie Sinclair despises the holidays, haunted by memories of a tragic event that shattered her world. Determined to escape the festive frenzy, she flees to her family home in Lake View. But fate has other plans when Nick Devereaux, a stranger, inadvertently crosses her path, leading to a snowbound stay in his family home, Heaven Sent.

As the snow piles up outside, Nick endeavors to show Maddie the joy of Christmas, despite her reluctance. Yet, amidst the twinkling lights and holiday cheer, an unexpected romance blossoms between them. But Maddie's past pain threatens that budding connection.

With Christmas fast approaching, Nick is on a mission to prove to Maddie that she is worthy of love and happiness despite the shadows of her past. Can he break through her defenses and convince her that she deserves a second chance at love, even amid the scars of tragedy?

Finding Mr. Valentine
Sweetheart Falls Book 5
(Clay & Luci's story)
Release Date: January 30th, 2025.

Lucida "Luci" Buchanan thrives in her fast-paced, independent life as an executive in the bustling streets of New York City. Content with her career at a prestigious marketing firm, she's taken aback when her best friend, Maddie, proposes a venture to oversee a new contract in New Zealand. Despite her reservations, Luci finds herself intrigued by the opportunity.

Clay Devereaux, a self-made billionaire with global business ventures, embraces the bachelor lifestyle, but years for something more meaningful. When he crosses paths with Luci, he's captivated by her fiery spirit and independence, envisioning a future together. However, Luci insists on maintaining a professional relationship.

As Clay introduces Luci to the beauty of New Zealand, and his home in Mackenzie, their connection deepens. Yet, Clay's attempts to surprise her are misinterpreted as control. With Valentine's Day on the horizon, they must navigate their differences and discover if their love can endure beneath the enchanting Mackenzie skies. Even after a plane crash threatens everything they've just begun.

Finding Mr. Unexpected

Sweetheart Falls Book 6:
(Jack Devereaux & Cora-Lea Wilson Story)
Step Back in Time
Released April 4th, 2025.

It's 1981, Prince Charles just married Lady Diana Spencer in a fairy tale wedding that held the world in awe, Cora-Lea Wilson among them. Within days though, she finds herself in a race against time, fleeing the clutches of her scheming uncle who is determined to marry her off for his own gain—everything but the fairy tale she just witnessed.

With only a bag and a desperate hope for sanctuary, she embarks on a journey from South Carolina to the Canadian border, seeking refuge with distant relatives in Ontario.

But fate takes an unexpected turn when she collides with Jack Devereaux, a wealthy businessman in the quaint border town of Sweetheart Falls. If she thought her uncle was a threat, Jack's intentions are a whole new level of daunting.

Despite her initial reservations, Cora-Lea finds herself drawn to the tight-knit community of Sweetheart Falls, craving the belonging she's been denied for too long. Yet, as she navigates Jack's world of privilege and power, she grapples with trust and the looming question: is it safer to flee once more, or to take a leap of faith and embrace the chance of a new beginning?

Short Stories

Spooky Going's On – 25th October 2024

All About Paul – 13th January 2025

Finding Mr. Happenstance – Gwen and Callum's story 14th April 2025

Step back in time – Jacques and Carlotta's story 30th July 2025

Finding Mr. Rekindled

Cover to be revealed soon

By Emmy-Lou James

Available on Amazon, Kindle, Kobo, Apple Books, Barnes & Noble, and other platforms from June 30th, 2024

Chapter One

FELICITY

FELICITY KIRSHNER'S jaw near hit the floor as she stared at her best friend, Savannah's beaming face, on the screen.

"YOU'RE GETTING MARRIED?" she blurted, unable to conceal her shock.

"I know, I know... Mac thinks I'm nuts too," Savannah admitted, her voice tinged with a hint of laughter. "But with all the events coming up, I *really* want to do this now."

Felicity shook her head in disbelief, the words taking long seconds to sink in. "I thought..." she trailed off, closing her eyes before opening them to fix Savannah with a mock-stern look. "I can't believe it. You're getting married?"

It was more of a statement than a question, and Felicity continued to shake her head as she spoke, marveling at how far Savannah had come this past year.

A year ago, Savannah had been rebuilding her life after a brutal divorce. Her ex, a prominent, now-disgraced, New York lawyer, had launched a vicious assault before she broke free. Mac, her fiancé now, had been there to pick up the pieces, and while Felicity and Savannah's siblings had worried it may be too soon, they'd been proven wrong.

Mac and Savannah were perfect for each other.

Since then, Savannah had spent most of her time in New Zealand, working on various projects with her twin brother, Clay, and Mac, who was also Clay's business partner. And now, she was talking about marriage—*again.*

"How do the girls feel?" Felicity asked, referring to Savannah's twin daughters, Jess, and Chloe, just as Jess popped into view, her excitement palpable.

"Isn't it the coolest thing ever, Aunt Flick?" Jess exclaimed, her enthusiasm infectious. "We're going to be Yan-Ki's."

Felicity couldn't help but laugh at Jess's excitement. "I'll let you explain that when you come home. In the meantime," she turned back to Savannah, her mind racing with questions. "How long to plan?"

Savannah's expression softened, and she glanced to her side, a smile playing at her lips as Mac came to stand behind her. Felicity couldn't help but feel a pang of envy at their easy affection.

"Three weeks," Mac chimed in. His chin rested on her shoulder as he hugged her from behind. Mischief danced in his eyes, and for the second time in as many minutes, Felicity's jaw hit the floor.

"You didn't get the best part yet," Savannah beamed, an expression Felicity knew all too well meant her friend was about to drop a bombshell.

"Go on," Felicity pushed, when Savannah drew out a suspense-filled silence, and she saw Mac nudge her. "Well..."

"We can't fly out until two days before the wedding, so we figured we'd hire you to oversee things."

Felicity blinked. "Sorry?"

"The resort opens in just over two weeks. I'm up to my eyes in planning here. I can't get away."

"And you still planned the wedding for three weeks?"

Savannah chuckled.

"Two weeks after, we shift into the next phase of resort openings, Clay's set tight deadlines. So, this way we at least get time for a honeymoon."

Felicity rolled her eyes, eying the paradise like scene behind. "Like that scene behind you doesn't scream of honeymoon already!"

Mac teased Savannah with that comment, placing a gentle kiss at her neck and she melted against him, closing her eyes on a sigh.

"Perhaps, but this way, we do it officially—and let's face it, the family are well overdue a big party."

"Like that's a reason to get married," Felicity blustered, hating that she felt the pang of envy at the easy display of affection. The last thing she wanted, or needed, in her life was a man. But for someone to look at her like that. To care for her...

Irritably she brushed off the thought, annoyed at where her mind had gone, forcing her focus back to the conversation. Aware that no matter what, she wouldn't let Savannah down. Their friendship meant way too much for that.

Five minutes later, Felicity disconnected the call and dropped her phone onto her desk, spinning her chair to stare absentminded out at the city skyline.

Since their debut fundraiser last year, the event management business had flourished so that they'd outgrown the home office back in Brooklyn. Where initially, Felicity had stepped in to help Savannah as a friend going through a tough time, Savannah had asked her to oversee things while she was travelling, and while Felicity had hesitated, she'd agreed. At least for the time being.

Early each morning, she'd satiate her side hustle, and passion for baking and decorating cupcakes, and supplying them to a local bakery, before going into the office to do what had become her day job. Keeping the dream of one day owning her own cupcake café alive as she rode the corporate waves of New York's busy event scene.

The ongoing success of the business had seen them occupy a suite of offices in Clay's Manhattan business headquarters.

They'd also grown their team of staff as they continued to flourish, so that now, with Savannah continuing to pick up business through her brothers resorts overseas, the New York arm largely rested in Felicity's care, along with the team of ten event's organizers.

"Three weeks," she murmured with disbelief. Three weeks to organize Savannah's dream wedding, and not in the city, but in Savannah's hometown of Sweetheart Falls.

The very place she'd avoided since that last visit a year ago.

Her phone vibrated again, and she snatched it up, half expecting to see Savannah's number again. Only it wasn't. The caller was Belle Richards, a realtor she'd spoken with recently in Seattle.

Felicity frowned, staring at the screen, then answered.

"Belle?" she greeted when the call connected.

"Hey, Felicity," Belle's warm voice greeted her. "An opportunity has come up that I thought you might be interested in."

Intrigued, Felicity pushed. "Go on."

"Knowing how interested you are in this kind of thing; I figured it would be criminal if you missed out."

Felicity's frown deepened.

"Ok, I'll take the bait," she replied. "What did you find?"

"How about an established cafe, about an hour and a half north of Seattle, in a small historic logging town called Darrington. Beautiful community, proper seasons, close to the US Canadian border." Belle's words came out in a hurry, as though she needed Felicity to hear everything quick.

She fell silent allowing Felicity to process what she'd said so far, before adding.

"It's nestled in the Cascade Mountains in Snohomish County. Stunning views of Mount Baker and the Snohomish National Forest. Snow tourists in winter, lake tourists, and hikers during summer, popular Fall festivals, tulip festivals, and the like in Spring, a hugely popular music festival in Summer, has it all. I've emailed you a link, it has all the information you need."

Felicity heard the rustle of paper, as her own laptop pinged with a message, and she clicked on the screen as Belle continued, as though reading from a prompt sheet.

"At this point I'll add, the Cascade Mountains Cupcake Café won awards for its cakes for five consecutive years and has grown its reputation with tourists since the pandemic, after its owners ran a social media series promoting the magic of cupcakes. The campaign went viral and put them firmly on the west coast tourism map."

Another pause, but Felicity's attention now directed at the screen in front of her, the images steeling her breath.

She'd dreamed of small-town living for her entire adult life, and now, she sat staring at the place of her dreams.

The cafe had a rustic cabin like vibe; the walls made of traditional pine, heavy beams holding the roof in place, and a stone fireplace in the corner housed a roaring fire. But that was where the cabin charm ended, the décor focusing on pinks and creams, curtains framing the windows like something out of the 'Woman's Touch' scene in Calamity Jane. The tables adorned with vintage teapots, and dainty pink and white floral arrangements, the counter a rainbow of decorated cupcakes, giving a magical feel to the space that resonated through the images on the screen.

"Unfortunately, the husband died recently, and the wife has been unwell." Belle continued, drawing Felicity's attention away from the pictures. "She's looking to retire closer to her grandbabies and wants whoever buys the cafe to bring the same love she did to its cupcakes—carry on its legacy. I thought of you the second I saw it."

For long seconds, Felicity didn't respond. Processing everything Belle had just said.

Her head spun.

This was it—her dream.

Could she continue this couple's legacy?

Until now, she'd provided cupcakes as a side-hustle never full time.

But it's your dream.

Is it the right time? Will there ever be a right time?

She closed her eyes, raking a hand through her hair as she played out the possibilities.

This has to be it.

Your moment.

Isn't it?

Savannah wouldn't begrudge her following her dream, and yet...

Glancing back up at the city skyline, she blinked, wondering just why she was even questioning this.

"Belle," she said, in a voice that was barely a whisper. "How soon can I look?"

Three hours later, and bristling with excitement, she checked in at JFK airport. She'd secured a cancellation seat for the early evening flight to Seattle and had panic-packed an overnight bag, with just one change of clothes. She'd be back in New York tomorrow night.

With no time to waste, she needed to see it with her own two eyes. With the wedding just three weeks out, she knew she'd need to decide before. Particularly if she were going to give Savannah chance to find her replacement. Not to mention, tie up any other loose ends that needed tying.

Was this the opportunity she'd been looking her entire adult life for?

As wheels-up time finally approached, she gazed out over the darkening city, smiling at the stars beginning to appear in the sky, the words of a song her mom had sung to her as a child playing over in her mind, whispering the second line into the ether, "wish I may, wish I might, have the wish I wish tonight."

She smiled wistfully, as the moon now became visible over the Empire State building, was it too much to hope that the cupcake café would be her wish come true?

She hoped so. That little slice of her own to build a future on, was the wish she'd wished for far too long.

GRAY

GRAY DEVEREAUX gaped in amazement as his mom dropped the bombshell, he'd least expected to hear.

"They're getting married. Already?" he gasped.

His mom, Cora-Lea, smiled fondly at her second youngest son. "It's been a year, c'mon now. You know how perfect they are together."

Gray couldn't deny it, they'd all thought so from the first time they'd seen Savannah and Mac together at her debut fundraiser. They were made for each other.

"They couldn't give us a little more time to organize it?"

"Apparently, Clay and Mac have brought forward the Whitsunday Resort opening, so they're on a limited window. They're coming back for two weeks before flying back out." Cora-Lea explained.

"The Whitsunday's are Australia—aren't they?" Gray asked, confused. "I thought Mac and Savannah were in New Zealand."

"It's a busy time for them."

Gray snorted.

"So, what you're saying is, we need to put together the entire wedding for them to come home to, right?"

"That's it in a nutshell, sweetheart. See, you're not just a pretty face."

Gray rolled his eyes at his mother's sarcastic retort.

"And to what extent is Savannah offering input?" he asked.

"We have a list to work to, she's organizing her dress, and the girls, the rest, she's giving us free rein."

"Us?"

Cora-Lea had the good grace to drop her eyes, her suspicious expression setting alarm bells ringing in Gray's head, and when she didn't answer immediately, he prodded.

"I'm taking it there's a sting in the tail to this proposal," he said, with characteristic cynicism.

The door opened, and his father, Jack, peered around the door. Perfect timing as ever. He glanced from Gray to Cora-Lea and back again, as though assessing how the conversation had gone, and when neither spoke, said.

"So, you told him then, Cora."

"Told me what?"

Jack's brows lifted, and he glanced back at Cora, head tilted to one side, waiting for her to speak.

"Not quite," his mother added, a guilty flush in her cheeks.

"Are you going to tell me what you're talking about?" he pushed.

For long seconds, Cora-Lea appeared to feign interest in her hands, playing with her nails, and when she looked up, he noted she struggled to hold his gaze directly.

"Spit it out, mom!" Gray growled.

"I'm in charge of the guest list," Cora-Lea spat out in a rush, hesitating, before she added. "You and Felicity will be in charge of organizing the ceremony and reception venue."

A charged silence settled through the room, and Gray felt as though he'd been punched full on in the solar plexus, winded, as he struggled to draw breath.

"Felicity?" he said on a low whisper.

Cora-Lea didn't speak, but slowly nodded her head.

"You mean *the* Felicity?"

"*The* Felicity," his father confirmed, and Gray's eyes slammed closed. Just the memory of her was enough to steal his breath. Those beautiful brown eyes, high cheekbones, the softness of her skin when he ran the backs of his fingers over her cheeks. The whimper when her lips parted on a gasp when he did.

Finding Mr. Rekindled

The last time he'd seen her, Savannah had been here. The date etched in his mind.

A year ago.

At least that was in person. She'd visited regularly in his daydreams, not to mention his deepest slumbers.

There was a time he'd thought they may have a future. But that had been dashed when she left, and he'd moved on, just the same as she had.

Except, just the mere mention of her name brought her rushing back through his mind, as real as though she'd been here just yesterday.

He shook his head, slowly, as though struggling to process what his mom had just said.

"So, she's going to be here?" he asked, frustrated at how tentative his voice sounded.

His mom nodded.

"She'll be arriving the morning after next, so get ready for a whirlwind couple of weeks. We've got a lot to sort if we're not going to let Savannah, Mac, and the girls down. Sweetheart Falls is set for the next chapter in the Devereaux's story, so make sure you've got your game shoes ready to go."

Twenty minutes later, Gray stepped out onto the ornate stone staircase that led down to the drive beneath the towering old mansion.

Heaven Sent, or Envoyé du Ciel, as it had originally been named by his long-passed ancestors. The French words still etched in the two white stones flanking the large front door.

Two centuries on, the home remained in the family, a testament to their journey. But that was another story.

His father stepped out beside him and wrapped an arm around his shoulder.

"Don't worry, mate, I'll keep her under control," he chuckled, referring to Gray's mother. "She has it in her head it's time to marry you all off—she just needs to remember that it's down to you all to choose your own life partners, not her."

Gray heaved a sigh.

"I'm taking it Sav is in on this too?"

Another rumble of laughter from his father.

"Like mother, like daughter. God only knows what the twins are going to be like. Two are a force of nature, double that, and I'm thinking we've got a whole helluva lot of trouble on our hands."

Gray shrugged his hands into his pockets, and rocked back on his heels, thoughtful for a long second. When he spoke moments later, his frown had deepened.

"Fact is dad, I'm not ready for anything serious. We've got too much going on here now. The last thing I need is a city-bound girlfriend—and one that isn't prepared to give an inch, let alone a mile," he shrugged. "It won't work."

"Then stand your ground, son. They can't make you do anything you don't want to do, no matter how much they wish it."

Gray chuckled.

"You ready to head into the office, old man?"

Jack cuffed him on the arm, rolling his eyes, as he added.

"Not so old you can talk to me like I'm a doddery old fool."

Laughing together, they descended the final steps to where Gray had parked his jeep.

"C'mon, let's get some work done before the chaos begins."

Chapter Two

FELICITY

Felicity was buzzing by the time she arrived in Sweetheart Falls. The past forty-eight hours had been a whirl of activity, and having checked out the beautiful Cascade Café, her mind was on overload. The fact it was the opposite side of the country, might have played on her mind, but right now, she had other things to worry about. The discussions with Savannah could come later.

As she steered the hire car onto Main Street, she pulled up alongside the expanse of green, sheltered beneath the dappled light of pines, maples, and oaks, she glanced at the Whispering Pines' Café, set back from the street, and grinned.

The sight, a reminder that in two short months, she too would own her own cupcake café.

Grinning, she killed the engine, and climbed out of the car, her gaze taking in the stillness of the town, the early morning quiet so different from the chaos of New York. At a little after eight, it was still waking, the warm spring day accentuated with the melodic song of black-capped chickadees, robins and cardinals, and the soft warbling of the Eastern bluebirds, somewhere in the canopy of trees of the park opposite.

Having shed their winter dormancy, each adorned with fresh green leaves, the delicate blossom of cherry and dogwood bringing a splash of pink and white, not to mention a sweet, delicate fragrance amid them.

Felicity smiled.

Idyllic was an understatement.

Somewhere in the distance, a dog barked, and she knew from her last visit that it was where the dog park was located.

The rumble of an old-fashioned truck bumping along the uneven road drowning it out moments later.

Yes, she loved Sweetheart Falls and had since the first time she saw it.

It's cobblestone sidewalk, the backdrop of nineteenth century historic buildings, steeped in a rich tapestry of tradition and time, of snow-capped mountains, like something straight out of a storybook.

Now, as she looked, a couple of young twenty-somethings walked down one side, engaged in animated conversation as they pushed strollers. Both wore fitness-wear, one, carrying a takeout cup in one hand, the other a water bottle hooked over the little finger of the hand holding the stroller.

An elderly couple looked through the window to the Pages and Petals bookstore and florist, a teenager walking a dog the size of a horse appeared to be dragged along by the exuberant pooch, its tail wagging with excitement, while a middle-aged man slid his keys into the door of the hardware store.

It was, a picture-perfect snapshot of small-town US, and everything Felicity had ever dreamed, except for one thing.

Gray.

His name played through her mind in a whisper of warmth, the inexplicable sense of longing infiltrating her mind in that same way it always did, and she brushed it away, fighting that all-too-familiar wave of sensation.

Gray Devereaux was anything, and everything, that she didn't need in her life, and she needed to remember it. Everything about him screamed danger, the very thing she'd spent her life running from.

She closed her eyes, shutting out the memory, turning her attention to the scent of freshly brewed coffee, mingled with the sweet aroma of freshly baked pastries, as she fought to steady the rapid beat of her heart.

Beautiful fire and ice-blue eyes that were anything but cold, the sharp jawline, that was too often emphasized with a scowl, and the... a shiver of awareness rocked her, and she growled, briskly shaking her head, at how easily he permeated her mind, allowing that last image of him shirtless, a sheen of sweat across his pecs, his biceps braced as he leaned over her.

She gulped back the lump in her throat, blinking away the memory, determined not to allow it any purchase in that moment. She didn't need him, or any man. Her life was her own, and she needed to stop this before it took hold again. Once she'd allowed him into her life. Once, she'd allowed him into her bed. That was more than enough. The momentary lapse of self-control, something she seemed incapable of restraining.

It wouldn't happen a second time.

She straightened her shoulders and turned to face the café nestled between the trees, grateful for the distraction of two toddlers playing on the swings outside as she strode forward.

Coffee, a breakfast biscuit, and Savannah's parents' home, in that order. She'd worry about Gray if their paths crossed again.

Moments later, she pushed open the door to the café, welcoming the tinkling of the little bell above that notified of her arrival.

Smiling to herself, she closed the door behind her; she glanced around the warm, inviting space, instantly comparing it with the Cascade Café.

It had the same welcoming ambience, only this was an entirely different architectural feel.

Where the Cascade Café was all timber, the fresh scent of pine still clear, despite its age, the Whispering Pines Café had a more contemporary feel. The tables were white, and almost clinical in their cleanliness, where flowers and antique teapots featured as centerpieces in the Cascade Falls, here, a miniature lantern in the shape of a cupcake was placed on each, with candles flickering inside.

Felicity grinned, what a cool idea.

She smiled at an elderly woman seated in the corner, her gaze sweeping round to where a woman fed a small baby, while fondly watching a toddler play with a wooden kitchen set in the corner. The ambience, so homely, she knew this was the environment she wanted to create. Homely, warm, and welcoming. The place anybody and everybody could come.

It wasn't until she completed her sweep that she stalled, her gaze meeting the blue-eyed gaze she'd least expected to see this soon.

Her breath hitched in her throat, heart hammering in her chest, the sound of blood pumping through her ears deafening.

"Gray," she croaked, as she watched his lips lift into a smile of surprise, unable to mask the way every muscle in his body tensed.

"Felicity," Gray replied, and Felicity wondered if she'd ever get over the way her entire body reacted to her name on his lips. The sound settling over her like a weighted blanket.

She moved aside as somebody else entered from behind, the handle of the door catching her on the hip as she did, and she winced.

A pale woman behind the counter, held out two keep-cups with the Sweetheart Falls logo she now knew so well.

"Triple, triple to go, for you," she said, as she handed them to Gray. "And a single for your dad, your ma will have my hide if he goes home wired at lunchtime."

"Thanks Abs," he flashed the woman a typical *Gray* smile, the same smile she herself had flushed in response to a year earlier, and which had led to this whole hell of a mess. "Not so sure dad will thank you, but..." He took the cups from Abbie. "You're a star, love."

Abbie flushed prettily, lowering her lashes, and reached for a paper bag, sliding what looked like two apple and cinnamon muffin into it, before handing them to him too.

"For the road, you flirt," she winked. "One for you and one for your dad, mind you don't eat them both!"

Felicity frowned, fighting back the unreasonable pinch of envy, at the familiarity, with which the woman smiled at him. The banter in no way going over her head.

She shouldn't feel this way, and yet... her teeth clamped over her bottom lip, as she straightened her shoulders, standing tall. She brushed down her skirt, before straightening her jacket.

As if she was bothered who Grayson Devereaux flirted with.

Gray, who now walked toward her, cups in hand, the muffin bag anchored by his little finger smiled, as though he was going to say something, but Felicity tugged open the door, gesturing for him to step through.

Then, as he stepped outside, shoved the door closed behind him. She ignored the look of surprise on his face when he turned to face her. Grinning with smug satisfaction, she turned and walked across to the counter, aware that he'd intended for her to follow.

Let him flirt. She was here to work, not get caught up in the magic of Sweetheart Falls, and its ability to crack even the toughest nut where romance was concerned.

She'd been burned by Gray Devereaux before, and she was darned if she would again.

She had every intention of organizing Savannah's wedding, and then getting the hell out of dodge, she had dreams to realize.

As she turned to glance quickly at the door, she didn't miss the annoyance on Gray's face as he stalked across the green.

The next few weeks were going to be entertaining, and she wasn't sure that was necessarily in the best possible way.

GRAY

Gray stormed into the office he shared with his father, grumbling to himself as he did.

What had started as a flicker of amusement had fast derailed into frustration as he realized Felicity had once again outmaneuvered him.

"What's the matter with you," he growled inwardly, resisting the urge to smack himself upside of the head. Every encounter with her left him feeling like a lovesick teenager, completely incapable of maintaining his composure.

Twice they'd been together, and twice she'd left him in the dust without a backward glance. It was a blow to his ego, not to mention his physical frustration whenever he thought of her.

"Twelve months," he cursed silently. A year since he'd last seen her, and he still couldn't shake her from his mind. Even after attempting to date other women, his thought inevitably returned to Felicity.

But it was the week of the fundraiser that changed everything. Felicity had shown him what he truly wanted in a partner, and it wasn't something he could find with anyone else.

His father's voice interrupted his reverie, pulling him back to the present.

"Looks like someone's got a big gray cloud over their head today. Need me to fetch some sunshine? No pun intended." Jack quipped, a mischievous twinkle in his eye.

Gray rolled his eyes in response.

"Think we both know the pun was fully intended, old man. Don't pretend otherwise."

Jack grinned back, his blue eyes twinkling with mischief. At sixty-five, he still had a playful streak that never failed to lift Gray's spirits, even on the darkest days.

"Aw Gray, feelin' a little shady, huh? Who upset you now?"

Gray shook his head, walking across to his own desk, and took a huge sip of the coffee in his hand before sinking into his chair.

"Can you believe she's in town and already gave me the brush off?"

Jack frowned. "Who?"

Gray shook his head. "Felicity-frustrate-the-hell-out-of-Gray's-my-middle-name-Kirshner. Who else?"

"Ohhh, so it started already, huh?"

Jack's understanding tone did little to soothe Gray's irritation. "What started?"

"Ah c'mon son, she's been giving you the runaround for more than a year. I know your ma has ideas, but the girl obviously grinds your gears. When you going to tie her down, or at the very least get her to take you serious-like?"

Jack's words hit a nerve, and Gray bristled with frustration.

"I've no intention of tying her, or anyone down," Gray retorted defensively. "I just don't understand why she's so... so damned stand-offish."

Jack grinned. "That's where it all starts, Gray. You've just got to figure how to break down those walls."

Gray shook his head in disbelief.

"I don't want to break down any walls, I just want to..." he trailed off, his frustration clear as he struggled to articulate the words.

"Maybe that's your problem," Jack interjected gently.

"Huh?"

Gray's confusion was clear as he searched his father's face for answers.

"Maybe you need to switch on that old Devereaux charm and show her what she's missing out on."

Gray's head tilted to one side, his gaze focused now on the coffee on his desk, the bag of muffins discarded, possibilities racing through his mind. Could it really be that simple?

"You're catching on my boy," Jack's encouragement spurred Gray into action. "Now why don't you go get started on Sav's wedding plans, see if you can't drum up a little romance for yourself. I've got things here."

Gray nodded thoughtfully; his determination renewed. Crazy as it seemed, his dad had a point. It was time he stopped dancing around Felicity, he needed to break down those walls, and show her what they could have together.

Except that was going to be no easy feat. But then, when had he ever run from a challenge?

He drummed his fingers on the desktop thoughtfully, then scowled.

It couldn't be that hard. Could it?

No longer dreading the next few weeks, he embraced the challenge before him with newfound resolve. Felicity Kirshner had blown his mind a year ago. Perhaps, now, it was time he repaid the compliment tenfold.

Chapter Three

FELICITY

Felicity arrived at Savannah's family home a little before lunch. She'd planned on going earlier, but an unexpected urge to explore overtook her, leading her on a detour through town.

As she wandered, memories flooded her mind—the last time she'd been here, watching Savannah's parents renew their vows, the laughter and joy that filled the air, had generated a magic like none she'd ever known before.

Now, with the town serving as the backdrop for Savannah's wedding, the atmosphere was charged with a different excitement.

With her coffee cup in hand, Felicity made her way down to the river, following the winding track to the falls. Sitting on the bank, she listened to the thunderous roar of the water crashing against the rocks, lost in the raw power of nature's display.

Nature, like men, was a force to be reckoned with, she thought bitterly, her mind drifting to a certain someone—the twinkle of amusement in those Devereaux eyes, the undeniable charm of their family dynamic.

On the surface, she admired their strength and unity, their unwavering determination to succeed. But deep down, she knew she could never truly belong among them.

Pushing herself up, Felicity brushed away a persistent fly, her gaze drawn to the majestic sight of a bald eagle soaring overhead. Birds always held a special place in her heart, a reminder of her love for nature and the freedom it represented.

Continuing her exploration, Felicity found herself in a glade beside the falls, the spot where Savannah envisioned her wedding ceremony.

Cora-Lea called it the Fairy Tale Terrace, a whimsical name that spoke to her belief in happily ever after's.

As far as Felicity was concerned, that was superstitious claptrap, but she'd never tell Savannah, or Cora-Lea, that.

Now, as she entered the old house, Felicity was greeted by a beaming Cora-Lea.

"How exciting is this?" the older woman asked as she led Felicity into the kitchen. The older woman's excitement was contagious, but Felicity couldn't shake the feeling of dread that settled in the pit of her stomach.

Felicity forced a smile, trying to mask her apprehension.

"Yes, it's quite the whirlwind. I...I can't believe they decided to get married so soon."

"Oh, I wasn't talking about that—although that's just as exciting! I was talking about you and Gray organizing it."

Felicity's heart sunk as she realized what was happening.

The legendary Devereaux matchmaking was in full swing, and she was powerless to stop it. She couldn't, wouldn't let Savannah down. But she also refused to become a pawn in the games of matchmaking-chess that both Cora-Lea and Savannah were renowned for.

"Oh, Cora..." Felicity began, the older woman cut her off with a cheerful grin.

"With, or without cream, sugar or sweet enough?" she chirped, holding out a cup of coffee.

Resigned, Felicity sighed inwardly. "White and sweet enough," she replied, bracing herself for whatever lay ahead.

An hour later, Felicity found herself seated opposite Cora-Lea at the worn wooden kitchen table, a laptop screen open, with Savannah's beaming face smiling out.

Pen in hand as she listened intently to Cora-Lea and Savannah talk between themselves, offering occasional remarks or opinions.

Finding Mr. Rekindled

It seemed strange to see the two of them discussing the event, and Felicity found herself inexplicably on the outside looking in. An unusual sensation that left her feeling uncomfortable.

"What do you think, Flick?" Savannah asked, breaking into her reverie.

"Sorry," Felicity blinked.

"Traditional band, or something more modern?" Savannah repeated.

"Oh, if I know you, you'll say something more modern, but traditional is good too—especially if you're going for the traditional ceremony."

Savannah frowned.

"Have you been listening to anything we've spoken about."

Felicity frowned and held up the pen and paper. "I've been taking notes, what do you think?"

"I'd say you're distracted—wouldn't you agree, mom?"

Cora-Lea chuckled.

"That's okay, love, there's lots to take on board. It's not as though you've dropped a wedding to organize in a few weeks."

"Mmmmm," Savannah retorted, her suspicious gaze shifting back to Felicity.

"Well, I need to call it a night. It's nearly ten, and we have another early start tomorrow. Felicity..."

Felicity cocked her head to one side, meeting Savannah's gaze, "Yes," she replied, when Savannah didn't immediately continue.

"You realize I trust you one thousand percent with this, right?"

Felicity nodded. "I'd hope so, I've been doing enough in New York!"

Savannah laughed.

"Yeah, but this is personal. You're one of the only people who knows me inside, outside, back to front and round the right way."

Heat rose in Felicity's cheeks, and she dropped her gaze, guilt flooding her as she realized she had yet to drop her very own bombshell.

"I mean it. I trust you to do this for me—and Gray. If there's two people in the world, I know can pull this off—it's the two of you."

"Ahem."

Cora-Lea coughed, and Savannah's grin widened.

"Yes mom, you are too. But I think we've got to trust Felicity and Gray to work the magic—don't you?"

The knowing glance between mother and daughter did not go missed, nor did Felicity's audible sigh.

"The two of you are incorrigible, do you realize that?"

Savannah rang off, leaving Felicity alone with Cora-Lea, and together they deliberated over the list they'd created.

"Ma," Gray's voice interrupted their conversation as he strolled in through the back door, a mischievous glint in his eyes. "Hard at it already, huh?" he remarked, helping himself to a cup of coffee and taking a seat beside Felicity."

"One—since when did you call me ma? And two, time waits for no one," she retorted, though there was a hint of amusement in her tone. "You were supposed to be here an hour ago."

"Work stuff, Ma" Gray replied, flashing a grin at his mother. His easy banter with Cora-Lea was a stark contrast to Felicity's own strained relationship with her parents, and she couldn't help but envy the comfortable dynamic between them.

As Cora-Lea updated Gray on the wedding plans, Felicity observed their interaction, feeling a pang of longing for the familial closeness they shared. It was a feeling she had never experienced with her own parents, whose expectations had always loomed over her like a dark cloud.

She'd been nothing but a disappointment to them. But that was something she refused to think of now.

"Now, what I'm suggesting," Cora-Lea interrupted Felicity's thoughts, turning her attention back to the task at hand. She outlined her their responsibilities for the day, delegating tasks to both Felicity and Gray with ease.

"You're both professional people. You've organized more than a few events before." Cora-Lea remarked, a playful smile tugging at her lips. "How about you go do what needs to be done and tell me when you need me?"

With that, she rose from her seat and made her way to the sink, where she rinsed her cup and placed it on the drainer. Felicity and Gray exchanged bemused glances.

"In the meantime, I have an appointment at the spa," she called over her shoulder, with a last grin before she disappeared down the hall, leaving Felicity and Gray to tackle their wedding planning duties together.

"Do you get the impression we've just been Devereaux'ed?" Gray quipped, a wry smile playing on his lips as he glanced at Felicity.

"You didn't just hear the conversation with Savannah," Felicity shot back, but didn't enlighten. She couldn't deny it, she had the feeling they'd well and truly been Devereaux-ed, and on the chessboard, she had the feeling they were dangerously close to checkmate.

GRAY

Refusing to allow Savannah or Cora-Lea's antics to gain any purchase, Gray turned his attention back to the task at hand, determined to steer well clear of any sensitive subject—at least for now.

"So where do you want to start, boss?" he asked, his tone playful, yet earnest. "The Falls like mom suggested? Or do you have something else in mind?"

Felicity regarded him with a hint of suspicion, and he knew there was more to his question than met the eye.

"I think we need to draw up a list for each of us and tackle them separately," she suggested, and he knew she was attempting to maintain a sense of professionalism despite his antics.

But Gray had other ideas, his blue eyes twinkling mischievously as he interrupted her with a sly grin.

"Oh no, no, no. That's not how we organize weddings in Sweetheart Falls, Felicity Kirshner," he declared, his tone dripping with playful authority.

Felicity's brows shot up in surprise. "Excuse me?"

"Didn't Savannah tell you?" Gray continued, enjoying the moment. "A couple have overseen every wedding that's ever been organized in Sweetheart Falls. It's an age-old tradition that is set in stone."

Felicity's eyes widened.

"We're not..."

"Yet," Gray interjected, his grin widening at Felicity's incredulous expression.

"Never will be," she countered.

"We'll see," Gray raised his brows, the grin didn't lessen any.

"You're impossible," Felicity declared, though there was a hint of fondness in her tone, and he didn't miss it.

"So, I'm told," Gray replied, effortlessly reclaiming Felicity's empty cup and rising from his seat. "Fact is, we have..." he glanced at his watch, the mischievous glint in his eye now utterly outrageous. "Four hundred and thirty-five hours, and thirty minutes to pull this together."

This time Felicity grinned, clearly enjoying his enthusiasm.

"Now let's get this show on the road—we've got a wedding to plan."

"It's a beautiful spot for a wedding," Felicity admitted several hours later, her gaze sweeping over the picturesque scene before them.

It wouldn't be long until sunset, and the light had already begun to shift toward twilight, the shadows far longer than earlier in the day.

Gray nodded in agreement, his eyes reflecting the same sense of awe.

They'd used a combination of sticks and stones to mark out the key aspects of the ceremony lay out, and now stood at the point Savannah and Mac would exchange their vows.

"Totally, although it's the history as much as anything that carries the magic," Gray remarked, turning his attention back to the waterfall. "When you have had generations pledge their love over the centuries, it leaves its mark, so that you can feel it just standing here."

Felicity nodded, taking in the significance of Gray's words without a reply.

"I used to think it was fluffy nonsense," Gray continued, his tone reflective. "I don't know how many times I've scoffed over the years at how ridiculous a notion it is to have this fairy-tale reputation, but as I've gotten older, it's hard not to see there's," he air-quoted, "something here."

He swallowed, walking across to one of the enormous old white pines that lined the open glade. It stood tall and proud; it's weathered bark etched with passaging time. Its' towering trunk reaching skyward with a sense of timeless grandeur that bore scars of decades past.

He rubbed his fingers across, showing the carvings, weathered, and faded with age, initials carved long ago by hands now lost to memory.

"See," he nodded when Felicity came to stand beside him. "Each letter here is a testament to a moment frozen in time, a declaration of love..."

He stood back, allowing her to trace the letters he had moments earlier. The JD and CW that were Jack Devereaux I and Cora-Lea Wilson, his parents' initials. The JD and ER, that were Jack Devereaux and Eleanor Reynolds, his grandparents, and the eleven other sets that traced his ancestral line back to the JD and CD who were Jacques Devereaux and Carlotta Dupont, the initial founders of Sweetheart Falls, and eleven times great grandparents of Gray and his siblings.

"So many Jacks," she murmured thoughtfully.

"Jack's the name of the first born of every generation, often they'd take on their second name in order not to confuse, with JD, we simply use initials though," Gray explained.

"This is such a beautiful gesture," she breathed, turning to meet Gray's gaze, her eyes shining with newfound understanding. "Are there others?"

Gray chuckled softly.

"We humans, if nothing else, love leaving our mark on nature," he remarked, leading Felicity to where the rock nestled beside the cascading waterfall, smoothed by the relentless flow of water over countless centuries. Like the tree, initials had been carved into the rock, but here, there were so many more. Some were weathered and faint, barely legible beneath the layers of moss and lichen that clung to the rock's surface. Others, fresh and bold, their lines still sharp and clear against the smooth stone. Unlike the tree though, many of these had dates too. A carving of each chapter in a love story, woven into the fabric of the landscape.

Felicity gasped in awe as she took in the sight before her, the etchings telling the stories of countless love stories embedded into the very fabric of this magical landscape.

"I get it," she whispered, her voice filled with wonder. "What a beautiful idea."

She gently fell to her knees, her fingers tracing the letters on the rock's surface as she read them aloud. Gray joined her, sharing the stories behind each set of initials, his enthusiasm infectious as he spoke.

"These aren't all 'D's," she said, glancing up at him, her eyes sparkling with wonder. "So, it's not only the Devereaux's?"

Gray laughed. "No, Sweetheart Falls isn't only about our family. It's about the town and the generations who've come before too. All stories of the townsfolk weave together to make the tapestry that is Sweetheart Falls. Here, look," he pointed to a new etching. "This RM and EF is Robin Marchant and Ellie Flowers," he said, showing the date beneath. "They were married here last Fall, and here, Caleb Reynolds, he was my grandfather's brother, married Edith Cohen, see."

For long moments, they remained there, immersed in the moment's magic, their hearts open to the timeless love that surrounded them.

"They ought to have a plaque here," Felicity said when she finally stood a long while later. Her gaze lingered on the carvings. "Something permanent that explains this kind of history."

"That would take from its magic though," Gray replied, staring out over the Falls.

"Why? It's clearly a historic place. Surely, to tell its story would be beneficial long term?"

"But it would also take from its natural beauty. The carvings do not tell you enough?"

Felicity frowned, thoughtful for a moment before she replied. "But, without you to explain them, they mean nothing."

"Really, you don't think if you'd found them alone, you'd have not done exactly as you just did?"

Felicity's head tilted to one side, her frown deepening.

"In what way?"

"You'd have traced your fingers over them, seen the dates, known they were couples because of the hearts that links each initial. Is that not enough?"

Felicity shrugged.

"I don't know. I guess…" she sighed. "I guess I like all the information to hand rather than having to ask for it."

She laughed at her own observation, waving a hand. "I guess I'm just an outsider looking in, huh?"

Gray narrowed his eyes. "That's how you feel?"

"An outsider?" Felicity's teeth clamped over her lower lip, hesitating before she answered with a small nod. "I am. I don't belong in Sweetheart Falls. I only visit intermittently. I have no investment here, emotionally, financially, or any other way. But—when I visit somewhere, I want to understand what that place is about. What its stories are, why those stories are told—don't you?"

Gray cocked his head.

"You don't feel that Savannah, the girls, my parents—damn it, even I—make you feel welcome here, a part of the…" His voice trailed off; his expression pained.

"Gray," Felicity began, but he raised his hand to stop her.

"Felicity," he interrupted, his hand reaching for hers. "A year ago, we—God I hate saying it like this, but I'm not sure how else... we shared something pretty darned special."

Felicity spluttered.

"Seriously, you're going there now?"

"Don't," Gray cut in. "Let me say this because if I don't, it's going to be the elephant in the room for two endless weeks."

She dipped her head in acknowledgement, allowing him to continue, but he could see her hesitation.

"There is no question there's," he hesitated, searching for the right words. "Chemistry between us. We've been here before, and you ran for the hills without giving us a chance... no, let me get this out, please." The pleading in his eyes rendered her silent, and he watched as her teeth clamped over her lower lip, her entire frame taut. "I understand why you hesitate. Honest. What I don't get though, is why you won't take a chance, see where..." he gestured between them. "This could go?"

"You don't think perhaps there's a legitimate reason I might want to pull back. Like, I'm not ready? Or maybe I'm not that into you?"

Gray baulked, shaking his head. "I think that's a lie," he said on a low whisper.

"You don't think that's for me to decide?"

"Of course I do, and I'd never take that from you, but you can't deny what we had was good."

Felicity's eyes widened, and a laugh of disbelief ripped from her on a gasp.

"Of course it was good, but have you never heard of the term friends with benefits?"

Gray froze, but she continued.

"Yes, we have chemistry," she blew out a breath. "Damned good chemistry, but I'm not committing to any man. Not now, and not anytime soon. I've too much to achieve before I saddle myself down to long-term commitments of any kind, let alone this."

Finding Mr. Rekindled

Release date 30th June 2024
Available on Amazon, Kobo, Apple Books, Barnes and Noble, and other online independent book sellers.

Dear Reader,

Thank you so much for reading the first in my Sweetheart Falls, Devereaux family series. I hope you enjoyed reading it as much as I enjoyed writing it.

The Devereaux's are proving to be so much fun to get to know.

If you enjoyed reading it, please consider leaving a review on Amazon, or Goodreads , or your choice of digital book store, as it helps other readers find my stories and please, keep an eye open for upcoming instalments of the series.

Have a great day, and happy reading!

Emmy-Lou James